TWIST OF FATE

TWIST OF FATE

D.L. Mark

An Aries Book

First published in the UK in 2023 by Head of Zeus,
part of Bloomsbury Publishing Plc

9 7 5 3 1 2 4 6 8

A catalogue record for this book is available from the British Library.

ISBN (PB): 9781803287744
ISBN (E): 9781803287720

Cover design: Mark Swan (kid-ethic)
Typeset by Siliconchips Services Ltd UK

Printed and bound in Great Britain by
CPI Group (UK) Ltd, Croydon CR0 4YY

Head of Zeus
First Floor East
5–8 Hardwick Street
London EC1R 4RG

WWW.HEADOFZEUS.COM

To my afternoon delights … Paulene, Merja, Rebecca, Tricia, the Lindas, Anne, Iris, Dorothy, Kim, Marguerite, Jane, Christine, Emma and the Goldster gang. You mean the world to me.

'*...a roaring lion fiercely threatened to tear him with its bloody teeth: then a bellowing bull dug up the earth with its hoofs and drove its gory horn into the ground; or a bear, gnashing its teeth and striking violently with either paw alternately, threatened him with blows...*'

Extract from Felix's *Vita S Guthlaci*, eighth century

Thirty Years Ago

The Church of St Wendreth, Little Mercy, Cambridgeshire

There are two of them. A him and a her. Neither of them should be here. They have partners waiting for them at home. Another *him*. Another *her*. They have responsibilities. Duties. Lives.

He's Sam.

She's Marguerite.

From here, in this light, it's hard to see where *he* starts and *she* ends. Their parameters are hazy, ill-defined; their forms slithering and interweaving in unions of limb and hair and spit. They move together like eels in a bag: all muscle and sinew and slime. In places *he* is *her*. She thrills to his touch: mould as damp clay beneath the firm ministrations of his palms.

Guiltless, wanton, they press against one another. Paw and claw and smear and lick. They grasp for one another as if looking for answers within one another's flesh.

Sam and Marguerite will die tonight.

They won't die well.

The building in which they shelter is no bigger than an outside toilet, its walls a collage of mismatched bricks and rotten wood. It's tucked into the 'L' of the low stone wall that surrounds the little church – itself encircled by a ring of ancient yew trees, their sodden leaves and tatty branches forming a scruffy canopy overhead. She hadn't known it was here. Had just held his hand and she had followed, meekly, as he shone the light from his phone down the pitted path and made his way towards the little church with its iron railings and big stone walls, its stained glass and listing headstones.

He'd seemed confident. Sure-footed.

He's been here before.

Take them off, he says, kicking at her mud-caked walking boots. *I need to get to you...*

She shivers. Shifts her weight, the cold air and the strong cider causing her world to softly spin. She feels dampness soaking through the seat of her jeans. Does as she is told and enjoys the lash of cold air across her exposed skin. Enjoys the smell of him as he begins to slip out of his clothes.

She splays her hand and reaches behind her for support. Pushes her palm down into a mound of cut turf. She drifts into him. Searches for him. He's not handsome, not really, but there's something about him. Something fresh and exciting. Something bigger than her little terraced house and her dying Vauxhall Nova and the bills and bills and bills. Something more than her boring bloody husband. She reaches up, grass and dirt upon her palm. Touches his cheek. His face, inches from hers, is damp. Pinkishly warm, like the belly of a cooked crab. His mouth, opening into hers, is aromatic with bourbon, with garlic, with the perfume and lip gloss of her face and her neck.

There is a fleeting contact; a dragonfly upon still water, as his embouchure forms the soft 'f' of safe. He is holding her the way she needs, his arms two thick plaits of rope around her waist and one hand a starfish against her back. She cannot fall. She is anchored here, pressed to him. She thinks for a moment of fossils and of wings, of brachiopods and footprints in ancient stone. She wonders what would become of their bodies if they could be left undisturbed. Has a fleeting image of their mortal remains becoming stone, their edges blurred; a monolith built of their fused forms.

Where are you? he asks, and his features are so close to hers that she feels dizzy searching for his eyes. She blinks, and he withdraws a little, as if chastened.

Your mind, he asks. *Where did you go?*

I was thinking of stones, she says. *Fossils. I'd like it if we turned to stone together. Have you seen the shapes barnacles leave on rocks? Or the patterns of leaf skeletons in soft rock? I'd like us to be like that. Do you think if we lie down long enough, we could just sink into the ground and it wouldn't matter any more? We'd just be together. One entity...*

She stops talking, irritated at her own inability to precisely articulate her thoughts. Since meeting him she has become increasingly aware of the gulf between emotion and language. She occasionally feels that her declarations of love will sound asinine to his ears. It is as if the language of her passion necessitates a more physical, demonstrative depiction. Sometimes she longs to crush a peach within her hand and hold it to his lips for him to lick. She wants to shake apples from a tree by swinging on the branches. Wants to say… I love you *this* much.

Like towels, he says, twitching a smile. *Neat, hotel towels, stacked on top of one another. We'd be like that. It's a nice picture.*

She smiles, her tongue poking out between her teeth and her nose wrinkling. He has told her before that her smile was the first thing he loved about her. She likes this lie. Of all the lies he tells her, it is the one she is happiest to believe.

Sam leans forward to stroke the tip of his nose against her warm, soft cheek. She raises her head to allow him the room to kiss the part of her neck he likes best. He runs his tongue along the fine, delicate bone beneath her throat. He has taken one hand in his and he closes his palm around her wrist so he can feel the quickening of her pulse.

Abruptly, he cocks his head: a gun dog hearing the fall of a bird. She looks at him quizzically, wanting his mouth back upon hers.

Did you hear something? he whispers.

I was in the moment.

He listens. It's the faintest of sounds. It's a soft, unctuous sort of a sound. Gloopy. Moist.

Is somebody there? she asks, quietly, her face so close to his that their noses almost touch. *You said there would be nobody here…*

It's fine, he promises. *Maybe a walker. Got lost. Made it home late…*

It's gone midnight, Sam.

He frowns, displeased at this sudden interruption. He listens again. A squelching, sucking, rhythm, like footsteps through thick mud.

I'll go see, he says, without enthusiasm.

No, stay here, she protests. *If they see you...*

I'll be quick, he says. *I can't concentrate. The car, remember? If somebody nabs it...*

There's no mistaking the sound now. He can hear the sound of mud slapping on mud. Out there. Beyond the small, low church, with its old timbers and its patterned glass and its monuments to the countless climbers who lost in their battles with the elements. Out there, in the little graveyard with the old bones and the damp tombs and petals bright as blood.

I'll be quick, he says, and slips from her embrace.

Sam...

He pushes open the rotten wooden door and steps out into the darkness.

He regrets his decision almost as soon as he has extricated himself from her grasp. He's not afraid of the dark. Doesn't mind graveyards. Doesn't believe in ghosts. But he is afraid of discovery. Exposure. Unwittingly he twiddles the wedding ring he always transfers to his right hand when he ventures out for their dalliances. Runs through some potential lies.

I was out for a walk...

Had a few too many...

Needed some air...

He holds his breath as he moves across the wet grass. The moon is almost full tonight, and it casts an eerie, bone-white light into the blackness. He's in the oldest part of the churchyard. Big Gothic monuments and mossy headstones, sticking out from the long grass and the dead leaves like shark teeth. He follows the sound as if hypnotised. He guides himself through the darkness with his hands, his fingers touching smooth stone, slimy stone, crumbling stone. He squints at names. Dates of birth, dates of death. Runs the pads of his fingers through the curve of an 'r'; some Latin inscription bemoaning the passing of a much-loved father, son, vicar of this parish...

The noise grows louder.

Suck, squelch, pull, suck, squelch, pull: a sensuous, dirty sort of a noise.

He crouches low. Runs, soundlessly, to the church wall. Looks back at the little groundsman's hut where he has left the woman he thinks he might like more than any of the others. Feels silly. Forty-three years old. A successful quantity surveyor. Owner of a four-bedroomed house with a grand view. Jeep Cherokee. Big telly and a hot tub. Three kids and a stepbrat and a plump little wife who doesn't give him more trouble than he can handle. Too old and too important to be scurrying about in the dark, investigating noises while a perfectly decent pair of tits grows cold not twenty feet away...

He peers around the wall of the church. Peeks out; a naughty child seeing whether the coast is clear before sneaking out with his pals. He squints, trying to get his bearings.

His gaze slides down. He blinks, eyes like the shutter on

an old camera. It takes him a moment to process what he is looking at.

A thin figure is bent over between two graves, plunging a shovel into the soft, wet earth. They are working in a fervour, their movements quick and practised. Their lower half is eclipsed by a black headstone with a curved top. The shadows cast by the screen of trees ripples the blackness around the figure, making it seem to Sam as though they are at the centre of some eddying, shifting collage; a spinning top painted in different shades of black and grey and darkness.

He steps back, unable to help himself. A gasp escapes his throat. His fingers contract, burrowing into his palms. Adrenaline courses through him. His head fills with a muddle of words and pictures.

Grave robber, he thinks, unbidden. *Burke and Hare. Dr Knox. Fresh cadavers. Leathery skin.*

His mind fills with pictures. Intestines, unspooling like ropes; big purple-grey innards; muscles and sinews and tendons exposed, pliers tugging at cartilage, electrodes pulsing against dead flesh…

He stops himself. Bites down hard. Begins to move away. He wants no part of this.

Time to go, he tells himself. *Slip away. Make a call later, if you must. Nothing for you here…*

He looks back to the groundskeeper's hut. Pictures her inside. Shivering. Scared. Waiting. Hoping.

He would like to leave her. Would like to walk briskly between the headstones and across the grass towards the lych-gate. Would like to run for his car. To drive home in the warm blue confines of his big, safe Jeep. Wants to drink brandy in front of his big TV then go upstairs and kiss the wife. But he can't. He's willing to be thought of as an occasional prick, but she doesn't deserve to be left alone. Doesn't deserve to risk discovery by the sort of person who digs up graves in the dead of night.

He listens, carefully.

The digging has stopped.

Sam suddenly realises how cold he is. Cold and damp. It's not quite raining but the air is misty, and his fleecy jacket is rimed with tiny drops of moisture. He pushes his hand through his sparse hair. It comes away wet. His breath gathers about his face. It looks somehow ghost-like as it clings to his skin.

He tries to remember what happened to the girls. Which came home and which did not. Finds his head filling with memories of Catherine and what she became the second he stuck a fucking wedding ring on her finger.

He walks quickly in the direction of the hut. Makes up his mind what he will do. Stick a hand over her mouth so she can't shout. Can't scream. Tell her with your eyes that this isn't a joke.

Not a sound, laddo, not a fucking sound.

He looks over his shoulder. Sees movement, as if the shadows are becoming flesh.

A small, pitiful yelp erupts from his mouth and suddenly he is running. Slipping and slithering between the gravestones, his feet going out from under him, casting frantic glances back the way he has come, hauling himself up, grazing his hands on the rough stone of a fallen headstone, sprinting for the exit, the girl forgotten...

*

From the doorway of the little hut, Marguerite peers out into the darkness. She sees her man, the man she wants, the man she thinks she loves. Sees him running and falling, slithering and tumbling, squirming feebly on the grass, scrabbling backwards towards a headstone the colour of bad meat.

She hears him shout. Hears him shriek.

She looks left. A tall, thin figure moves between the graves. Their face is half obscured by the folds of a black hood. Watches as they stride into a circle of watery moonlight. Feels her gorge rise as she glimpses something strangely pig-like – an intimation of snout and tusk and tanned leather. Sees something that makes her think of dried-out meat and snuffling tusks and the stink of bacon fat in the bottom of the pan.

Man, she decides. *Big. Strong. Capable…*

They have something in their hand. It glints silver in the milky light.

Her eyes pan right: a sniper glaring through a telescopic sight.

And her Sam is on his back. He can't seem to find his feet. She wants to help him. Wants to run to him. But the fear holds her where she stands, one fist in her mouth, biting through her skin, mouth filling with the taste of liver and pennies.

The figure does not pause in their stride.

She sees her man raise a hand. Hears him try to speak: shrill and alien, cracked syllables, broken by fear.

The words carry to her on the breeze.

No.

Please… please…

I've got kids…

Don't.

She closes her eyes too late. Her mind, spiteful, makes the connection. Gleaming metal and old wood. A spade. The suck and squelch and pull. Spade. In a graveyard. Bodies. Corpses.

Meat.

Meat.

Meat.

And then she is watching the figure in black bring the shovel down into the belly of her man, cutting through skin and fat and innards as if shovelling snow.

Her teeth meet through the flesh of her index finger. Blood trickles onto her skin, thick red caressing the blue veins at her pulse.

Marguerite feels her heart slow. Watches her breath rise like steam. For a moment it feels as if she is fragmenting, as if she is coming apart and being put back together by a force more powerful than her own will.

She hears herself breathing hard. Becomes aware of the dryness of her mouth; her heavy, dilated pupils; the goose pimples on her flesh.

Marguerite steps out from her hiding place.

The darkness engulfs her like a mouth.

PART ONE

I

October 6, 6.06 p.m.

Mount Carmel House, Thames Embankment, London

'Lovely, exquisite... ex-animo, perhaps *ecrasant* – that is acceptable, yes? Ecrasant. Overwhelming. Not a croissant, ha, haha... that's something else. But loveliness, yes? No? *Non*, perhaps... non, erm... *mignon*, non *seduisant*... ah, formidable! Yes, formidable! That is how you appear, *oui*, if that is the intention. However you wish to look, that is most certainly how you look. Was that wrong also? Forgive, *je me ridiculise*, forgive...'

He pinches his nostrils shut: a diver clearing their tubes. Tilts his head as if encouraging dirty water to run from his ears. Slaps the smile on again: bog-brown teeth and split gums: skin missing from his lips.

'Claudine?' He pushes the word at me: a dog nosing a ball towards its owner. 'Sister?'

I can't make myself speak. I'm one of the most important communications consultants in the country and I can't even get my mouth to form the right shape for a 'hello'. There's dead air between us – an invisible wall of things unsaid. A scent rises off him – that stale, whispering odour of buried memory, muddling my senses in a rush of olfactory images.

I don't let my face show what I'm feeling. I feel dizzy and sick – memories rising and popping like marsh gas.

He peers at me as if I were at the far end of a microscope. Glares past the make-up and the scowl. Sees the little girl he half remembers.

'It is you, yes, *Moineau*… sister, zus, *sorella*… sister, yes? My little sister.' He's blinking as he speaks, as if mentally flicking between files in his big, muddled brain – seeking the right language, the right words.

My heart's thudding so hard I expect it to be visible through my top: a maniac head-butting their cell wall. There's a pain low down in my stomach. I'm picking the shellac off my thumbnail; gnawing the Rouge d'Armani from my lower lip. Why here? Why now? I've already got too much to carry. I'm already full to bursting – a plump sponge saturated with unspilled tears. One more drop and I'll burst.

'Moineau… don't be cross, don't be, it pulls down the corners of your mouth and you become a marionette, a dummy, something unreal, and you are real. I know it, I cling to it…'

His accent changes. For a moment he's a public schoolboy again: a fine English gentleman-in-waiting. He's suddenly ebullient, eloquent – gleeful as he glances around him and takes in the majesty of the big, bright reception area. Then something passes over the lenses of his eyes; some strange milky film briefly occluding his pupils. When he speaks again, he has a rural accent. Fenlands. That little green world where Suffolk and Cambridgeshire slap wetly against the lowest reaches of Lincolnshire: an ancient, watery vastness of rivers, marshes and reeds. Home, for him. Home for me, too, when I still believed in such things.

'I don't know which Tube to get on,' he mumbles, thickly. 'I had a ticket but the wind took it. Are the taxis expensive? Everything is expensive. And they don't stop when I wave. Would they take a cheque? I tried to buy my tobacco with a promissory note and the young lady just laughed, and…'

God help me but I'm ashamed of him. There's a journalist upstairs – a twenty-something in flared cords and retro trainers, busy writing a profile about the movers and shakers in the Westminster bubble. I'm holding it together for long enough to validate the lies spoken about me. I've earned the right to hide behind a persona, haven't I? I've given up so bloody much to become somebody of consequence.

I'm sorry, Esme. I don't blame you. I know you'd have stayed if you could. It's not your fault. None of it is your fault. But look. This would have been your uncle. He's a good-hearted man. More than that. He's pure, I guess. Entirely untainted by self-interest. He'd give you the skin off his back if you were cold and said you needed a jacket. Better than me. I'd have been more than I am if you'd stayed. But you didn't. And now I'm thirty-eight and single. Childless, despite my best intentions. An orphan, if you can be such a thing in adulthood. I've got my house in Southwark and my career and I've made my peace with it.

But I have a brother. I have Jethro, tucked away in his tumbledown cottage like a mad wife locked in the attic. I pay for his life, his occasional care, his bouts of medication. All he has to bloody do is stay there. Read his books, write his stories, indulge himself in his enthusiasms.

I suddenly hear the echo of our last conversation. Hear him pleading with me to come and see the thing that he's found, the thing that's making him giddy and stopping him from sleeping, the thing that's making him forget to take his tablets and not eat the meals that his neighbour brings for him each day and for which I pay a grand a month.

I'll visit, I promise. I swear, Jethro, it's just so busy, but I'll come see you, I will. Of course I love you, but there's so much on at work…

My lip wobbles as I look at him. He deserves better. Deserves a hug and a smile and a few words that map out my delight at seeing him and my amazement that he made it all this way on his own. I can't give it to him. There's not enough kindness left in me. Not now. Not here.

I don't know what to do with my face. If I scowl at him he'll burst into tears. If I'm mean he'll dissolve and then I'll have to be kinder to him than I'm capable of. I can't meet his eyes or my own lip will start to wobble so I just stare past him and out into the chaotic, rain-jewelled darkness beyond the glass. Every surface seems to have been transformed into a funfair mirror: each surface throwing back concave reflections; streetlamps and headlights are turning the night air into a collage of gaudy shimmering spheres.

He's rambling, now. Making a show of himself. He looks wrong here, in this big, broad, brightly lit space. I can see our reflection in the darkened glass of the huge front doors. Can see myself with my hands on my hips, huffing and puffing like a mum at the school gates, trying to get him to lower his voice. He's much taller than me but he's stooping to accommodate the hefty, tatty rucksack on his back. He looks like Krampus, hobbled beneath the weight of his bag of naughty children.

I open my mouth to tell him that there's a café down the road, that he should head there and buy a hot chocolate and thaw himself out with the hand dryer in the disabled toilet. He doesn't let me get the words out. Catches his own reflection in the glass of a modern-art print on the wall behind me and raises his eyes. He cannot stand to see himself. Cannot stand to see what he has become.

I step back: kitten heels loud on the faux-marble floor. Take a moment to digest the full scale of his shabbiness. He looks bloody awful. It's nothing new, but Christ. I'm standing here in a grand's worth of Misha Nonoo and LK Bennett and he looks like he's been covered in glue and kicked around in a skip. There's a stink about him too: something fusty and bad, like yesterday's jellied eels or parsnips on the turn.

It's not the clothes; I'm not that shallow. He can wear what he likes. I'm all for self-expression and if he feels comfortable in his patched-up vagabond cords and stained anorak then good for him. But he doesn't look eccentric, he looks mad. And Jethro isn't supposed to look mad – not if he wants to stay in his little house and take care of himself the way he says he wants to. All he has to do is stay home, take his tablets, eat the food I have delivered for him and get himself to his appointments without a fuss. It's not a lot to ask.

'Mercy, Jethro,' I mutter, looking him up and down. My smile appears unbidden: a carp rising to snatch a dragonfly from the surface of a pond. 'It's a good job I changed my outfit. I was wearing that same ensemble this morning.'

He grins, dirt-streaked cheeks creasing into familiar folds. He's red-faced, blue-eyed; pupils little more than pinpricks in the glacial mist of his irises. His shoulders shake for a moment as he gives in to a torrent of silent tears, and then he's sniffing and smiling and making fun of himself again. He has been this way ever since the accident. Has been my problem since Mum gave up and went back to France and left me the responsibility of keeping him alive.

'I didn't think... I had a clean jumper, I think, but then I thought I'd need a shirt, but you wouldn't see it was clean if I put it under the jumper so I wore it on top, but then I thought that might look odd so I put a waistcoat on but that had a cherry brandy in the pocket and I thought it might slosh when I walked so I drank that and then I felt bad and realised I should have poured it out but then that would have splashed my shoes so I changed into the rubber plimsolls but I hadn't cut my toenails so I had to cut through the plimsolls to reach them with the scissors and then they were broken so I used the gaffer tape...'

I put my face in my hands. It's like he's made up of half-finished projects: the oddments snatched from a mound of other people's discarded eccentricities. His beard's not really a beard, just a patchy smattering of vaguely pubic spider legs. It only seems to grow with any degree of luxuriance around his Adam's apple, where it sprouts in an absurdly thick patch of coarse whiteness. His glasses are an amalgam of two different pairs of spectacles, held together across the bridge with a twisted paper clip. One is thick as the bottom of a pickle jar: the other a more feminine frame with a feline sleekness. And the hat! Jesus, the hat. He's sewn ear flaps onto a flat cap and they dangle loosely down the side of his face, fluttering and flapping whenever he turns into the wind and looking a lot like a spaniel on a speedboat.

'He's looking at me,' says Jethro, jerking his head towards the reception desk. I step into his line of sight, bringing his attention back to me. I glance behind me. Sure enough, the security guard's staring. He's got his arms folded. He's broad across the shoulders and there's a tattoo climbing over the collar of his blue, logo-embossed V-neck jumper and up the bovine thickness of his neck. He's regarding Jethro with a sort of mild detachment: paying attention but displaying no outward signs of any urge to get involved.

The Spanish girl on reception keeps flicking her eyes over to where we stand: tucked away behind the huge vase of lilies and the horseshoe of luridly coloured chairs. I can't help but wonder what she's thinking. I'd fought an overwhelming need to explain myself to her as I clip-clopped across the wooden floor and flicked my security badge over the scanner. I almost wanted to make sense of him for her.

I could have made it easy. *He's my brother. He's brilliant. He's got an IQ of 188 and three doctorates. He's a kind, caring, slightly batty man and London scares him. I haven't got time for him and I'm horribly embarrassed that he's come to my place of work where I've spent the past two years cultivating an image of a polished professional and if you tell anybody about this, I swear I'll follow you home and hurt you in your sleep.*

I don't say any of it. I don't explain myself to anybody. I don't apologise unless there's mileage in it for me. I don't show weakness until I'm alone. And then I cry until there's nothing left.

'Could we talk, Moineau? I will try, I swear. I will keep on the straight and narrow path. It's important. Perhaps, at least. I don't know what's going on... It doesn't make sense...'

I don't take in any of what he's saying. He's so much bloody trouble and I'm too damn busy to listen as he explains some incredible thing he's found in some archive or textbook or dusty old grimoire. He keeps making the same discoveries over and over. He writes symphonies I already know. He finds paintings that he scribbled in his youth and imagines he has discovered some unappreciated master. Each day is full of new and wondrous discoveries for him, and he always wants to share them with the one person he never seems to forget. But he's never come all the way to my workplace before. Never shown me up like this.

'Jethro, why didn't you call ahead?' I say it with my eyes closed, trying to keep my tone as bright and carefree as I can. 'I mean, it's lovely to see you – it's always lovely, of course – but this is my place of work and I really do have far too much...'

He's nodding, his glasses slipping down his red-veined nose. He pushes them back up with his middle finger: a dirty Elastoplast covering the nail. His hands are filthy. There's writing on the back of them but he's moving his fingers so quickly that I can't make out what he's scrawled into the grime. I glance down at the floor. He's left a trail of muddy water behind him on his way from the double doors to the reception. I can't help but think of it as a snail trail: a line of ooze marking his passage.

'I didn't know,' he's saying. 'Wasn't sure, I mean. Sorry, sorry, I can't seem to get the words into the right order. It's been a little... Well, what's the word – I mean, it's more than unsettling, but rather less than debilitating. Is there a word for that? The Germans will have a word for that. Marvellous language. *Teutonophilia* – that's a word I rarely get to employ. A love for all things German. Though, of course, how can one have a love for all things. One must leave room for doubt...'

He stops. Scratches at his throat. I see that every one of his fingertips is wrapped in masking tape. He sees me looking and puts his hands into the pockets of his raincoat. I hear the clink of a glass on glass, and he gives me the twitchy little smile that makes him look, for a moment, like my big brother. And then it's gone.

'You don't look well, Jethro,' I say, flicking my hair behind my ear. 'You're taking the tablets, yes? And the lady – she's checking on you? You don't look like you've been eating.'

He ignores me. Looks me up and down. 'You don't look like you,' he says, accusingly. He reaches forward and for a moment I think he's going to do what he used to and start poking his fingers into my mouth and tugging at the skin beneath my eyes, looking for whoever's wearing me as a mask. He stops himself, twitching another toffee-toothed smile. 'Black. *Preto. Schwarz. Noir.* Black, yes? Why's your hair black? Your hair isn't black. You're a sparrow, not a crow. And you don't look comfortable. Those shoes will hurt your feet. Where are your glasses? You know contact lenses are dangerous. And the air around you – it hasn't got any colour.'

I wait for him to finish. Even like this, his mind astounds me. There's a colossal library of knowledge in his head but he has no control over which books present themselves for inspection at any given moment. His genius exhausts him. He stops talking, panting for breath. He looks all sad and sorry for himself. His bottom lip starts to go. I feel the sudden bloom of sympathy open up inside my chest; feel parts of myself threatening to come to life.

No, I tell myself. *No, you let yourself care and you'll let yourself down. Stop. Don't feel. Kill it. Push it down and kill it...*

The double doors open again as one of my colleagues pushes inside, letting in a blast of cold, rain-speckled air. I get a whiff of the river, of exhaust fumes and spilled oil, of beer and fried food and the low, sonorous hum of the rain-disturbed sewers. My colleague does a double take as she spots him. I can see her working him out. An activist? A new client, perhaps? An eccentric genius? She gives me a toothpaste-advert smile, manic and bright, then scurries across reception and swipes her pass against security. She makes a face at the guard, and he gives a reassuring nod. *Don't worry,* it says. *I've got this.*

I force myself to keep my hands at my sides. If I touch him I'll want to hug him, and if I hug him I'll cry. And if I cry then everything will come crashing down and I can't deal with that. Not yet. Not now. I'll break some other time. I'll crumble when it's convenient.

'I recognised him, you see,' mutters Jethro. 'Not who I thought. Or who I thought wasn't who he was. Sorry, sorry, that's all gobbledygook, isn't it? First used in 1944, gobbledygook – used by a congressman to describe politicians. Said it reminded him of turkeys gobbling. You'll know that, of course. Sorry – I'm not mansplaining. That's a new word, isn't it? Explaining, when one is a man.'

He twitches, his face contorting in pain. 'I don't know what I thought you would do. I look a little silly, I'll be bound. I shouldn't have... no, I'm sorry, I just didn't know where to...'

I take a breath. I know that if I were any kind of decent person, I would take him to one of the chairs and fetch him a tea and listen to what he has to tell me. I should get my coat and take him home, feed him and clean him up and find out what on earth he's doing here. I should be a decent sister or at the very least, a decent person.

'Okay,' I say, softening my voice and forcing myself to look into his eyes. 'I don't know what's happening but we're going to...'

He turns away from me mid-sentence. A shrill noise is spilling in through the open doors. I don't register it at first: the world outside is dark and cold and full of other people's business. But Jethro doesn't know London. Jethro lives alone in the dank green silence of the Fens. So the scream means something to him. The scream is a cry of distress, of fear, of somebody in need.

'It's okay, Jethro,' I say, reaching out instinctively. 'It won't be important...'

He turns back to me. There's something like disappointment in his eyes.

There are raised voices. Shouts. Screams building up layer on layer, different voices overlapping like roof tiles.

Jethro drops his bag and totters towards the front doors. The Thames is fifty feet away, across four lanes of static traffic. I raise my wrist to my nose, breathing in my perfume before the reek of the river can climb inside me. For a moment I'm on the bridge again, staring down into the darkness, breathing in the high, silvery reek of the water. I can taste my tears, taste the blood in my throat. I'm looking out through a caul of tears, swaying, swaying, my grip on the cold black metal slipping, slipping...

And then there is a man in the doorway. There's blood on his face and down the front of his bright yellow coat. Blood on his hands, too. Blood pooling on the impeccably clean floor.

Jethro puts out a hand; raises it up, palm-first, as if commanding a car to halt. There are four paces between them. Jethro says something that I can't quite make out, but it doesn't matter because suddenly all I can see is the knife in the bloodied man's hand.

I try to speak but the word dies on my tongue. The man looks towards me. Looks past Jethro and directly at me – his face twisting, contorting. For an instant it seems there are a multitude of creatures twisting within the bones and tissue of his face, as if beasts and demons were writhing within the prison of his skin. When he speaks, his tongue seems to twist in upon itself like a burning serpent. I don't know what he's saying, but I know the words are ancient. Powerful.

'...*pedes vermes, vermitudo interet...*'

He comes towards me in brisk, unhesitant strides, raising his arm, his coat flapping open to reveal the red, scarred tissue of his chest...

Jethro pulls him back. Puts his hand upon his shoulder and turns him around.

I cover my face as it happens. Fold in on myself as the man sticks the blade into my brother's belly. Slide down onto the cold ground as he carves upwards to his neck. Slashes across his chest.

I don't see what happens next. Don't see him stick the blade in the security guard's neck. Don't see him slip and tumble in the great treacly ocean of fresh blood. Don't see him run back out into the road, stumbling his way through the cars that can't part to let the fleet of police vehicles through. Don't see him stick one last victim: a young man jogging along the embankment, pausing to film the commotion on his mobile phone. He's stabbed twice in the chest and once in the side of the head. And then the attacker is up on the railings of the bridge, staring down into the waters, and police gunmen are telling him to drop the knife, drop the knife.

From the floor, I hear the shots. Hear the screams. I think, faintly, I even hear the splash.

When I finally open my eyes it's because the blood is lapping at my cheek.

2

La Forchetta, Bethnal Green Road, London

His name's Billy Dean. *William* on the birth certificate, but he's been Billy since he was a lad. He looks a Billy, too. Bright eyes, strong jaw, bit of a twinkle about him when he's in a good mood. Likes a pint, likes his football, knows which boxer would win in a pound-for-pound clash between the greats. He's heard all the jokes. Knows how to laugh at himself, though nobody pushes him too far. He's got a temper, has Billy.

It was Billy that she fell in love with; Billy who made Francesca Steadman giggle and squirm. Billy who made her eyes gleam with his romantic gestures and his silly sayings and his absolute belief that she would become all that she wanted to be. Billy who bent so far backwards to accommodate what she wanted that he very nearly broke in two.

It's William who's going to have to sign the divorce papers. William Michael Dean. And he'll do it, too. He'll definitely sign them. Just not now. Not here, in the moment, when she's sitting there looking so bloody perfect and cool and insisting he make both of their lives '*easier*' by simply ripping out his heart and placing it, still bloodily pumping, upon the piece of paper in front of her. Here, as she tells him that he's got one last opportunity to make her happy; to give her what she wants – to free her from something that has come to feel like a cage. To let her go.

He's willing to give her his whole life. He's willing to love her and walk by her side until the day he dies. But she doesn't want that. Doesn't want him as Billy, or as bloody William. Instead she wants a graphic designer called Adrien. Adri*en*, with a fucking 'e'.

Detective Sergeant Billy Dean chews on this thought. Chews on it like a wad of tobacco and forces himself not to spit. His stomach's sour and grumbling, hot acid rising up his oesophagus and burning his throat. The smells wafting through from the kitchen of the quiet little Italian restaurant are making him salivate, but he feels too sick to risk putting anything in his mouth. He can't seem to keep anything down these days. Nothing tastes right. His mouth always seems to be full of the taste of blood. He has to keep his hands in fists or they'll start to shake, but holding them so tightly leads to stiffness in his shoulders, which climbs up into his neck and across his head and across his broad, lined brow.

By early evening he always has a headache and is gasping for a drink that will numb the pain. But if he takes a drink, she wins. If he bristles at her use of his full name, she wins. If he threatens to harm Adrien, she wins. If he signs the divorce papers, she wins. He hasn't worked out a way in which he can avoid losing.

She's sitting across the table, looking so effortlessly beautiful that it fills his chest with a hot, tight pain. She's got a sparkling water with a wedge of lime and four ice cubes neatly balanced on top of one another. She looks slim and elegant in a cream suit over a silky, deep-blue blouse. She drank cider and blackcurrant in pint glasses when they met. Wore flared cords and little crop tops, dyed the tips of her hair purple and smoked Silk Cut. She preferred Blur to Oasis but liked Pulp best of all. She played bass guitar and used to Tipp-Ex little patterns onto her leather coat.

He can't remember when she became the person who sits across the table looking a proper grown-up. They're only forty-seven, for God's sake. He'd thought she was just pretending; just doing what she had to in order to fit in and give herself the best chance of advancement. But somewhere down the line she stopped being who she was and became who she is.

She makes him feel like a vagrant in comparison. His suit's a three-piece but the buttons strain a little over his stomach. There's a blob of something unidentifiable on his tie. The collar of his shirt is slightly folded in on itself, like the ear of a spaniel. He shaved this morning but it was a half-hearted affair, and there's a distinct shadow on his cheeks and neck. He got wet on the walk from the Tube and his thinning hair has dried flat. He's drinking a non-alcoholic beer. It frothed up when he took his first sip from the bottle, spilling over his hairy knuckles and creating a little pool of syrupy liquid. She mopped it up with a coaster. Didn't say a word.

'I know this is hard for you,' she says, in the detached way she's adopted since she stopped loving him. 'This is the last little power you can assert over me. But, William, you have to ask yourself, is this really the way you want the final chapter of our story to go? You have an opportunity here to be a real adult. To do something that hurts, okay, but which is the right thing for all involved. You have the chance to walk away from this with dignity and a genuinely fair settlement of our finances. I don't understand why you want this last little bout of petulance to be the legacy of our relationship.'

Billy screws up his eyes. Rubs his forehead. Pushes his hand through his hair. He's never been very good at finding the right words, but he's never had any trouble making himself understood. He just doesn't know how to turn all the hurt and rage and sorrow that's thudding inside his brain into a sentence that does it justice.

'I don't want a divorce,' he says, his teeth clamped together. 'I don't want it to be over. I don't want half of the equity in the house or a settlement of our joint assets. I want you, home. I want to wake up in our bed, roll over and see you there, smiling at me.'

'That hasn't been our life for a very long time,' she says, with a little shake of her head. 'You're remembering a life that died years ago.'

'And whose fault was that?' he asks, sitting forward on the uncomfortable chair. 'I tried! I never once stopped trying to make you feel like you used to…'

'Please,' she says, words wrapped around a sigh. 'Let's not go through this again. We grew apart. We had good times but what was there has gone. There's nothing to be gained by delaying the inevitable.'

'Life is about delaying the inevitable.' He scowls, biting down so hard that he hears something pop in his jaw. He lowers his head, feeling the heat behind his eyes. Even now, even after all that's happened over the past few months, he wants nothing more than to hold her. He wants to reach across the table, take her hand and make her look at him properly. He needs to look into those blue eyes and see if she's still in there, to try and connect with the last vestiges of the woman who loved him and loved him and loved him and then didn't even like him any more.

She shakes her head, exhausted by his stubbornness. She removes one of her pretty little gold earrings and rubs at her earlobe, pulling it, elongating it. She closes her eyes. He hopes that when she opens them again there will be a sheen upon her lenses: something that suggests this pains her, something he can cling to, some whiff of hope. There's nothing. She just stares at him, icy and detached.

'Please, Fran,' he says, sitting forward and trying to take her hand. 'Please, I can try harder. I can be whatever it is that you need me to be. I've tried so hard, you know that. All the galleries, the plays, the exhibitions, the dinner parties – I took up golf just because your mate's husband plays. I'm in a Hugo Boss suit, for God's sake. Brown-and-white brogues, even though I keep slipping over and they make me feel like I should be at a bowling alley. I love us enough for both of us. Just come home, please, Fran. Don't do this, don't do this...'

The tears start to fall. He starts jiggling both legs up and down against the table. He feels ashamed of himself, disgusted by the sight he must present. And the shame becomes anger as quick as it did when he was still drinking. He feels himself about to smash his fists down on the table, to scream in her face through locked teeth, to tell her that she's a whore and a bitch and a slut and froth a great spray of venom in her perfect face.

'There he is,' she says, scorn curling her lip. 'There's my Billy Dean. That little flicker, that flash of who's underneath. That's why all the things you tried to change never made any difference. It's because it was all pretend. It made no difference to who's underneath. You're the same person you were twenty years ago. God, Billy, you could have been a detective superintendent by now.'

He sits back, throat dry. 'How could I, Fran? If we'd put my career first, then you wouldn't have had the opportunities you've had. We made a choice. You're the career animal – you're the one with those ambitions. I want to catch villains. That's what matters to me most. I achieved all my dreams when I married you!'

'Oh for God's sake, Billy…'

There's a moment when something flickers in her face, as if a petal has landed upon the surface of a still pond. There's a flicker of something he recognises, the merest whiff of true emotion. And then she's shaking it away, distracted and irritated with herself. He becomes aware of the sound of buzzing: her phone, in the expensive handbag on the back of her chair. He feels his own phone, damp in the pocket of his clammy, itchy trousers. Feels it vibrate against his leg.

She holds up her hand in the faintest gesture of apology. Pulls out the phone.

'Detective Superintendent Cesca Steadman,' she says, her voice sounding clear, clipped and professional.

Billy scowls into the neck of his beer. He didn't mind that she kept her name when they got married. But she used to be Fran. She started calling herself 'Cesca' around the same time she took up Pilates and started thinking of hummus and edamame beans as an actual lunch. That was when she first began introducing him to her friends as 'my husband, William'. He'd played along, thinking they were both enjoying the same joke. By the time he realised she was serious, she was three rungs above him on the career ladder and had come to the conclusion, quite independently, that they weren't ever going to have children. He'd been willing to accept those terms, provided she continued to love him. To be his Fran, like he was 'her Billy'.

He pulls his own phone from his pocket, irritated at the interruption. As he does so he gives a quick glance in the direction of the handful of other diners. Have they seen him make a show of himself? There's a couple at the nearest table, ploughing through a pizza and a carafe of house red. She's eating with a knife and fork – he's folding the slices with his fingers and eating them by hand. They're talking about stair carpets, talking about seagrass and hessian and whether or not the kids could be trusted with a lighter shade. Billy feels a surge of jealousy.

He turns his attention back to his soon-to-be-ex-wife. Her face is inscrutable as ever but there's a tension in her voice that he knows of old. This is important.

'...and how many injured?' she's asking, tucking the phone under her chin and retrieving a pen from her jacket. She starts to scribble on the pristine white napkin. 'Situation still live, yes? Yes, I know the building. The underwater search unit... right, no... and it was a foreign accent, you're certain... well, yes, of course. No, pays to be careful... sensitivities, of course... I've got a good relationship with the counter-terrorism lead, yes... yes, sir, of course...'

Billy stares at his phone. There are little icons on the screen, capital letters screaming headlines under the banner 'BREAKING NEWS'.

He answers the call. It's DCI Jim Mosley, his friend and boss.

'Billy, mate, it's Jimbo. Suspected terrorist attack down by the river, embankment way. Multiple dead. Borough commander is pushing for us to take it, but we might be underneath the wife, as it were. You cool with that before I confirm?'

He looks across the table. At Fran. At Cesca. At the divorce papers lying unsigned on the beery tabletop.

'I'm in,' he says.

THREE DEAD AFTER ATTACK BY MASKED MANIAC SHOUTING 'IN FOREIGN TONGUE'

Live report by **Chief Crime Reporter Lis-Jayne Bingham** and *London Echo* staff

TERROR returned to the streets of London today when a masked attacker stabbed three people dead and left an unknown number of others fighting for life.

Armed response officers are understood to have

opened fire on the suspect as he attempted to flee the scene of the slaughter.

Confusion now surrounds the fate of the suspected attacker, who was seen to plunge from Blackfriars Bridge into the Thames just moments after specialist firearms officers ordered him to drop his weapon. Witnesses report hearing four gunshots.

Information received by this publication suggest that the mayhem began in Victoria Embankment Gardens – an area of Victorian parkland popular with London's large homeless community. A spokesman for the Metropolitan Police was unable to confirm or deny reports that the victims of the atrocity were congregating in the area waiting for their daily meal to be served up at the nearby soup kitchen.

Police received their first report of violence at 4.31 p.m. The final shot was fired at 4.46 p.m.

It is understood that the second wave of violence took place in the reception area of Mount Carmel House, a large office building on the Thames Embankment, which is home to a large publishing house and a communications agency. Police have yet to rule out a terrorist connection and witnesses report that the attacker was shouting in a foreign language as he lashed out at passers-by.

Lawyer Devon Subramanian, whose office overlooks the area where the bloodshed began, told this publication: 'It will stay with me forever. There are always lots of homeless people in that little area. They don't do any harm and there's never any real trouble. It just flared up out of nothing. One moment there were half a dozen of them just sitting around and trying to stay out of the rain, and the next this madman is sticking a knife into people. I heard the shouting and looked out of the window, and he was on top of this poor guy who was just laid out on his back with his arms out and the attacker was pushing the knife into him. When he looked up it was like something out of a film. He had a mask on, I think, but it was getting dark and with the rain and the blood it was impossible to say. I know what he was shouting sounded like it was in some foreign tongue.

'Somebody tried to grab him and he stuck the knife in them without a word. People started running. Screaming. There was blood everywhere. A couple of workmen looked like they were trying to get near enough to grab him, but he was swiping with his knife, screaming something I couldn't understand. Then he just sprinted off. We all heard the shots a little later. What we didn't know was that he'd dashed in at the big building by the bridge and gone for the first people he saw. It was genuinely horrific.'

Among the injured is security guard Kenzie Hamilton, 31, who used his body as a human shield to protect bystanders caught up in the slaughter. He is being treated for life-threatening injuries. A 52-year-old, believed to have been sheltering within Mount Carmel House, was pronounced dead at the scene.

Politicians are already under fire for their perceived failure to come down harder on suspected terrorists after a string of high-profile attacks in London and across the UK.

Reports just in suggest that the attacker slashed a passer-by across the throat while attempting to flee the police and that the deadly incident was streamed live on the victim's mobile phone. A spokesman for the mayor's office said...

3

Sixty-eight hours later. I think I've slept for three. The rest of it has been statements and interviews, hospitals and police stations; showers and endlessly trilling phones.

It was a madman, they say. A *random*. A nutter off the street. He killed three others before he made his way into our building: a moth heading for the brightest light. Committed acts of unspeakable violence because the voices in his head told him to. Snatched away lives because he forgot to take his medication, and his local mental health team hadn't had enough phone operators to talk him out of bloodshed. Unsullied by facts, the story's writing itself. There'll be answers, in the end. There'll be an explanation. There'll be lessons learned. But Jethro will still be dead.

Jethro.

My big brother.

My hero, once upon a time.

The last person to love me.

Is there a name for somebody orphaned of tenderness? They're all gone, now. Mum, Dad. Two ex-partners, long since married to better people than me. You – the daughter who never took a breath. I called you Esmerelda, though nobody else ever will. Six pounds seven ounces of perfectly inanimate child. Blue and pink and fair in your stillness: exquisite in my immaculate failure.

Jethro too, now. The last to love me. The last to wish me well. Dead on a slab, empty and grey: a Y-shaped incision in his flimsy chest and absolutely nothing inside the raw red fist of his static heart.

There was a newspaper on the table on the train. It looked odd, sitting there: an anachronism – something from a different time. Who still buys newspapers? Magazines? Books? I hadn't been able to help myself from picking it up and rubbing the pages between finger and thumb. Jethro's picture was on page five. Another tribute piece. This one from Reverend Struan Talbot. Said Jethro was a 'brilliant, kind and troubled soul' who could have become anything he wished had he not suffered with such ill health.

It was a thinly veiled euphemism. So too 'the accident' that occurred when Jethro was in his final year at Cambridge. He fell from the roof of a little village church, St Wendreth's – his survival the cruellest of miracles. We always knew that he jumped. Jethro didn't remember any of it afterwards – why he'd done it or how he'd got up there. Didn't remember much of anything after a recovery that wasn't far short of a resurrection.

He was still the cleverest person I'd ever met but he couldn't get his thoughts in order. Couldn't see things through. Couldn't concentrate. Couldn't live without help. Had it been Dr Talbot who helped with the money for his care? The name sounds familiar. A memory stirred as I sat there, holding the paper open as if reading a map. He'd been one of Jethro's lecturers at university, I think. He came to the hospital several times while Jethro was on life support. Sat with him. Held his hand. Prayed.

I was just a kid at the time. They called me out of boarding school to tell me what had happened. One of the pastoral staff drove me to the hospital. Told me it was okay to cry. Told me she had an uncle who'd done the same thing. Told me that mental illness was no more to be ashamed of than cancer or arthritis. She was nice. I wish she'd been my mum.

I blink it away. Shake off the memory and look back to the road.

I shouldn't be driving. Haven't been behind the wheel in months and these heels get stuck in the rubber mats when I stamp on the brakes. Shouldn't be wearing them. Shouldn't be dressed for work. Black trousers, black top, mulberry-coloured bag – I look like I'm on my way to a meeting. Should have put on something comfy, something casual, but then people might think I'm local, or a tourist, and I'm neither of those things. I need to be passing through. Need to be somebody from London who's popping back to complete a burdensome task before zipping back to where they belong.

I think I might still be a bit drunk from the two cans of whisky and ginger that I downed on the train. I could use some food, but my stomach feels like it's full of eels and the thought of putting anything solid on my tongue makes me retch. So I squint through the rain and hold the wheel as if strangling a snake. I tried to apply some nail polish on the journey up but my hands were trembling so much and the little droplets of red were too hard to look at, so I wiped it off with a napkin. Same with the lipstick. It looked too stark against the paper-whiteness of my face, the crow-black of my hair. My reflection in the train toilet showed somebody unfamiliar: all freckles and burst capillaries, dark shadows and sunken cheeks.

I'm on a road I half remember, somewhere between Wisbech and the little village with the funny church. I remember some of the landmarks, but everything seems to have been turned about and rearranged since I was anything approximating a local. I slow down instinctively as I approach a gap in the thick line of trees to my right. My muscles remember even if my brain is too muddled to keep up. There's a farm here, half a mile down a rutted track, barely visible through the skein of hazy rain. I'm an *enfant* again. Lonely. Scared. A French girl trying to be English after a lifetime of feeling English in France.

I feel something rising inside me. It's not just grief, it's deeper than that. Something that's all shame and rage and impotence. I screw up my eyes before my mind can fill with pictures of my brother: pictures from life where I treated him as burden and a nuisance, or images of his death: his body emptying redly across the white floor of the lobby.

I open my mouth as wide as it will go: a silent scream that makes my jaw click at the hinge. Fumble for the wipers as the rain doubles its assault on the glass. This is Jethro's car: a boxy blue Volvo with a dent in the passenger door and a crack running all the way down the windscreen. There were two parking tickets under the wipers when I picked it up from the rear of the bus station where he'd left it. He could never handle motorway driving – the fact that he'd passed his test was largely due to a brief period of mental clarity and a kindly examiner. Sliding onto the driving seat had felt like sitting on his knee. It smells of him.

Looks like him. The seats are ripped and there's stuffing poking out between gaps in the gaffer tape. The back seat is all books and Tupperware containers, random animal treats and carrier bags full of photocopied pages. I haven't looked in the boot yet. Haven't rummaged through the glove box. I can't face any of it. Can't do the one thing I'm here to do.

I play with the radio. It's tuned to Radio Three. Jethro didn't drive very much but, when he did, he liked to listen to sounds that soothed him. Talk radio made him cross and he didn't have a taste for modern music. Radio Three was safe – bland but intellectual conversation interspersed with music that felt like stroking a cat.

I can't find any London stations on the dial. I rummage in my handbag for my phone. Four missed calls and too many emails to contend with. I fiddle with the screen and find LBC, but the wireless connection won't pick up and I'm left listening to empty air.

I wind the window down, an action that feels oddly comforting: some nostalgic whiff from a kinder time. I feel the rain and the cold air on my face. Breathe in deep, trying to let the breeze sweep the dust and cobwebs from my mind. I fill myself up with the scents of the Fens. Of childhood. Of home. The old fens are gone, drained long before I first drew breath. But the air carries their echo, the atmosphere somehow tainted bottle green. The air here smacks of ancient wilderness – the flat green fields seeming no more than a quilted blanket thrown over the ancient marshes beneath. The world feels bottomless here: a place of tall reeds and deep, rotten darkness. I smell marshes and decay beneath the clean crisp ozone of the falling rain.

Beside me my phone blasts into life as it finally picks up

a signal. There's a cattery a little further ahead – a once-grand farmhouse transformed into a hotel for pampered pets. They let Jethro work there, for a time. He enjoyed it at first. Loved the responsibility and the chance to care. It was letting go that hurt him. He disliked the act of giving the animals back to their owners. They were happy where they were, he'd claimed. Happy with him. I had to make a donation to the charity of the owner's choice when he befriended a three-year-old Korat and took it home.

'...police are still searching for the man behind the murderous rampage carried out in the shadows of London's Blackfriars Bridge.

'Police believe specialist armed response officers shot and killed the man thought to be responsible for the gruesome knife attack that has rocked the capital. However, the suspect fell from the bridge after the brutal five-minute killing spree and he has not yet been identified, or his body found.

'Police have been unable to rule out a terrorist motive and admitted at a briefing this morning that they have no leads as to who the man was, or what sparked the bloodshed.

'Four people were killed and a further five injured during the incident. One of the dead has been named as twenty-four-year-old Alexander Lomas, whose death was streamed live on his mobile phone in the moments before the Blackfriars Bridge shooting. It is understood that another of the victims was fifty-two-year-old Jethro Cadjou. Cadjou, older brother of Claudine Cadjou, a former director of communications for the failed Vote Remain campaign and a well-known political lobbyist.

'Questions were asked in the Commons yesterday about recent police budget cuts and...'

I lose the signal as I turn off the winding road, edging left through a gap in the hedgerows, and the tyres find the familiar grooves in the muddy road that runs beside the little river. The landscape is entirely man-made but there are places where the river still follows its natural course. This little patch of waterway, shielded by a spear wall of reeds, drifts into a darker, older part of the marshes. Nobody comes here unless it's where they're looking for. And nobody comes looking.

There's a house set back from the trees about half a mile down the track: a dark, soot-smudged old vicarage with a mossed-over roof and a scribble of black smoke rising from the red chimney. There are dogs running around and barking in the front yard: a colossal ridgeback standing with its front paws on the bonnet of a little white car.

I should stop, really. She'll want to know the latest. Will want to know if they've caught the person who did it. She'll offer tea and kindness and I can't face any of it. I touch my foot to the accelerator and carry on up the sweep of road. Memories fall like leaves. For an instant I'm – a kid again and *Maman* is telling me that this is where we live now: a place of witches and frogs and chattering magpies, tucked away where nobody will find us and nobody will look. It will be her and me and Jethro, and Jethro will get well, here. It will help him feel safe and peaceful and close to nature and, because I love him, I will be a good girl and won't cry and won't ask to go home to Papa and the cats and the apartment with the ceiling rose and the smell of fresh-cut roses and warm madeleines.

And then I'm looking at our house: Glavers Cottage. It's derelict. Slack-walled and neglected, as though the last owners walked out one day and simply didn't come back, leaving it to the elements and the birds and the creeping nearness of the deep black water. It's got worse since the last time I visited. There are more holes in the roof tiles, a true waterfall of dirty rain spilling from the blocked gutters. There's barely any paint on the rotten wooden door and there are mildewed squares of white fabric nailed up in front of the slitted, squinting windows. A scraggle of ivy rises from a mess of nettles. Bramble bushes climb up the sodden brickwork towards the roof; its uppermost leaves almost touch the tuberous roots of some unidentifiable plant that has started sprouting from a hole.

There's a little barn and an outhouse around the back: rust-and-red corrugated panels sagging inwards and the door hanging from one hinge.

The silence when I switch off the engine is absolute. It's as if I've been wrapped in a thick muslin cloth, uncomfortably swaddled by air so thick it seems to hold me in my seat. My hands tremble as I reach for the door handle. I start to hear my own breathing. Hear the soft buzz of the insects, the soft whisper of the leaves. There is an overwhelming feeling of awkward reunion; a sense that the house is squinting down at me, accusing, asking where I've been, how I could let it come to this – wanting to know whether its custodian will return soon, if he's well, if he will soon be back where he belongs.

I stand for a moment half in and half out of the car. I shouldn't have come. Should have sent somebody on my behalf. Should have stayed in London. Should never have come back.

A grey cat slinks out from behind Jethro's long-idle

motorcycle: a collage of rust and leather leaning against the little brick outhouse just beyond the far wall. The animal looks well fed and healthy: green eyes and the sort of face that makes me think of a jewelled sultan in a harem. She pads towards me, stepping between puddles and cracks without taking her eyes off me.

'Hello, Bibi,' I say, softly, bending down to pet her. She purrs. Rubs her face against my bare leg; soft, damp fur against my skin. I tickle her under the chin. She drops something at my feet. I let out an unexpected laugh as I take in the unwelcome gift – a dormouse head, perfectly bitten through at the neck, face preserved in a look of astonishment and fright.

'What do you expect me to do with this?' I ask, scooping her up and holding her, pressing her face to mine. 'You know already, don't you,' I mutter, in her ear. I feel her claws pricking at my skin through the light material of my sweater. 'I'm so sorry, Bibi. He won't be back. He's gone, he's gone.'

She lets me hold her as I make my way to the front door. Nuzzles against me until the moment my hand is on the cold metal of padlock beneath the door handle. Then she bites me. It's so unexpected that for a moment there's no pain: just the sensation of skin being tugged and torn. I drop her like a sack of old cloths, hissing noiselessly as I register the sudden sharp sting of her teeth closing around the webbing between my forefinger and thumb. A perfect crunch that draws an instant circle of brimming blood. I think of rubies, of Mum's garnet chain. Think of all that has been taken from me these past years. All that I've given up, all that I've lost.

I raise my hand to my mouth. Suck on the copper-and-offal reek of my own spilled blood.

The pain leans against the dam of my defences. I feel the prickle of hot tears. The constricting of my throat. The gooseflesh rising on my shoulders and behind my knees.

The dam breaks. The tears fall.

Only now do I sob for him.

Bibi climbs back into my arms. Lets me hold her. I feel her rough tongue upon my pierced skin. Stroke her neck as I weep.

'Thank you, *ma chérie*,' I say, softly, through the sobs and the snot. 'Thank you.'

4

A small, dark, sticky little space on the second floor of the British Transport Police HQ, Camden Road, London.

'This is Billy,' says Jim, distractedly, one hand on his forehead and the other jabbing a message into his mobile. Billy stands next to him, unsure whether there will be more. His DCI briefly gives both men a moment of his attention. Seems to recall that he was in the process of introducing his detective sergeant to the plump-faced, soot-eyed constable who sits behind the bank of computer screens with an air of pathological gormlessness. 'Detective Sergeant Dean, as it were. He's a good chap. Don't upset him. Could you give him a quick update and he can filter back what I need to hear? Yeah. Right. That'll do, ta.'

Billy casts a quick glance around the dark, joyless space. It suits his mood. He throws angry eyes at Detective Constable Gordon Remus and concludes, based on first impressions, that he's an irritating twat. Remus has been sitting here for the past three hours, working his way through a pile of disks that contain the security footage from the car park at the rear of the investment bank behind Mount Carmel House.

There's a huge unit of digital forensic officers scanning through endless hours of CCTV and speed camera footage but they do so on relatively up-to-date machines and can access the recordings digitally. Footage obtained from private companies and individuals can usually be transferred via a compressed digital file. But occasionally, the recordings are pressed straight to a disk and there's only one little office with the facilities to play them. It has VCR and MiniDisc facilities too, as well as tape decks for audio files. The last time Billy was here he'd seen somebody wearing a Sony Walkman. It's like a little museum to obsolete technology.

'Billy Dean?' asks Remus, his accent pure West Midlands. He grins, as something strikes him as funny. 'Shouldn't the tiles light up when you walk on them?'

'What's that, son?' asks Billy, who's heard it all before.

Remus grabs his crotch. Says something that might be *'shamaw!'* He follows it up with a high-pitched *'hee-hee!'* when Billy doesn't smile. Pulls a face. 'Jacko? Billie Jean?'

'Shall we crack on?' asks Billy, pulling up a chair and sitting down. He hasn't been to sleep yet. He's dressed as he was in the restaurant. He and Fran departed in opposite directions, bound for different offices. They'd stopped talking about themselves the moment they heard about the atrocities down by the river. They didn't get the chance to speak again, just fielded calls and absorbed information and slotted into their natural place within the chain of command.

Fran gave orders into her phone. They filtered through the system and arrived, heavily augmented, on Billy's mobile moments later. They left without saying goodbye. As a detective superintendent with British Transport Police,

Cesca Steadman is a major part of the senior leadership team, heavily involved in making strategic decisions, apportioning manpower and implementing agreed protocols across the multi-agency task force. Billy, as a detective sergeant within Murder Investigation Team C, doesn't have to consider such things. He just has the job of catching the bastard who did it.

'Anything yet?' asks Billy, nodding at the screen.

'Not a sausage,' says Remus, making a face and shaking his head. He reaches across for a can of pop. Puts it to his lips and growls his dissatisfaction. 'Run aground,' he mutters, and throws the empty can into the bin in the corner of the room. It misses by three feet.

'Can I help?' asks Billy, rubbing his jaw. The headache is there already, rising up into his temples, bulging behind his eyes. He managed to consume some chicken soup around four a.m., sitting up, wide-eyed and drowsy, in front of the TV in his cold, half-empty living room. He had one of her coats wrapped around him. It's lost her smell, but it still brings him comfort. He can't get into their bed without her. Doesn't like going upstairs unless he has to. Just sits and watches whatever he can stomach, throat afire, eyes leaking tears as if his brain were a leaking sponge.

'You can yell the DCI that I'm wasting my bloody time, if you like,' grumbles Remus. 'We've got the bugger's movements. No car. No alternative route. We've got him nigh on every second of the way.'

Billy decides he definitely doesn't like the junior officer. Up close, he's got a whiff about him: bacon crisps and body odour. Billy's here to act as a liaison between the DCI and the team under his direct command. He's got a dozen detective constables and more civilian staff at his disposal and it's Billy's job to make sure that those higher up the chain are kept informed of developments while not being overloaded. He's good at it. He's been involved in almost thirty murder investigations, and he's held in some esteem by those above him and below. He doesn't hide the fact that he's married to a very senior officer. He's always been proud to tell people that the trainee PC with whom he went through basic training is not just his wife, but also somebody he has to officially call 'ma'am'.

Only Jim and a couple of other old pals know that the marriage is over. He'd love to overhear somebody gossiping about it, would love to hear what people really think. He doesn't know how he'd react. Temper, probably. Always temper.

'Briefing's at eight,' says Billy, giving his attention to the screen in front of him. It shows an underground car park: expensive vehicles parked in wide spaces, big enough to open both doors without the risk of dinging the next vehicle over.

'More of the same, no doubt,' says Remus, stifling a burp. He performs an elaborate stretch, his arm coming uncomfortably close to Billy's face.

He wonders if Jim's put him in here as some sort of wind-up. Or worse, whether this is a test. Is he okay? Can he keep himself from losing his cool in the face of provocation? Jim knows, almost as well as Fran, that Billy Dean has a rage within him. He's prickly. Fiery, even. He doesn't mind a scrap, if the situation calls for it. He'll get stuck in. He doesn't want to fight, not really, but if the opportunity arises, well...

'You sound bored, Constable,' says Billy, glaring at him. 'Somewhere you'd rather be, is there? More important things to do? Brutal multiple murders ten-a-penny in your world?'

'Leave off,' says Remus, his face twisting. 'I'm doing my job aren't I? I've been awake nineteen hours. Can't I have a bloody grumble?'

Billy doesn't reply. Licks his lips and jerks his head towards the screen again. 'Run all the plates, I presume?'

'Not on my list.' He shrugs. 'Can do it if you tell me to, but when there's a review talking about duplication of workloads, don't go blaming me.'

Billy takes a moment to chew on his thoughts. Decides that he probably shouldn't punch the chap in the side of the head just yet. He wants something to look forward to later in the day.

'He didn't make it, if you're wondering,' says Billy, his eyes boring into the younger man's ear like a drill. 'Still touch and go on the security guard.'

'The one in the office, you mean?' asks Remus, showing a whiff of interest. 'Did you see the photographs of the wounds? He was never going to survive that. He was half empty.' He leans over the keyboard and logs in to the database, images reflecting on his glossy face as he flicks through the crime scene photographs. 'Neck to nuts,' he says, jabbing a fat finger on the screen. 'Another across the middle. Opened him like a box.'

Billy hasn't seen any photographs from the scene yet. He sits forward in his chair. The image on the screen shows a large, brightly lit reception area; yellowy tiles stained crimson with still-wet blood. A man in too many layers of mismatched clothes lies on his back, arms out as if crucified. Among the mangled skin and bisected flesh, Billy fancies he can see bone. He swallows. Closes his eyes and wishes the world were different.

'Stills from the bodycam,' adds Remus. 'Frame after frame and none of it pretty.' He flicks forward, showing the tactical officers and paramedics slipping and sliding in the spreading pool of blood. Billy sees a woman in an expensive suit. Dark hair, dark eyes. She sits with her legs drawn up, feet bare, hugging her knees. There's blood on her face.

'Who's that?' asks Billy, narrowing his eyes.

Remus reaches down and picks up a sheaf of papers, flicking through the hastily assembled briefing notes. 'Sister,' he says, jabbing at the screen. 'Claudine Cadjou. Thirty-eight. Works at…'

'I know her,' says Billy, chewing the inside of his cheek. He rubs his eyes. 'Political something-or-other, I think. Journalist, maybe?'

'Consultant in public affairs,' reads Remus, pronouncing the words as if they were a foreign language. 'Worked on Team Remain during the referendum. That might have been where you saw her. Looker, isn't she?'

Billy doesn't reply. Scowls at the screen, itching his tongue on his teeth.

'Wouldn't have them down as siblings, would you?' muses Remus, flicking from one image to the next. 'Family liaison took a statement last night. Cool as a cucumber, they said. Recovered sharpish, by the looks of things. Apparently he'd never been to her place of work before.'

'That's her office, is it?'

'Public relations, media management and whatnot. High

up. Plenty of money. Three-bedroomed house in Cheam. Company car. Important, if you can actually be important in that line of work.'

Billy rubs at his jaw. Grinds his teeth. She seems so familiar to him. He isn't sure if it's her he recognises, or just her general air. She looks slick; well-groomed; self-assured, even as she stares at the leaking body of her brother. There's a coolness about her that makes him think of Fran's new friends. He doesn't think he would like her. Fancies she would make him feel uncouth and messy and nowhere near good enough.

'Did I hear he lives out in the middle of nowhere?' asks Billy, looking again at the dying man. He's skimmed the briefing documents, trying to get up to speed as quickly as possible. Everything is still a mess. They haven't recovered the body of the man who fell from the bridge yet. They haven't got a full ID for the first two victims. They know that the man killed in the atrium of Mount Carmel House is one Jethro Cadjou, but there's barely enough hard intelligence to put out a press release and the politicians are already demanding answers.

'South Holland,' says Remus, looking at his notes. 'Lincolnshire, not Netherlands. Glavers Cottage, Dead End Lane. Nearest place with a postcode is called Little Mercy. Christ, we live in a weird country, don't we?'

'Really?' asks Billy, managing a grimace of a smile. 'Dead End Lane?'

'The sister said he's been back there a few years. Bit of a hermit, apparently. Never comes to London. Lived in a sort of sheltered housing place for years then moved back into this place. Couldn't find it on Google Maps but it's almost off the edge of the map. Satellite images show its all reeds and marshes. Not far off a swamp.' He moves his fingers over the keys and pulls up an image that is all greens and browns. A stretch of water forms a wiggly outline around a little lump of land, accessible only over a rickety bridge. 'If the wife booked that for a weekend away, I'd reckon she was planning on doing me in,' says Remus, stretching.

Billy rummages in his inside pocket and pulls out a handful of soggy pieces of paper. Receipts from the pharmacy and Tesco Express, a parking fine, a letter from his mobile phone provider insisting he and Fran are locked in to a joint contract for the next nineteen months and their separation will not change the status quo.

He picks up a loose pen from the desktop and jots down a couple of things he wants to make sure he remembers. He has a good memory. He doesn't like taking notes in public. He's slightly dyslexic and doesn't like the idea of people writing him off as a halfwit just because his spelling isn't perfect. He always makes sure he types up his notes as soon as privacy permits. The approach has come in handy on several occasions. Even the most assiduous of police officers occasionally needs to write down things as they should have happened, rather than as they did.

'Sheltered housing?' asks Billy, looking up.

'I think Helen is working on the victim profile,' says Remus. 'Do you know Helen?'

'Savage?' grunts Billy. 'Yeah. Big hair. Sweet. Mumsy sort.'

'That's her. She'll be reporting to you, I'd imagine.'

Billy shrugs. He knows from past experience that the biggest problem a large investigation faces is how unwieldy the operation can become. Too often work is duplicated or assumptions are made about whose remit a certain task falls within. Leads aren't followed up, or else they're completed in triplicate by officers following different lines of inquiry.

'IOPC will be trampling all over us after nine, no doubt,' grumbles Remus. 'Nowt worse, is there?'

Billy grunts. He's been investigated by the Independent Office for Police Conduct before. The discharge of the police firearms guarantees its immediate involvement, ensuring a difficult inquiry will be even more heavily scrutinised.

'Let the arguments commence,' mutters Billy. He has no doubt there will be rows as the different strands of the investigation overlap. He remembers the riots of a decade ago, caused in no small part because the IOPC, ever eager to be top dog, omitted to tell the family of a well-liked Londoner that he'd been shot and killed by police.

'Hello there,' says Remus, brightly. On the screen, Claudine Cadjou is walking through the car park. She wears gym clothes: trainers, leggings, a hoodie. She stops at a parked Mercedes and the lights flash twice as she presses the button on her keys. She retrieves a bag from the boot and then climbs into the rear seat. Three minutes later she emerges, dressed in an elegant black dress and a short velvet jacket. She glances upwards. Billy leans forward and pauses the video. She's done her make-up. Dolled herself up. He glances at the timestamp in the corner of the screen. 'Four hours?' he asks, doing the maths.

'They'll have bagged her clothes,' says Remus. 'She'll have changed into her gym stuff or her running clothes, I suppose. Maybe just wanted to feel like herself after all that she'd just seen.'

'She didn't go to the hospital? She wasn't at the hospital with her brother?'

'Busy giving a statement,' says Remus. 'Helpful enough. In shock, according to the first responders. She confirmed what the witnesses said down at the little park where it started. Foreign language. You reckon it's a terrorist?'

'I don't reckon anything,' says Billy, glaring at the well-dressed, coolly beautiful woman who stares up from the screen. God, she reminds him of who Fran's trying to be. 'I do my job and gather the evidence and see where it takes us.'

'Witnesses said it didn't sound Muslim.' Remus shrugs.

'Muslim isn't a language, you dickhead.'

'Eh? Oh well, you know. *Allah Akbar* and all that shit – the sort that puts the fear of God, or Allah, I suppose, into us infidels.'

Billy looks across at the junior officer and wonders whether he's trying to be provocative. Has he been told by Jim to push his buttons and see how he reacts? Another thought streaks through his mind. Perhaps Fran has insisted upon this little union. Perhaps his wife has insisted he be kept out of the way in a quiet little cubbyhole with an officer guaranteed to wind him up. Is this what she wants? Is she trying to get him to lose his temper and smack the prick; lose his job and his pension and end up on the streets so she can move Adrien into the house and start shagging him in the marital bed? He grimaces, sick rising up his throat, headache pounding in his head. He won't have it. Won't let them. Won't stand for being treated like an arsehole when all he wants to do is go back to how things were. They made vows! Swore that it would be for better or for worse.

'You all right, Billy?' asks Remus, looking at him.

Billy realises he's kneading his temples with his fingertips, eyes closed, face locked in a sneer. He shakes his head, trying to make the thoughts fade. But he's left with the echo of an imagined betrayal. Feels hungry and weak and nauseous all at once. God how he wants a drink. Fourteen months sober, just to prove to her that he needed nothing to fill the gaps in himself except for her. She'd smiled that nasty smile when she told him she was leaving him. Told him that at least now he could get himself back on the vodka that had sustained him through his thirties. He's so far refused to give her the satisfaction. But the thirst is growing.

'Billy?'

Billy shakes his head again. Stands up sharply, his chair clattering back behind him. 'Yeah, right, cheers…'

He stumbles from the room, his vision shredding as if somebody were tearing a photograph into pieces before his eyes. Clatters down the long corridor and into the toilets, stumbling into the first cubicle and lifting the seat. He falls to his knees and dry-heaves into the bowl, the agony in his head briefly receding as he emits pitiful strings of watery bile. His guts twitch. His throat burns. He holds his tie in his fist as if throttling an eel.

Presses his face to the cold porcelain and cries, silently, until he's empty. Then he stands, wipes his eyes, and flushes the toilet. Walks, unsteadily, to the sink and washes his face. There are no paper towels in the dispenser so he looks in his pockets for something he can dry himself with. Finds his notes. Looks, through blurry eyes and a mist of water, at the few words he jotted down. '*Cross-shaped wounds. Crucifix? Sheltered housing. Never been to London before. Sister too cool by half...*'

He wipes his face with his sleeve.

Goes back to work.

5

The rain starts coming down harder while I'm fiddling with the padlock, the haze of damp air abruptly reassembling itself – thickening, dilating – immaculate in its rearrangement of form, shape, texture. Tiny pixels of moisture tremble and burst and in a moment I am drenched by a billion billion raindrops – air shimmering with the fury of the tumbling skies. There's a noise like applause as pearls of rain slap down upon the cracked ground, the muddy track, the ancient water beyond the reeds. I let it soak me. Let myself feel briefly clean.

I like the rain. Always prefer to run when it's tipping down. I have a quiet fantasy about running naked down the South Bank during a proper torrential downpour, zipping pinkly past the bewildered tourists and footsore commuters as they huddle beneath awnings and umbrellas. I find myself giving a strange little smile – the way you do when you spot a deer slipping between the trees or a random toddler grins at you on the tube. It's a strange feeling and the salt crystals on my cheeks feel like cheap make-up, cracking around my laughter lines.

I let the rain clean my face, looking up into the colourless sky, clouds hanging so low I feel as though I could reach up and scoop a handful of their melancholy air. I let myself imagine Jethro at my side. He loved the rain too. Loved to feel nature upon his skin; to lean forward, posing like a ski jumper, in the face of the hard easterly wind. I realise how much of what I like and don't like has been influenced by my big brother. Realise, in a moment of quiet oblivion, that he will not influence me again.

The key turns easily, and I unhook the big silver lock from the rusty loop. I place it in a little cave where the mortar has fallen away between the stones of the front wall. I don't make a show of opening the door. Don't take a breath or steel myself. Just turn the handle and push.

The smell's all him. Wood polish and TCP, glue and compost, and the low, sonorous hum of damp clothes aired in damp rooms. There's a dusty rag rug covering the bare brick of the corridor, a picture of the Holy Mother on one side of the narrow hallway and a picture of David Bowie in full Ziggy Stardust regalia on the other. The roof has always been low but now it positively sags: the floorboards having given way in places to droop precariously into the gloom of the corridor. I have the absurd sensation of lying in a lower bunk, looking up at the lump of some unknown room-mate – weight pressing the bedsprings perilously close to where I lie.

I try the light switch on the wall by the living room. Nothing happens. I squint into the gloom and pull out my phone, turning on the garish blue light of the torch. The room has been given over to tomato plants. There's a thick roll of clear tarpaulin covering the rotten carpet and perhaps forty or fifty dead tomato plants in a variety of containers: empty paint tins, jam jars, an iron kettle black as night.

I crouch down and look at the nearest plant. There's a label halfway up its stiff, dead stem. Jethro's hand. It reads: *Gwendoline. 08.06. Coffee grounds, grebe eggs and Elgar. Disappointing.*

A memory stirs. Had he told me about his experiments last time we spoke? I'd grown so accustomed to not really listening – to getting on with work, or dinner, or dyeing my hair – the phone on loudspeaker somewhere within easy reach and his words coming out in a great spurt of enthusiasm. He rarely stopped to let me talk. Only needed the odd grunt or 'wow' or 'I see' from his little sister. His new enthusiasms left me cold. Everything left me cold.

I walk backwards into the hall. Make my way down to the snug little kitchen. This is the room where he lived. There's a little camping stove sitting on top of the big black Rayburn; his solitary saucepan, tin opener and fork neatly placed on the Formica counter at its side. There's still a carpet of sorts on the uneven floor but it's rotten through, and there are stones and bare earth visible in places. The centre of the room is taken up with the huge old table: a genuine eighteenth-century piece worth a fortune to a collector with a decent eye. There's a white plastic garden chair pulled up at the head of the table, split down the seat.

Something tickles my hair and sends a shiver down to my toes. I look up through the damaged plaster and sodden timbers and through a hole into the duck-egg blue of the bathroom. There's a staircase at the end of the hall, which leads to the snug top floor, but Jethro hadn't risked the wooden steps since he put his foot through the rotten timber and cut his calf down to the bone. These last months he lived almost entirely in the kitchen. Slept in his plastic chair, wrapped in his blanket, lit by the gas fire; writing his pages, his thoughts, his scattered recollections and conjectures; sipping at his fungus-reeking broth and reddening his teeth with whichever home-made spirit he had remembered to drink before it exploded or ate through the container.

The voice – the one that still runs reptilian fingers up and down my neck. I hear it. Hear him. Hear the stern and joyless tones of the priest as he instructs that I look inside myself and hold out my sins for his consumption.

You disgust me, Claudine. How did you let it get to this? You knew. You knew this was how he was living. Knew and did nothing but send more money. You are wretched. Sinful. Selfish. Shameful. He was ill and he needed you and you let him shiver and starve in this pitiful place. And then you lay still and watched as the devil stuck his talons in his belly and bathed in his sainted blood...

I shake the voice into silence. Force myself to mumble and hum, to fill the void with cheerful inanities. I swish the phone around, the circle of light drawing shapes in the dark air. It's a clutter of twist-tied carrier bags and sodden boxes full of mildewed paper. There are tins of cat food and shining empty tuna tins placed on every surface. The deep old sink with its solitary tap is full of cold water and rimed with a soapy scum, a pair of trousers and a mustard-coloured vest sticking out of the grey foam like a sandbar.

'Jesus, Jethro,' I mutter, closing my eyes. I open two of the lower cupboards. Cleaning products spill out alongside an avalanche of paperback textbooks and ream upon ream of creamy linen paper inscribed with indecipherable but familiar handwriting: great cursive loops and swirls descending into a frenzy of something that might be musical notation and might be nothing at all.

I reach for the lantern on the wall, hanging where it's hung for the best part of thirty years. I don't think about my actions – just let my fingers go through the familiar action of twisting the wick, lighting the match, holding it within the glass bauble until a soft yellow light begins to flicker. I close the slide. Lock it in place. Watch the flame grow and the shadows lengthen.

I become aware again of the silence of the place. The walls are still thick in the places where they're not crumbling. The roof still muffles the outside air, even with the big gaps between the tiles. There's still something homely, sturdy about this old cottage – already more than two hundred years old when Mum bought it as a place where she could go when the sadness took over. Three years after going to university, Jethro became sad too. Became so sad that it nearly killed him. So she let him have the cottage. Moved us from our home in Normandy and into this dank, green wilderness and insisted I try and fit in while she and my big brother attempted to take care of one another's sadnesses. Daddy was still back in France. I'd have stayed, if he'd asked me to. He never did.

I hold the lantern at arm's length. Try and make sense of the room. It seems emptier, somehow. Feels as if unfamiliar hands have already riffled through the meagre possessions mounded on the tabletop and inside the sagging cupboards. I haven't stood in the kitchen for nearly four years; but I remember it being fuller, more haphazard. There are fewer books. Fewer lever-arch files. And the lectern. The cabinet of curiosities.

I look to the metre square of bare wall by the window. It's a sickly colour, malarial and garish. There should be a plate rack there, stuffed full of his little glass specimen jars – his finds from the Fens. There should be toads and bats, shrew skeletons and tiny brittle magpies bobbing in murky liquids, stoppered and labelled in black ink. The lectern, too. It's stood at the end of the hallway since I was a girl: a massive great wooden affair adorned with cherries and gargoyles: curlicue scrolls of artful fretwork intertwining with leering Pagan goblins. It has held the family Bible since before Napoleon. It's missing. The Bible, too, is nowhere to be found.

I feel a panic rising. I only came to do one thing for him, only came to safeguard that which mattered to him most. Am I too late? Have thieves already taken something that they can't even begin to know the true value of?

I'm standing still, tugging at my fringe in the way that used to irritate Mum, not sure what to do next. I try and work it through rationally as if it were a challenge at work. Force myself to stay calm. To work through it one step at a time. I could use a drink, suddenly. Could use a cigarette or at least a place to recharge my vape. There's a generator in one of the outbuildings. I could find an instruction video on YouTube, work out how to get some power to the house, get some proper light on the subject, search from top to bottom.

I look at my phone, noticing again the missed calls and emails. I have to make fists with my hands in order to not reply. I've been told to switch off, to take some time for myself, to do what I must, to grieve. They value me at work and they're right to. I'm their biggest asset. I'm good at what

I do. The best, in fact. I'm one of the one hundred most influential women in media and PR. I matter. The thought of them getting by without me feels like a foot across my throat.

I make my way back towards the door. I hear a familiar sound drifting across from the water: a guttural croak, a pencil dragged over a serrated surface. The frogs are singing. Fen nightingales, they're called. I can picture Jethro's face as he told me this delicious little fact. Can picture the absolute delight in his eyes as he held up a great fat toad for my inspection and approval, its bulging eyes and scabrous green skin filling me with that wonderful mixture of revulsion and delight. Is there a greater thrill? Does anything feel better than the ecstasy of delicious disgust?

I pull the door open, feeling lost, feeling dizzy, feeling sick…

I jump back as if slapped, my heart in my throat, heart thudding, blood rushing in my ears. She's standing a couple of paces away from the front door. She's wearing a dark hat, wide-brimmed, and rain falls onto shoulders swaddled in a slick black gown. For an instant she's a woodcut of a witch. A stooped crone carrying the reek of the Fen, grey-haired and wolf-eyed and fringed by the damson and coal of the gathering dusk.

'Oh, I'm so sorry, I must have scared you half to death!'

I hear myself gasp. Hear the silly little half-laugh half-cry as my cheeks turn crimson and my pupils become pinpricks. It's his neighbour – the lady from the bigger house down the lane, a lady I'm supposed to know better than I do. And she's standing in front of me, her face a cartoon sketch of kind little eyes and a sort of glazed-pastry skin; a figure of assembled spheres, round and soft and warm. She's holding a basket out in front of her, and I give a little snort as my mind fills with fairy-tale images. I've never bothered to ask her age, but she must be seventy if she's a day. Even so, for a moment she's Little Red Riding Hood skipping off to see Grandma.

She steps forward and pulls me in for a hug that I would never have imagined I wanted, and which I can't bear to break.

6

She bustles around in the kitchen, huffing and sighing and making the little noises of somebody whose bones always ache in damp weather. She rummages in the chaos of bags and boxes with the easy familiarity of somebody who knows where everything is, where it isn't, and where it should ideally be. Occasionally she says something audible, some muttered pronouncement about men in general and Jethro in particular.

'...of course, Jethro, of course you'd keep the spoons in your plimsoll...'

I lean against the wall, smiling and frowning and looking down at the floor. She's nice to look at, in the right light: messy hair and pink cheeks and a mess of scruffy grey-blonde hair. Her big woolly coat is covered in dog hair and there's mud up her jeans, but she had the decency to take off her boots before entering the kitchen. I didn't think to. Didn't think to do anything besides shrink into myself and try to touch as little as possible. She's wearing odd socks, a hole in the big toe, and the sight of her pink-painted toenail makes me feel absurdly pleased that she exists.

She's suspended the lantern from the hook on the beam above the table and the room is filled with flickering, mazy shadows as she sets about making me the hot drink that she seems to think I need. I'm reminded of an old-fashioned zoetrope: her image a series of painted silhouettes, twitchily moving in a crude form of animation. Mum had one when we were small. I think Dad took it with him when he left. Took it or burned it, just for spite.

'Should have a quivering,' she says, brightly, lighting the camping stove and pouring gin-clear water from a jerrycan into the black cauldron sitting above the blue flame.

'A quivering?' I ask, and my voice sounds all slurry and wrong. 'I don't think I know...'

'Best done at midnight,' she says, accent local. 'Heck of a thing to witness, so I'm told. You lay him out on his bed in his best clothes. Make him look as presentable as he ever got. Brush his hair, shave him. Prettify him. Light some candles and give him a good scrub. You ask those who loved him to come and join the chorus. You wail and sob and proper make a din. Bang the floorboards, rattle your bangles, do whatever you need. You drive the devils out, see. Scare the buggers off. My grandmother even had a quivering stick: metal rod with wooden rings around it. You make the house proper rattle.

'Then the men do their thing. Grip the mattress he's laid out on and shake the very Dickens out of it. You're shaking out their sins; their wrongdoings, see. My grandmother went to one when she was a girl. Some maiden aunt who drowned in the Lode. Swore blind that she could see the poor dead woman's sins hanging in the air above her. Like ash above a fire, so she said. Your Jethro was a bugger for wanting to hear that story. Like a kid with a favourite nursery rhyme, I swear.'

'I don't know if I believe in any of that,' I say, pushing my hair back behind my ears. 'I think I'm an atheist.'

'Doesn't really matter what you believe,' she says, smiling. 'It's what believes in you that's important. Some people don't know if gravity's real, but they don't go floating off the surface of the earth, do they?'

I make a face. 'Who doesn't believe in gravity?'

She leans back against the sink. Closes one eye and probes in a back tooth with her tongue, ruminating on something. 'Bad example,' she concedes, with a grin that sits comfortably among the ruddy skin and happy wrinkles. 'He'd like it, that's all.'

'You think?' I ask. I don't want to shrug. It seems horribly rude. But I also don't really know what to say or do. I know with deep-down certainty that I shouldn't have come. Should have stayed in London. Should have stayed where the only air you breathe in is what somebody's just breathed out. There's too much space, here. Too much openness. I don't like feeling so small, so inconsequential.

'A man with a lot of beliefs, your brother,' she says, testing the side of the pot with her knuckles. 'Some of them flagrant contradictions, of course. Zealous about one thing one day and its total opposite the next. Perfect apostle on a Tuesday morning and militant atheist by Wednesday afternoon. Depended what book he'd just read or conversation he'd just had. Some days it was just the wind changing direction.' She looks down at the floor as a tremor of quiet grief passes through her. 'Wish I'd known the man he was before…'

'I find it hard to remember,' I say, and this time I really do shrug. 'He was a lot older than me.'

'Loved the bones of you though,' she says, staring right

at me. There's no accusation in her expression but I still feel cold and uncomfortable, as if she's outright tearing a strip off me for neglecting him as he shivered and starved in this bleak, damp place. 'Loved you right through. Some things would stay in his head and some would fall out, but he always talked about little Claudine, his *moineau* – big deal in the city, took care of him, sent money so he could stay in his own place and not have to go back to the hospital where the walls were crushing him flat. Proud to be your brother, he was.'

'I don't think I deserved it,' I say, and I rather hope she'll offer me some comforting platitude.

She doesn't. Just turns back to the pot.

I glare at her back, ashamed of the show I made of myself when she arrived at the door. I don't know what made me hold her the way I did. We've barely had anything to do with one another save the occasional email and phone call. She's an employee, if anything. I've spent a small fortune keeping Jethro fed and clothed. She's made a tidy profit on three meals a day and she certainly hasn't troubled herself with tidying up or keeping him clean. I should be demanding to know what had happened to him over the last weeks and months of his life. Instead, I just stare at her – at this little round woman in her long coat with its bulging pockets, her hat dangling from her pudgy neck on a length of twine.

I feel so far out of my comfort zone I don't even know how to begin. Her name would be a help. Christ, I've seen it on my bank statements for long enough. Seen it on her correspondence. And yet I can't draw it to mind.

'I've no doubt you're quietly going mad over there trying to remember my name,' she says, as if reading my mind.

'Mrs Goodall, if you're ringing from an electricity firm and trying to get me to change supplier. Margaret, if it's a Sunday and I'm trying to impress. And it's Peg, if we're friends.'

'I did remember,' I lie.

'Course you did. Anyway, Peg's fine.'

I stand quietly, wishing I had a nickname or some friendly sobriquet I could permit her to use for me. I don't. I'm Claudine. Jethro called me Moineau, but nobody else ever has.

'You'll be wanting to tear a strip off me, I'm sure,' says Peg, opening a cupboard door and unearthing two glass jars. She splashes water in both and empties it into the sink. Reaches into the pockets of her coat and unearths a little square of fabric. She stretches it tight across the aperture of the bottle with one hand and lifts the pot of boiled tea leaves with her other. If the heat of the handle pains her she doesn't show it. She pours the boiling water through the fabric. I watch, mesmerised. It takes me a moment to register what she's just said.

'Tear a strip?'

'Come on, you must have a million questions,' she says, a slightly sharper note to her voice. 'What the chuff was he doing in London? Why wasn't I keeping an eye on him? Why was he so skinny? Maybe they'll have done the post-mortem examination by now. Maybe not. Either way, you'll soon enough be wanting to know why he wasn't taking his pills. So come on – get cross. You're in communications, apparently, and I'm not seeing much from you that makes me think you're very good at it.'

I can't help but bristle at the accusation. Indignation flares through me. I harden my features.

'Oh, there she is.' Peg smiles, wrapping her palms around the jar of black tea and raising it to her mouth. Wisps of steam rise up and into the gaps in the roof. She places the jar down on the table for me and sets about making another for herself. 'Drink that while it's painful,' she says, brightly. 'It'll do you good. You look just about ready to fall down. I'll do you a decent brew back at the house, but you won't make it back in that state.'

'Make it back?' I ask.

'You'll be staying with me until you're done,' she says, as if we've had this conversation already. 'I've got the spare room already made up.'

'No, no,' I say, trying to sound gracious rather than horrified. 'No, I'll get a hotel. Or I can just head straight back when I'm done. I'm not staying. I just wanted…'

She stands still and nods at the glass on the table. I do as she commands. Pick it up with my fingertips and take a sip. It's scalding hot but there's something good about the tingling pain on my tongue and fingertips. It doesn't taste like any tea I've drunk before. There's a depth to it, an earthiness that makes the back of my tongue ooze moisture. 'What is this?' I ask.

'Medicine.' She smiles again. 'Your brother made it. Helped him sleep.'

We stand in silence for a second. I force myself to look at her the same way she looks at me. She's damn right about the questions I should be asking. I know I should be insisting that she tells me about Jethro's last days. I think I'm just too frightened of the answers to ask the questions. I already feel like I'm being eaten alive with pure cold grief and guilt. To know more might be too much.

'You've come to take care of his things, I gather,' says Peg, rummaging in another pocket and pulling out a little leather pouch of tobacco. She rolls herself a little cigarette, not even looking as her pudgy fingers pinch and twist and roll. She lights it from the flame on the campfire, her face lit by hot blue flame.

'His things?' I ask, and I realise that I'm becoming an echo.

'That's what you're doing, isn't it? Sorting out his stuff? I don't envy you, but I'll help as I can. It might make more sense to you than to me. The useful paperwork's all laid out at my place for you already. Birth certificate, qualifications, diplomas, doctorates, driving licence. Deeds to this place too,' she says, drawing a circle around me with her eyes. 'The will's with Honey and Dobson in the village. All to you, of course.'

I sip the tea. Watch her through the steam. 'I'm not after money, if that's what you're implying.'

'I'm implying nothing, chicken,' she says, with a big smile. 'As I say, he loved the bones of you. Wouldn't hear a word said against you.'

'Who was saying words against me?' I ask, as I feel the drink slip into my stomach and spread its warmth all the way to my fingers and toes.

'My husband would be one,' she says, without apology. 'You'll maybe remember Everitt. He was doing some work on the barn roof when you were here last. When was that, now? Two years, maybe? Bit more?'

I look down. 'I phoned,' I say, cheeks burning. 'I wrote.'

'Yes, the letters are at my house too,' she says. 'Five of them, I think. Eight pages in total. Lovely paper though.'

I shake my head, feeling the tears prickle. 'I did my best.'

She shrugs, mimicking my own display of insouciance. 'Do you think?' she asks, sucking her cheek. 'Only you can know, I suppose. I know you were generous. Everitt and me probably wouldn't have been able to keep our place without your contributions. I'll miss them. I'll miss Jethro more though.'

I finish the drink. My tongue feels numb, my throat tight. I know that if I start to speak, I'll burst into tears. I pinch the bridge of my nose, breathing hard. Bibi slinks into the kitchen and starts to wind her way between my legs, purring happily. I reach down, glad of the distraction, and press my face to her fur.

'Everitt's allergic,' says Peg, apologetically. 'We can't have her. Lady at the cattery might take her back. Maybe you'll want her with you? Do they have cats in London? Seems a bit selfish to me, having a pet in a city like that, but maybe I'm wrong. Where is it you live? I asked Jethro but he'd never seen it.'

I put Bibi down. 'You've made your point,' I say, sounding a little more like myself. 'I wasn't a good sister. I should have seen him more. Should have done more. It's too late now – I get that. And yeah, I'm sodden with guilt. Coming here, seeing this place, sorting out his things – I guess it's something I thought I could do for him that might...'

'Make you feel better?' she asks, eyebrows raised. She sucks the last half-inch off her cigarette and throws the butt in the sink. 'Not working, is it? You look around, see how he was living – see all the evidence of his problems. No wonder you were crying in my arms on the doorstep.'

I pull a face, childish and embarrassed. 'You gave me a fright...'

She puts her hands in her pockets. Breathes out a great plume of grey. 'Shall we start again?' she asks, a softness in her voice. 'I'm sad, see. Such a silly little word for such a big feeling, isn't it? And you're sad too. There are other feelings as well, but it comes down to sadness. So maybe we should be nice to each other. See if we can't answer one another's questions. I'm not a one for sobbing, but I've fair emptied my eyes out this past couple of days. When I heard his name on the news...'

'I should have told you myself,' I say, with another stab of guilt. 'I haven't known what to do. I only came here because it felt... oh I don't know.' I stop, unable to articulate it. 'He died right in front of me. Just stab after stab after stab. There was so much blood.' I close my eyes and see it again – see him staring, emptily, across the spreading lake of red. 'He didn't even cry out. Just went from alive to dead and that was that.'

She moves across the room without a sound. When I open my eyes she's there in front of me, tears veneering her bright eyes. 'Was it, though?' she asks, with a quiet urgency. 'You know what he thought: the one belief that he kept coming back to. You know what he wanted. Did you see it? Did you see it rise?'

Incomprehension shows in my features. I don't know what she's talking about. She looks momentarily crestfallen. Closes her eyes and cuffs at her cheeks in case any tears have dared to make themselves known.

'You really didn't know him at all, did you, chicken?'

'I'm sorry?'

'We'll go back to my place,' she says, briskly. 'It might make more sense for you to see it yourself. See what he saw.'

'What he saw?'

She lets out a little huff of exasperation. 'Where he went the last time,' she says.

'The last time what, Peg?'

She stands still, hands on her hips. Glares up at me as if I'm a terrible disappointment. 'The last time he died.'

7

I can hear the low, mournful song of the frogs. *Croak-creek-craa-ack*. A swollen door dragged against a flagstone. The sound makes the swaying reeds seem ever more alive, as if the Fen were breathing through constricted lungs.

We pull the door closed behind us and lock up. I sway a little bit, hungry and sick. The rain's eased off a little but it's still coming down hard. The track to the house is slick with mud, and the trees are all a couple of shades darker than when I arrived. It must be early evening but I've no memory of seeing the sun. The sky's a great block of violet and grey, the colour that water goes when you clean your paintbrushes. I squint up into it, feeling the rain on my cheeks. I realise that my face is flushed, my cheeks feverish. I feel a little strange; drowsy and high, as if I've stood up too quickly in a hot bath.

'Red barn,' says Peg, nodding in the direction of the low building with the sunken roof. 'He called it The Chapel. So did his pals.'

I follow her towards the outbuilding. I glance down at the mud as the rain starts to fill in the hollows and cracks. I can just about make out the outline of bare feet: arched soles and flat toes pushed into the damp earth, too many to count.

'Take a peek,' says Peg, pushing the door open. I do as instructed and poke my head into the darkness. It takes a moment for my eyes to adjust.

He's built a nest. He's woven sticks and reeds around a circular raft so that he can climb inside like a bird.

Peg squeezes into the doorway beside me. 'Shame,' she grumbles, jerking her head towards the far wall. It's been whitewashed. 'Painted over it. Maybe it scared him. Was amazing, honestly. Like the ceiling of the Sistine Chapel, but with more demons and death. All very godly, but the right kind of godly. Old Testament, I guess. Real good, real evil. He saw some terrible things when he had his bad dreams. Everitt and me would hear him screaming all the way over at our place. He could never really put it into words, but he could paint it. Beasts with fangs and tails and claws. The saint with the flayed skin. He put himself in it too. Him and his pals. It helped him. They helped him. But he hadn't been right – not these past few months. Not even by his standards. I don't want to lay it at your door but, by God, he missed you. And after the tragedy...' She nods at my stomach, where you should be. 'He'd have done anything for you, girl.'

I can't think of anything to say. *I came apart after you left me, Esmerelda. I couldn't take care of myself.*

'Anyway, he's with his angels now,' says Peg, rubbing her hands together. 'I bet St Peter's got a migraine already.'

Unexpectedly she slips her arm through mine and gently steers me back onto the track.

'I wish I'd known,' I mumble, grateful that the rain is masking my brimming eyes. I desperately want to tell her about you, Esme. I want to explain myself. Want to scream into the grey air that my baby was born without a pulse and that every moment since has been an agony; that the entirety of my energy has gone on not coming apart like damp paper.

'You can bring his car but it's as like to get stuck in our driveway,' says Peg, slipping the keys into her own pocket and fastening herself up. 'We can talk as we walk, if you're all right in those shoes. Not the best choice, were they?'

'I wasn't really thinking,' I mumble, apologetically. 'I don't even know what I'm doing.'

'Grieving, I'd imagine,' says Peg, her hand on my shoulder as she steers me around a puddle and onto the muddy track. She cocks her head as she hears the croak of the frogs. 'Fen nightingales – that's what they're called. Did you learn that when you lived here?'

'I don't know if I ever really lived here,' I say, huddling into myself. Peg slips her arm through mine. She's warm and soft and she smells of baking and coal.

'You don't give much in the way of a straight answer, do you?' Peg nods me in the direction of a rock that stands proud of the muddy water in the track. I step onto it and make a little leap towards the soft wet grass that leads down to the edge of the marsh. I stop for a moment, looking through the mass of reeds, listening to the pitter-patter of raindrops on the ancient water, the eerie croaking of the frogs.

'I did know that, yes,' I admit, as Peg appears beside me and resumes her position at my side. 'I think I'd forgotten until you said it, but I knew it.'

'That sounds like the sort of answer that a smart kid gives when they don't know something,' she says, and gives me a little push, as if we're old friends and she's able to tease.

'I only really lived here for a couple of years,' I say, picking another safe space to put my feet and trudging into the green gloom of the track. Tree branches form an archway overhead. 'Mother worried about Jethro. She and my father were already living separate lives. She had a chance to be near Jethro – to give him what she thought they might need. It was Jethro who found the house for us. Said that he really believed he could feel better about himself if life became more simple, more quiet, more…' I waft my hand around. 'More like this.'

'Didn't work, did it?' says Peg, quietly.

'Maybe it did,' I say, unsure how much to say. 'I think of this place and I think of him smiling. I think of Mum smiling. I even think of myself, collecting frogspawn, making tree swings, sitting in the little boat on the water reading my books. It was peaceful.'

'He never spoke much about what happened before the accident,' says Peg, as the ground gets harder and we're able to move a little quicker through the wall of rain. 'Snippets. He was forever reading his old diaries and looking through your old albums, trying to get his brain to reattach itself to the past. All he did was fill it with more images. They were no more real to him than the things he read in books. Everitt did his best with him, towards the end. Did his bit to help him reconnect to the past. That was their thing, not mine. Sometimes the past is too painful to look at, don't you think? I know Everitt sometimes found himself frightened by the things Jethro described to him.'

I stop, swaying slightly, feeling too hot and too cold all at once. 'You spoke about the last time he died,' I say, and I make sure I meet her gaze when she looks up at me. 'He and I – we never spoke of it.'

'You didn't speak of much, Claudine,' she says, flatly. 'I don't blame you for it. You've had your own life to live, and it looks to me as if in some ways, you've lived it well. A big brother in and out of mental hospitals is a hell of a burden to put on a child. I've seen pictures of your mother and she doesn't look as though she were useful for much more than draping herself about the place looking pretty.'

I don't argue. Don't feel any desire to defend her. She left me in England and went back to France within six months of Jethro's suicide attempt. Closed the door on Glavers Cottage and didn't look back. Married an economist called Luc and moved to a country house more suited to her delicate constitution. Died of cirrhosis the day I turned eighteen.

I got a letter from a French solicitor a year later. Dad had died too. I was on my own. The two inheritances were split between Jethro and me, with me designated as the responsible adult with legal accountability for his assets. I had to make all the decisions about his care. Had to come up with the plans that would keep him housed and safe and cared for once the grant he'd received from the benevolent fund at his university had been used up.

Residential care bills ate through Jethro's savings inside six years. It ate through my own in another four. Soon we couldn't afford to keep him in the nice facility where he'd been doing so well. The mental health team suggested moving him to a 'more modest' institution and from there he began to take steps towards independent living. He spent almost a year living in a block of flats on the outskirts of Peterborough, proving himself capable of independence. That's when he made the decision to move back 'home'. Packed his things and trudged overland to the abandoned cottage in the last little pocket of fen. Stayed put until he came to visit his sister in London and got himself stabbed to death for his troubles.

'It was coming back to him,' says Peg, nudging me forward. I can see the little wooden bridge that leads over the water to the shingled driveway of her house.

'What was?'

'What he saw,' she says, a little out of breath. 'You must have seen the change in him. I don't know what the hell he was thinking heading up to London without so much as a word, but there was a mania in him the last few days. I was frightened, if I'm honest, and I don't frighten easily. He wasn't eating. Wasn't sleeping. When he talked it wasn't just the usual eccentric stuff – he was genuinely spouting things that made no sense. You know how he got with the different ways he expressed himself – French one moment, local yokel the next – mimicking his dad, his mum, his lecturers at university. You never knew what he was about to say. But he was speaking a language that sounded like something out of a film. It made the hairs on my arm fairly stand on end – I swear to you. You know how clever he was: Latin, Greek, all these ancient languages that he picked up when he was small – they'd just spill out of him.'

'They said it was a side effect of the injury,' I say, staring at my feet.

'Aye, well, it made him interesting company right enough but towards the end he seemed to be really going somewhere dark in his mind. I did my best by him and, I promise you, I called the crisis team and told them about his history. All they could do was put him on a waiting list. I mean, my God, this country…'

'You said he remembered,' I prompt, not wanting to hear a rant.

She sighs. Pulls her hat from her pocket and pulls it over her wet hair – too little, too late. 'When he *"died"*,' she says, quietly. 'After the accident. After he fell. His heart stopped, didn't it? That's the way I understood it. He spoke to Everitt about it more than me but from what I could tell, there were ten minutes or so when he simply wasn't here any more.'

I nod. Look away, into the gathering gloom of the marsh. 'Thirteen minutes.'

'Miracle he came back at all,' says Peg, in wonder. 'We're lucky we got so much of him back, when you think about it. He never spoke about it. Didn't remember much of the before or the after – not until a few weeks back. And then it was all he could talk about. Angels. Demons. The little devils with their split tongues, St Bartholomew, flayed skin. It was all a nonsense but his eyes fairly gleamed when he spoke about it.'

I want to ask her why she didn't tell me. I stop myself. I have no doubt that she tried. I'll have voicemails, I'm sure. I'll have letters and emails, and I won't have looked at them because they won't have been as important as whatever I was doing at work.

'Did he suffer?' asks Peg, unexpectedly. 'I hate to think of him being upset at the end. He had such a sweet nature. That chap in the newspaper had him pegged right. Did you see it? Lovely tribute.'

It takes a moment for me to catch up. 'Struan, something?' I ask. 'I glanced at it. He knew Jethro when he was at university. He was kind to us after the accident, I think. I don't really remember.'

'Did he suffer, Claudine?' she says, again.

I can't give her anything but the truth. 'He didn't cry out,' I say.

'And the man who did it,' she says, with more urgency in her voice. 'Did he speak? The papers make it sound like he was some random nutter – that it could have been anyone.'

'Random targets,' I say, screwing up my eyes as if not wanting to look too closely at the memories. 'Nothing to do with race or colour or gender. They think he might have been one of the homeless people who sleeps in the park near Somerset House. Stood up and stabbed the nearest person. Didn't say a word, according to some witnesses. Another said he was screaming something in a foreign language. He must have just come into our building because the lights were so bright.'

'Did Jethro try and tackle him?'

I shake my head. 'The police asked me that. I think they wanted to have a bit of heroism in there, to make the story have something less bleak at its heart. Jethro didn't even raise his hands. The security guard tried to tackle him, but he never stood a chance.'

'I've seen the video,' says Peg, water spraying off her lips. 'The poor young man out for a run. He got a close-up of the attacker but it's not going to help, is it? There was so much blood on his face it's no wonder people can't make out his features. But those eyes…'

I nod. 'I've not seen the video. I can't bring myself to. But I remember the eyes. Black as coal.'

'You've been through hell, Claudine,' says Peg, and rubs my arm. 'Come on, let's get warm. I've some

84

decent elderberry cordial that goes nicely with gin and hot lemon barley. I've baked, too. I know you're all out of sorts and you want to get going but please – let me look after you.'

I can't resist the offer. I already feel intoxicated by her warmth, her nearness, her kindness. For a little while, I want to be cared for. I want to be cosseted, mothered – I want to be treated the way I'd have treated you, Esmerelda, had you just been allowed to live.

I nod. 'Thank you,' I say, softly.

And I follow her through the gloom, a moth pursing the soft flickering warmth of the flame.

Behind me, Bibi slinks through the blackness. Mews, faintly, at the thing that slithers up from the water's edge.

Leaps, silently, and pierces the green foulness of amphibian flesh.

CALL FOR BETTER SECURITY AT ANCIENT CHURCH AFTER NEAR-FATAL 'FALL'

By Julie Crawford

19.11.1993

A HEART-broken vicar has vowed to 'move Heaven and Earth' to provide better security at historic St Wendreth's Church in Little Mercy.

Paramedics and police officers were called to the site of the ancient church on Monday morning after a 23-year-old local man was found unconscious at the foot of a newly dug grave.

A witness, who declined to be named, said: 'It was a miracle he was found at all and incredible to think he survived. There was so much blood. A grave had been dug ahead of a funeral service, as is common practice, and it was pure luck that I had a little peek over the edge while I was laying some flowers for my nan. He was half covered in mud. I was genuinely terrified and had to run half a mile to the nearest house to use the phone. I didn't think for a moment he might wake up, but I felt I had to try.'

An investigation by local police has confirmed that the man, believed to be a divinity student at a prestigious Cambridge college, had fallen from the spire of the church.

Inspector Simon Dickerson of Cambridgeshire Constabulary said: 'We can confirm that we are not looking for anybody else in connection with this incident. There are mental health issues involved and it would be inappropriate to say more. Suffice to say, the paramedics and police officers who arrived at the scene within minutes of the initial call deserve great credit for saving this young man's life. We understand that his heartbeat stopped several times during their desperate battle to save him.'

Rev Caleb Bonasso, vicar of St Wendreth's, said: 'We're still trying to make sense of it. Somehow he got inside the church and made his way up the staircase to the little flat section at the top of the spire. There's barely enough room there to stand with your feet pointing forward and I wouldn't go up there if you paid me a fortune. It's absolutely heart-breaking to think that this man, who is somebody we are most familiar with at St Wendreth's, faces such a long and difficult road back to health. I'm happy to respect matters of privacy but suffice to say this young man has endured some difficult times. People reach out to God for any number of reasons, and I just wish I could have been here to talk to him and perhaps encourage him onto a different track.

'We will definitely fence off the spire as soon as funding permits, and we shall move Heaven and Earth to find a way to add extra security. Already some of our most generous parishioners have begun to offer donations to the cause and also to provide whatever medical care the young man may need on his journey back to health. We shall pray for him.'

It is the second time in 12 months that police have been called to the picture-postcard spot. Last November, officers searching for missing Peterborough man Samuel Parris, 43, found his car abandoned in the grounds. His wife and two children have previously told this newspaper of their fears that he has come to harm, despite reassurances by Cambridgeshire police, which scaled down the investigation in January.

A church has stood at the spot in the tiny hamlet of Little Mercy since the ninth century, though the current place of worship dates back to the fourteenth century. It is dedicated to St Wendreth, second sister of the semi-legendary St Guthlac: a monk who lived a life of abstinence and prayer on a tiny island in the Fens and who battled with 'demons' before being rescued from the mouth of Hell by St Bartholomew. Among those interred in the grounds is Nicolas Hobekinus, an English herald and antiquary, Whig politician and decorated army officer who was a fellow and president of the Society of Antiquaries. At the time of his death in 1756, his library of religious antiquaries was said to be among the finest in Europe.

8

Peg's house is a grander affair than Jethro's cottage. Bigger and older and better maintained. But it's far from cheerful. It's dark and poorly lit, the frontage stained the colour of bog water and the windows looking like angry eyes. It's got a melancholy about it, an air of neglect. I can't help but think of *Wuthering Heights*, half expecting some brooding Heathcliff to stamp across the muddy yard with his pack of hunting dogs.

I had the same feeling when I first saw it all those years ago. It was empty then. Jethro and I sneaked inside from time to time. He'd read to me by candlelight, wrapped up in one of the big old mantles we found in one of the abandoned chests on the first floor. He'd tell me whatever he'd just learned. Saints. The names of the demons. The true nature of the story of creation. Sometimes he'd recite the entirety of a page of the gospels, all from memory. He was exceptional. Frighteningly clever. And when he got sad it was his little sister that he wanted. I could usually make him laugh and if I couldn't, I gave him a safe place to cry.

Peg tells me the history of the house as we stand in the front yard, shivering under the endless onslaught of drizzly rain. It was built in the seventeenth century by a

London eccentric sent to manage the draining of the Fens. The project ended in failure for his backers but with some degree of personal success. He found himself a wife and was able to swindle enough money from his benefactor to pay for the construction of a decent family home, tucked away in the densest pocket of the marsh.

He built several cottages nearby and placed advertisements in the great city newsletters encouraging poets, philosophers and the great thinkers of the age to come and join him in his new community. Few came. Of those who did make the journey into the misty green marshes, none stayed long. One essayist, who would later find fame for his musings on melancholy, spoke of the 'eternal sadness' that pervaded the wetlands and the troubling visions that would plague his sleep.

Creditors claimed the property and the attendant lands. Few owners have stayed long. Tenants have rarely prospered. Our cottage had stood empty for a decade when Mum bought it from a local firm of land managers. Peg's house was empty too: the property latterly used by the diocese as a place for burned-out clerics to recuperate and spend some time in communion with God.

Peg lived in the next village at the time and was a housekeeper of sorts. Everitt was a young vicar who had witnessed a brutal assault within the grounds of his own church. He was sent to the Fens to heal and restore his faith. He found a different type of love instead. The diocese permitted him and his new wife to serve as custodians for the property, provided they offered lodgings and a peaceful place of prayer and reflection to any priest or pastor who might need it. Of the few who have been to stay, none have returned.

Peg tells me all this as she leads me down the flagged corridor and into a warm sitting room. The open fire has been eating itself to cinders in Peg's absence and she gathers up a handful of pine cones and dumps them onto the smouldering ashes. They begin to snap and crackle at once. She arranges a little cross-hatch of split logs and artfully arranges lumps of black coal in the crevices, talking all the while.

I take a slow, heavy-lidded look around me. It's a low-ceilinged room, exposed timbers blackened by centuries of smoke. The walls are a shade of soft yellow that makes me think of churned butter in Enid Blyton stories. They're haphazardly plastered, bulging here and there as if big, gilt-framed pictures have been absorbed by the brickwork. There's a huge three-seater sofa beneath the single leaded window, a dead oil lamp on the wonky windowsill. The floral curtains are open but the last of the light dies against the dark glass. The sofa is covered in random antimacassars and crocheted blankets. There's a flagged stone floor beneath a threadbare, colourless rug and the horse brasses by the fireplace catch the light of the rapidly gathering fire.

It's a cosy mess of a place: piles of paperback books, ripped-open envelopes, bills with red letterheads, half-finished crossword puzzles. I would love to live like this. I can't live like this.

I sit without being told to, sinking into a huge leather armchair covered in hairy tartan blankets and soot-smudged cushions. I lie back, resting my head on the squashy leather.

'That was Jethro's favourite chair too.' Peg smiles. 'Loved to warm his feet by the fire. We had to light a scented candle or two, of course. He did have a habit of carrying the smell of the marsh.'

I give a weak smile. Offer up a confession as if in payment for her kindness. 'I was thinking that just moments before he died,' I say, softly. 'I was so embarrassed to see him there. The way he looked – the way he smelled. God, I can't let go of it. I cringe when I think of it – my shame at seeing him there, at people thinking we were associated somehow...'

Peg doesn't speak. Just nods. 'He wouldn't want you to be hard on yourself, Claudine. He knew himself better than a lot of people do, even with his problems. He'd always apologise to people when he met them for the first time – explain himself, like. And he knew who you had to be in London and didn't judge you for it.'

I pause a moment, searching her words for accusation. 'Who I had to be?'

She hauls herself up, bones creaking. Gives a shrug that looks familiar. 'If you were ever in the newspapers, he'd want us to keep a clipping. If we saw you online, he'd have us print it out for his books. He was really proud of what you were trying to do in politics. And when you went into the other line of work, well, he had no doubts you had good reasons.'

'The other line of work?'

'You know, all that communications and corporate nonsense – blue-sky thinking and pushing the envelope and such. You tried your hardest to make a difference, I'm sure. No shame in feathering your own nest for a while. If you can't beat 'em, join 'em, that's what Everitt muttered from behind his newspaper.'

I feel sick at the thought of people discussing me and my

motivations, feel sick at being judged so unfairly by people who didn't understand. But I'm warm and I'm comfy and she's spoken of a drink and a meal, and I don't particularly have the energy to argue or to move.

'I'll lay out a change of clothes for you,' she says, brightly. 'The Wi-Fi password is written on the inside leaf of that book to your left. It's not a bad signal, surprisingly enough. Your room's at the top of the stairs. Most of Jethro's stuff is in the big wooden chest outside your room so you can leaf through it at your leisure. If you're anything like your brother, you'll doze off sitting there but I'll go rustle up some treats just in case your hunger kicks the backside of your tiredness.'

I don't really know what to say to her, so I just give my best meeting-a-new-client smile. She sees through it. Holds my gaze for a moment too long and gives a tiny, almost imperceptible shake of her head. Then she's gone and I'm on my own, sinking into the old leather and imagining my brother; picturing him sitting here, wet socks damply steaming, a look of contentment and peace on his face.

I fall asleep with tears on my cheeks.

9

'Still no sign?'

'Not a dickie bird. Divers are struggling with the current.'

'He couldn't have survived. Two bullets, in him, according to witnesses.'

'Stranger things have happened…'

'Name one. Name fucking one.'

'Mick bought a round. How's that?'

Billy tries to tune out the back and forth between the constables situated around the bank of desks. There's a nervous energy to their voices, almost a sense of wonder. Could the killer be alive? Could they have really survived the fall into the Thames? Could they have somehow hauled themselves out and slunk away? Could they, perhaps, strike again? Billy can't blame them for their excitement. This is a big case. It could be a career maker if handled right. And if the person responsible does somehow come back from near certain death, they might, somehow, be involved in catching a live villain rather than fishing a dead man out of the river.

'Nutter, I reckon.'

'How fucking astute! Cos sane people go around stabbing people to death every day of the week, don't they?'

'No, you know what I mean. Lone psycho, voices in his head told him to do it...'

'Religious thing, if you ask me. Honouring God or Allah or Buddha or Vishnu or whatever.'

'I don't think you get Buddhist fundamentalists, do you?'

'He was speaking in a foreign language though.'

'I had a girlfriend when I was a teenager and her stepdad was a proper born-again Christian. He spoke in tongues, actually.'

'Spoke in tongues?'

Billy turns his head, interested. The speaker is Dan Hornsby, a Northern lad who doesn't tend to join in with the more loud-mouthed banter. He looks a bit embarrassed at getting such a hard-eyed stare from his sergeant.

'Sorry, Sarge, I'll get on...'

'No, go on,' says Billy, trying to remember how to smile. 'Educate them.'

'I think the real name is *glossolalia*,' he says, wincing at how silly he fancies he sounds. 'It's where people start speaking something that's kind of a language but they don't know what it means. It's got the right shape and sound to it but they're not words with a translation. I think there's a specific religious one. Is it maybe xenoglossy?'

Billy doesn't need to pretend he understands. It's one of the areas that Fran has prattled on at him about. But he doubts the others have a clue. 'Go on, Dan.'

'Apparently it's a gift from God. There are videos online of people doing it. The Bible talks about it. I don't know much more than that. But, like, the language he was speaking didn't sound like anything the witnesses recognised. It was like a language, but not, y'know? Sorry, I'll shut up.'

The other officers look to Billy. When he doesn't laugh, they decide to treat the contribution as worthwhile rather than ridiculous.

'You're a dark horse, Dan. Like Black Beauty.'

'Worth knowing, that.'

'Shame you never do the pub quizzes...'

Billy turns back to DC Helen Savage as the laughter starts to build again. She rolls her eyes, and he manages a ghost of a smile. He's worked with Savage before. She's thoughtful, determined and very likeable. She has three children, teenagers now, and she'd be a lot higher up the career ladder if she hadn't taken time off to raise them. She hasn't quizzed him on why he wants her to repeat the briefing she has already delivered to the DCI. She does what her superiors ask, unless the request is stupid or illegal. It's an approach that has so far served her well.

'Jethro Cadjou,' she says, starting again. She'd already got two paragraphs into her report when they became distracted by the rising volume from the rest of the unit. She looks to Billy, who nods his assent. He wants to hear it again.

'Born 1970 in Hastings, Kent. Mother, Madeleine Cadjou. Aged sixteen. No father on the birth certificate. From what I got from the family liaison who got a few moments with the sister, Madeleine's linked to one of the old French noble families. You know the sort – can trace their lineage back to before the Battle of Hastings. I've found her obituary in a French newspaper and passed it through the translation app. Still reads like nonsense but I got the gist of it. Very Bohemian, put it that way. Ran away to Paris and then to London. Did some modelling, posed for artists – there's a photo of her sandwiched between Mick Jagger and David Bowie on one website that I saw. Anyway, got pregnant, couldn't exactly keep up with the party scene, had a kid she called Jethro.

'Next thing she's back in the bosom of her family. Raises the lad at the family chateau – am I saying that right? – and gets herself back on the social scene. Lands a husband – another French chap from good stock who doesn't mind her keeping her aristocratic name. Jethro goes off to boarding school at seven. Little Claudine comes along a few years later. I'm waiting to hear back from a dozen different sources about the major gaps in the timeline but at seventeen he was offered a place at the Sorbonne in Paris. Stayed a couple of years then transferred to a divinity college in Cambridge, with a view to eventually getting a PhD. Bilingual, like his sister… He was twenty-something when Mum and Claudine moved over to England. Bought the little cottage in the Fens. A year or so later there's the accident…'

'Accident?' asks Billy, flicking his eyes towards her.

'Post-mortem's happening as we speak and the DCI's there with the pathologist, phoning across updates as he goes. Terrible head wound, long since healed. Matches with what the sister referenced in her statement when she talked about him being a really gentle person, incapable of hurting anybody or anything ever since the accident. Reading between the lines, it was a suicide attempt. Jumped from the roof of St Wendreth's Church in Little Mercy. Coma for months and then he went into a sort of sheltered housing set-up in Suffolk. A place for clergy. Priests and vicars and people with illnesses or mental health problems. He wasn't ordained but the college and the local diocese picked up the tab for the first few years. Mother went back to France. Died not long after. Dad too.

'The estate was split between them and it's all gone on his care since. Sister's been picking up the tab since it ran out. He was there for years. Suffered seizures. Fugue states, if you know what they are. Memory loss. Not your Hollywood version – just holes in his recollections. Spent a bit of time living in a flat in Peterborough to see if he could hack it and decided he wanted to go back to the place that had made him happy in the short time he'd spent there. Sounds fishy to me, but he was an adult and they didn't have the power to keep him against his will. Lived in this tumbledown little place ever since. Writes and reads and draws. Helps out at a soup kitchen from time to time. Cleans at the church. Looks after animals. No harm to anybody.'

'And then one day he comes to London and gets himself murdered?' asks Billy, scratching his head. 'There's bad luck, and then there's something else.'

Helen Savage raises her hands, palms up. She wouldn't like to hazard an explanation. 'The sister will hopefully be able to give us a fuller picture when we talk again. She's at the family home at present. Turned down the offer of a FLO. Got her mother's looks, hasn't she? Decent sort though, under the lipstick and the Chanel. Been paying for her brother's care her whole life. Pays a good lump into the account of one Everitt Goodall each month. He and his wife, Peg, live in the house next door. They bring him his meals, make sure he looks after himself as well as he can. We'll be getting a statement somewhere down the line, no doubt, but if anybody knows what made him suddenly get in the car and drive to the train station…'

'He drove?'

'Big old-fashioned thing.' Savage nods. 'Still in the station car park at Wisbech. British Transport sent the footage through. They're a good unit, aren't they?'

Billy doesn't respond. He isn't sure whether she's goading him. He senses eyes upon him. Feels the familiar burn in his gut.

'Ah, there he is!'

Billy turns at the sound of an ebullient, upper-class voice. He recognises Detective Superintendent Argyll; head of MIT C. He's a tall, straight-backed and grey-haired copper who looks as though he should be wearing green wellies and a Barbour jacket rather than a plain grey suit. He's holding a mug of coffee and looks remarkably fresh, despite fielding calls and gathering supplemental manpower since four a.m. He's a good officer whom Billy rates highly. Argyll rates him back.

'Thought I'd find you skulking,' says Argyll, perching himself at the edge of the desk. 'Did my heart a good turn when I saw your name on Jim's list. I know you're meant to be shuffling papers, but the PCs are still wet behind the ears and the DI on the ground can't make a decision without having to get fifteen different signatures. Could you pop down and see if you can turn a rabble of vagrants – sorry, the homeless community – into something approximating a group of witnesses?'

Billy takes a moment, swallowing bile. Argyll's voice sounds wrong, as if he's hearing it underwater. 'Sorry, sir?'

'The church by the park where our chap started his little stabbing spree,' explains Argyll, all smiles. 'That's where half of London's homeless mill about waiting to be fed. The church nearby – not St Martin's, the other one... they provide a hot meal each evening. Good church, that one.

Dentistry, haircuts, bit of basic medical care. That's who our killer targeted before he ended up in the office and before our lads had the presence of mind to shoot him. None of them want to give names, half the witnesses are trying to slip away, the others are claiming they did it so they can get a nice long prison stretch and a warm place for winter. It's bedlam. Can I trust you to pour oil on the waters?'

He looks past Billy. Smiles at Savage, who gives a grin in return; a child hoping to be picked for a major part in the school Nativity. 'Take young Helen here too, eh? She's a safe pair of hands. And you can learn a lot from this grumpy bugger, Helen. Don't let the scowl put you off. Get him on the ale and crank the karaoke up and he's an absolute star.'

Billy manages a nod. His mind is full of memories; his mind is full of *her*.

'Splendid. Good man.' He walks away, slaps a DC on the back and tells him he's doing a first-rate job.

Billy stays still until he's sure he can stand without falling. By the time he turns around, Savage is already wearing her coat and holding out a coffee for him. He takes it with a grunt of thanks. Takes a sip and swallows, cautiously.

'Black, yeah?' asks Savage, pleased to have got it right. 'No sugar.'

He nods. Tries his best. 'I'm sweet enough.'

'Sorry?' she asks, looking puzzled.

He shakes his head. Glares at his stupid shoes. Shrugs. 'It doesn't matter.'

10

There's a wetness on my chin, a sensation of warm drool spilling from the corner of my slack mouth. I want to wipe it away, but my arms don't respond to my command. I'm embarrassed. I feel like I'm being watched, as if I'm making a fool of myself, but the end of the thought seems to lose itself in a swirl of nothingness and instead I feel empty, numb. I have half a sense of you, Esmerelda. I feel your kick against my palm as I lie flat and clasp my fingers and make a cradle for your tiny unborn toes to tickle. I see a bedroom, painted in yellows and pinks; a mobile made of coat hangers and scraps of my old clothes.

Then your foot is pushing through my skin and I'm listening to the tearing of my flesh as talons perforate my belly, gnarled claws ripping me open as if something were digging through dirt. For a moment I see nothing but teeth and hair, hear the screech and hiss of something dying in a pan of bubbling water, and then there is nothing but a long tuberous tongue, splitting, twisting, wrapping about my neck, my wrists, my ankles – worm-eaten and frog-skinned – breath foul against my cheek. And I am folding in on myself as if made of paper; creasing, reducing, folding; an agony in every cell; a sudden glimpse of raw, dripping, excised flesh; a great furl of puckered flesh; frog eyes and the taste of iron, and...

I jerk awake as if the chair is on fire. I throw myself forward, a crumbling cliff edge behind me. I hear my own haggard breathing, the locomotive thud and wheeze of my heart, my rushing blood. I open my eyes wide, my index and mid-finger instinctively rising to take the pulse at my neck. I feel sweat. Tears. Drool. I wipe my hands across my face and they come away sopping, even as I shiver and my teeth begin to rattle inside my head.

It takes a moment to gather myself, to chase the monsters from the shadows in the room. I lower myself back down into the chair, talking to myself as I purse my lips and blow out a slow lungful of air.

'Bad dream?'

I jump at the sound of the voice behind me, leaping up and looking over the back of the chair. A man in pyjama trousers and a tatty blue jumper is leaning against the sloping wall by the window, positioned to stand sentry as I slept. I recognise him as Peg's husband. He wears thick spectacles but they're a little bit too far down his nose to serve much purpose. Thickets of thin white hair stick up wildly atop his weather-beaten and balding head. There's a soreness to his skin: a sort of flowery rosacea, mottling his features like lichen on a stone wall. He's barefoot, his feet filthy.

I gulp once or twice, still breathing hard. Manage to find a smile for him, to make fun of myself. I wipe the back of my hand across my chin. 'Awful,' I say. It doesn't seem enough. I start bawling, feeling silly. 'I used to suffer with night terrors when I was small. Horrible things – the sort you get when you've got a high temperature. Hallucinations more than anything.'

He peers at me over his glasses. 'What did you see?' he asks, and there's a hoarseness to his voice. As he cranes his neck, I see a patch of roughed skin: a perfect line of puckered flesh beneath his Adam's apple.

I give a shake of my head. Wave a hand. 'It's fading,' I say. 'Nothing nice.'

He looks down at the floor. He seems surprised to see his feet naked and dirty. 'Sorry,' he mumbles. 'Not used to guests. I think I was sleeping. I heard a noise.' He jerks his head at the pile of papers to my right. 'See,' he says and I realise that my hearing has been muffled, as if I've been underwater. Suddenly I can hear the bright trill of my phone.

'Sorry, sorry...'

I rummage through the papers, spilling letters and statements, adverts and bills. I spot my mobile and make a grab for it. There's movement out of the corner of my eye, a smell of damp earth and brick dust and then I'm alone again, holding my phone with slick fingers and staring at the screen through blurry eyes.

'Claudine Cadjou,' I say, grateful for something to cling to.

'Ms Cadjou,' comes the reply, slightly breathless and mightily relieved. 'I'm calling from the Investigation team. It's regarding your brother. I'm so pleased to finally get a hold of you. Your colleagues were of the opinion that you've left London. Is that correct?'

'I've come to my brother's house,' I explain, airily. 'There are things to pack up, things to arrange...'

He clears his throat. Takes a sip of something as if

composing himself. 'Ms Cadjou, you're a witness to an incredibly serious crime. We are at the most preliminary stage of the investigation and really do need you to be here to assist with…'

'I'm here now,' I say, cutting him off. I'm good at this. I can get members of parliament and the most senior of civil servants to stop talking when I'm tired of listening. 'I heard on the train you still haven't found the body.'

'No,' he says. 'No, but that's only a matter of time. We're reviewing the security footage and have an expert in tidal patterns assisting with potential retrieval sites.'

'So how can I help?' I ask, my whole body stiff, my teeth mashed together at the back.

'It's regarding your brother's injuries,' he says, with as much tact as he can. 'Some of the findings in the post-mortem examination are a little, well… we could use some background, I think.'

I let out a sigh: somebody who has been through this too many times already. 'He was ill. He suffered with paranoid schizophrenia when he was a student. There was a suicide attempt and he survived it. He wasn't well and spent most of his adulthood in a care facility. The past few years he chose to live alone, with some financial aid and under the care of his neighbours and myself. I don't know why he was in London. Pure bad luck, I think. As for the injuries, I didn't see the knife, so I don't know…'

'The older injuries, Ms Cadjou,' he says, a note of unexpected steel entering his voice. 'His chest. His back. There's evidence of severe and sustained trauma. The pathologist has seen similar injuries before when she attended a conference in the wake of the war in Angola.

They are the injuries you might receive were you to be repeatedly beaten with what you or I might refer to as a scourge. A cat-o'-nine-tails, but with hooks and barbs. The injuries have healed poorly. No medical treatment as far as we can see. More than that, he was in extremely poor physical condition. Malnourished, parasitic ringworm in his skin and in his gut. We've taken samples for toxicology but what's really interesting is the contents of the stomach. We've found scraps of vellum in his gut: vellum and what appears to be goatskin leather...'

'Please stop,' I say, and I hate how feeble I sound. I can't stand to hear any more but he's not stopping. I can hear a ruckus in the background – the sound of excited voices, fingers on keys, the rustle of paper. He sounds triumphant when he speaks again.

'Ms Cadjou, as you can imagine, we have a lot of conflicting theories about how the perpetrator selected their victims and in some of the security footage from immediately prior to the attack, there's some suggestion that the figure we believe to be the perpetrator, is in conversation with another gentleman who very neatly matches the distinctive figure of your brother. We will be sending police officers to your brother's house to conduct our own search so I must really ask that you leave things precisely as you find them. I also need you to think again upon the description you gave us of the man who did this. You spoke of scar tissue on their chest. We really need you to think hard and...'

I'm not really listening any more. I feel sick. Hungry. I can't work out whether I've been asleep for an age or a few moments. I look around for the drink that Peg had promised me but there's no mug or glass anywhere nearby. No food either. I don't like the feeling on my skin, the sensation of animal hairs and unfamiliar flesh against mine. I can't shake the sensation of the great serpentine tongue touching my own skin. But to stop thinking of the dream is to engage with what the police officer is telling me, and that's a worse place for my thoughts to be. I find myself yearning for a place to go, a sense of sanctuary, of retreat. For a moment I just want to opt out of all of it – to withdraw from reality and find a place of quiet solitude and abstinence – a place where nothing can intrude.

'Here's that book,' says Peg, brightly, bustling into the room behind me and making a face when she notices I'm on the phone. She's got a steaming mug of something in her left hand and a bowl of some kind of sponge pudding in the other. There's a book under her arm. She lays down her burdens on the little table in front of the fire, mouthing more apologies while I tell the police officer that now isn't a good time; I'll call back.

'Book?' I ask, hanging up and giving her a look of incomprehension.

'The one your brother was reading,' she says, reminding me of a conversation she thinks we've had. 'By that pal of his. Struan whatshisname.'

The name is printed in gold letters on a leathery purple cover. It's a paperback but it's been professionally bound. The title is *Golden Lies: Radical Secularisation, Revelation and Silence*. I take it from her and flick through the pages. It's a dense read, the font a little too small and so full of footnotes and citations that I feel a migraine prickling at the base of my skull. I try and find a description – something to tell me what it's about. At the front there's only a signature and inscription: *To Jethro. A goodly, godly man. Ever, Struan T.*

'Held it like a baby with a favourite toy,' says Peg quietly, taking it back from me and placing it on top of an avalanche of papers. She picks up some envelopes from the stack by the fire. Twists them, the action making me think of a wrung neck. 'Could you?' she asks, holding out a thick sheaf of papers. 'Makes it easier to get the fire going if there are some twists already made. You'll find some newspapers under the tray, too. You'll enjoy tearing the *Daily Mail* down the middle if you're anything like your brother.'

I'm a bit surprised to be asked but I'm glad to have something to do. 'Of course.'

'There are some slobbing-about clothes on the bed for you, like I said. I'll run you a bath when you want one. Have a bite of this first, get your tummy settled, eh? It's good. Bramble and elderflower. Sinks into your belly like hot coal.'

I kneel in front of the fire, sweat drying on my skin. I smell the burning pine cones, the singed paper. Smell my own sweat and damp hair. I start making twists of paper, determined to do a good job. I have half a memory of doing this as a child, back in France, lighting the fire in Father's study one morning when the lady who helped us couldn't make it to the house because of the snow on the roads. Mum was ill. Jethro was in England, studying for the great future that awaited him. I remember the feeling of paper against my palm, the inexplicable delight at the flaring of the match-head, the sense of absolute achievement as the paper began to flame and curl and to slide its dancing flames onto the body of the pale spears of kindling, the rough logs, the raven-dark coal.

I'm so consumed by doing what I'm doing that I almost miss the number on the sheaf of paper in my hand. It's a phone bill – a list of calls made and received from the landline. I emit the softest laugh, amazed that people still exist who request such old-fashioned things as a paper phone record. I smooth it out. Check the date. It's recent. The last call recorded was just two days ago.

I trace my finger up the list of calls until I see the one that had caught my eye. It's my number. My own mobile. It doesn't matter, of course. There's nothing significant in that. Jethro has been a regular visitor to this house and has made many a call on this phone. But it's the volume that seems off. I count eighteen phone calls over the course of three days – each to my mobile number. Some are in the morning, others late at night. I don't recall him ringing me that often. There were voicemails, I'm sure, but I tended to flick through them without ever listening to the whole message. Why had he been trying to get in touch with me? I look at the other numbers on the list. Some are local but there are two London area landlines and a further mobile – each phone call lasting no more than a few seconds and each made at around the same time he was trying to get in touch with me.

I can't help myself. I don't know what I'm suspicious of, but I know that it matters. I fold the piece of paper and slip it inside my trousers. The alternative is to put it on the fire, and I can't seem to bring myself to do that.

I sit back and watch the fire grow. Take a sip of the hot, syrupy cocktail and feel the warmth spread through me. I raise the ceramic bowl of cake to my nose and decide I'm not really hungry. It looks heavy and English and really not for me. Afraid to be rude, I scoop a handful of it out of the bowl with a fold of paper, twisting the top and dropping it on the fire. It flares, briefly, and then the flame devours it.

I pick up the book. Read the opening lines. Close it again. If it mattered to Jethro, then I'll try to make it matter to me. But for now, I can't pretend I'm interested. Instead, I'm thinking about what the police officer said. I'm thinking about the scars. I'm thinking about my brother's wasted body and the way he greeted his attacker without fear.

It was almost as if he had been expecting him.

11

'Hell of a thing, ain't it? I can barely lift the lid. Ugly, too. Can't tell if it's medieval or Javanese.'

Peg's prattling is quite a pleasing sound. I've tuned in to the lyrical way she talks now – noticing the imprecise gaps between her words: strange little hitches and misdirections in the inflection of her syllables. I realise that she's becoming more comfortable with me – dropping her brief pretence at cut-glass newsreader pronunciation.

'We brought it from France,' I say, softly, looking at the huge chest that takes up one whole wall in the hallway outside the guest room. It's far too big for its place here, at the top of the stairs. 'Mum brought some things that mattered to her. This, the Bible, some oil paintings. There was jewellery too, but that's all gone.'

Peg is remaking the bed in the spare room. It's already made but she seems the type who needs something to do with her hands. The clothes she's laid out for me are draped over the metal footboard. They look warm and comfortable: a thick cable-knit cardigan and a pair of denim dungarees. I'd definitely add them to my basket if I spotted them on a vintage clothes app. There's a big lumberjack shirt too, which she recommends I wear to bed. It gets damn cold after midnight, so she claims.

'Jethro said your mother was some kind of royal,' she says, conversationally. 'It was always hard to know what was true and what was something he'd just read, but I reckon that might be true.'

I smile, tiredly. 'Old money,' I say. 'Very little of it left by the time she married my father, and he did his best to waste it as quickly as he could. She didn't really care about money when she had it, but once it was gone she realised just how fond of it she really was.'

Peg stops what she's doing to give me a kindly look that almost makes me cry. 'You have the look of her. More than Jethro.'

'Maybe that's why Father thought of me the way he did,' I say, stifling a yawn. 'Perhaps I reminded him of her.'

'Jethro never spoke much of your father.'

I stare past her at the darkened window. There are seashells on the windowsill and a little black-and-white etching of a country church. I take a moment before I feel able to answer her in a way she might understand.

'Different fathers,' I say, looking down at the old wooden floorboards. One of the knots in the old wood looks back at me; a hooded eye, staring up accusingly.

'He never mentioned that,' says Peg, with something like an apology. 'God, it must be awful to think of police officers picking over all of this. Jethro would hate it. I'm so sorry this is happening, Claudine.'

I give a nod of thanks. Look back to the huge great wooden chest. The wood is stained almost black, and the carvings have been deformed by years of inattention, but it's still a glorious piece of furniture. I think Mum said it was sixteenth century but I'm no expert. Jethro would know, of course. He'd be able to describe every single feature. I just know that it used to scare me when I was small. I always had a terrible fear of waking up trapped inside it, the great rusted hatches locked shut and me hammering and screaming on the thick lid. We used it for blankets when I was little. The linen always emerged from its depths smelling like something from another age: all camphor and lavender and mildew.

'I suppose it's all evidence now,' I say, running my hand across the surface. Beneath my palm are ancient carvings of sprites and cherubs, cherries and leaves. For a moment I'm a kid, a stranger in an alien landscape, curled up in Mum's big luxurious shawl, running my fingertips over the smooth rises and dips of the absurd antique, wedged in the hallway at the little cottage that Mum insisted would help Jethro feel better. I recall with absolute clarity the anger that flooded me, that hot prickle of indignation as I pushed the pads of my fingers against the ancient wood and cursed my brother for his weakness, his feebleness; his damnable hold upon Mum's heart. I remember staring into the shapes on the lid, tears making my vision shimmer and blur. The cherubs twisted, contorted. The faces of blessed saints seemed to twist themselves into new, ghoulish forms: jawbones dislocating, eyes sinking, tongues rolling free of slack jaws and splitting down their length to flicker and hiss, lapping against the webbing of my little warm hands as if searching for nourishment.

'Claudine?'

I step back from the chest, overwhelmed by a flood of recollections. Christ, how had I forgotten that? How had I never taken it upon myself to unpick the strands of that childish imagining?

'Sorry, zoned out, I think. I'm going to have to sleep. I'm so sorry…'

She's looking at me, head on one side, a hand on her hip. If I were sitting, my legs would be jiggling up and down. I'm trying not to pick at the skin around my nails, trying not to bite the skin of my lips. I feel hot and cold at once. There's a feeling a little like fear kneading chill fingers at the nape of my neck but there's something else too – some sense of a thing not quite forgotten, some memory trying to drag itself out of a locked room.

'I can help you,' she says, gently. 'Police won't be any the wiser if you want to go through his things right now and decide for yourself what they've got the right to see.'

I'm tempted by the offer. I've no doubt that Peg has already rummaged through Jethro's possessions plenty of times. I know I would have done if I were storing books and papers and family albums for somebody else. Who wouldn't?

'In the morning,' I say, pretending to stifle a yawn. 'I can't face it now.'

She nods, understanding. 'So much of his stuff got ruined when the ceiling came through,' she says, again. 'This is really all we could save.'

'It must have taken some getting up the stairs,' I say, in an awkward attempt at small talk. 'Your husband must be stronger than he looks.'

She pauses for a moment, a strange look on her face, one

eye momentarily closing. She looks as though she's digging something out of a back tooth with her tongue. 'It was a couple of Jethro's pals, as it happens,' she says. 'Nice lads. Quiet. Peter and Thomas, I think.' She smiles at a memory. 'Always a bit hard to tell one from the other when it comes to the Apostles.'

I let my confusion show in my face. 'Apostles?'

Peg laughs, smoothing down a crease in the bedspread with the flat of her hand. 'That's what Everitt and I used to call his pals when they stopped by. Barefoot hippies, mostly, and even those with shoes on looked as though it was under sufferance. Long hair and beards, Rosaries and those shiny eyes you see when somebody's been on the festival circuit since Woodstock. Nice lot. We said they looked like disciples when they wandered along past the house on their little rambles. Harmless, of course. Like minds are drawn together, aren't they?'

I don't answer at first. I'm thinking again of the police officer. I know there are going to be questions and I haven't got anything like enough answers. I'm going to be cross and upset and end up feeling like the worst sister in the world. I didn't know my brother at all. This nice lady, his only neighbour, would be of more use to the investigating officers than me, his only relative.

'We'll tough it out, don't worry,' says Peg, squeezing my arm as if reading my thoughts. 'You and I know the truth, don't we? Jethro was a lovely, sweet, troubled man and he lost his life through nothing but bad luck. Wrong place, wrong time – or maybe right place, right time, depending on your point of view. I heard you on the phone. I wasn't eavesdropping, I just heard what you were saying. And you don't know, do you? Not really. Don't know what might have happened if Jethro wasn't there. Maybe you wouldn't be standing here now. I don't like to take refuge in platitudes but maybe things really do happen for a reason.'

I nod politely, eager for her to be gone. I'm so tired. My limbs ache as if I've been swimming through mud and my scalp is throbbing as if I've worn my hair in a too-tight plait. I need sleep. Need silence. I need to talk to you, Esmerelda – to sing you a lullaby inside my mind and imagine the life I would be living if my body had done what it was made for instead of betraying us both and killing you. I need to weep for a while – for me, for Jethro, for you. Always you.

'Your bag's on the back of the door,' she says, looking around as if trying to find a new reason to stay. I can't hear any sound of Everitt from downstairs. Can hear nothing but the rain and the occasional creak of a settling timber. I should go downstairs with her again. Sit in front of the fire. Read and chat and offer some company to this lady who was so much better to Jethro than I ever was. Instead I give a tight smile of thanks and watch as she lets herself out, pulling the door closed behind her.

I don't even wait until she's gone a respectful distance before I slide the bolt across at the top and bottom of the door. My bag is hanging from a nail, crudely hammered into the old, white-painted wood. I lift it down, cradling its familiar heft and bulk. Slide out the laptop again and throw it on the bed. I change quickly, pulling on the thick shirt and wishing I had some bedsocks. I always slept with my socks on as a child. Always knew that my toes would look appetising to the monsters at the foot of the bed.

Only when I'm sitting up in bed and, sinking into the soft

pink pillows, do I return my gaze to the back of the door. There are scratches scored deep into the paintwork: layer upon layer of harshly scored grooves, a lattice of lines dug into the wood and have been half-heartedly painted over. I climb back out of bed. Cross to the door. Raise my hand and touch my fingertips to the scored wood. I feel something sharp against the pad of my index finger. A little bead of blood bubbles up from beneath the punctured skin. I suck it instinctively while I dig at the wood with my other hand. I feel like an archaeologist scraping through compacted sand.

Suddenly a big sliver of wood slips free and in the crevice beneath it I can make out the object that has pricked me. I pull it free with forefinger and thumb and lay it reverently on my palm. It's a fingernail, perfectly excised, yellowed and thick and pinkly bloody at the root. Somebody clawed at this door as if trying to pull themselves free of the grave.

I switch out the light and stumble blindly back to bed, the nail still clutched in my fist. I push the laptop down towards the foot of the bed and curl myself up as tight as I can. I listen to the rain and the wind and the soft shushing of the swaying reeds.

Sleep comes before the tears have a chance to fall.

12

'Bloody hell.'

'Yeah, I think that just about covers it.'

Billy and Helen are lingering in the darkened entrance to the little church. The buildings are tall, the road narrow. The streetlights are already on. The rain is coming down hard, drumming on the bonnets of the handful of parked cars and rippling the surface of the grimy water that gathers between the kerbs and reflects back a blurry replica of the old and creaking street. They've finally disentangled themselves from the melee of London's homeless community. They're cold and wet and confused but neither wants to grumble about it. What they've just seen makes their own suffering seem of so little consequence. They'll both sleep in warm homes tonight. They'll sleep without fear of death coming in the night. And they'll wake up to warmth.

'You should buy a proper coat,' says Savage, pulling a face as Billy shivers beside her. He's soaked to the skin, his suit clinging to him. He's trying to suppress a shiver. Savage, clad in a sensible alpine coat, walking boots and woolly hat, is fighting the urge to take care of him. He doesn't look very well. He's shaking as if he's a drinker in need of a shot. She wants to pop down to the convenience store and get him a hot chocolate and a bacon roll. A blanket would be good too. One of the homeless men had certainly thought so – offering the shivering detective sergeant a damp, tickly covering and telling him he could keep it if he promised to find who killed his mates. Savage hadn't known where to look. Billy had declined.

'I've got a proper coat,' growls Billy. 'I'm just not fucking wearing it.'

'Ask a PC for a spare. You're going to freeze to death.'

'I'm all right.'

Savage doesn't argue. She's married to a stubborn man and knows that there are times when it's better to let somebody suffer than to keep having offers of help rejected. It's a truth that causes her daily dismay.

'The woman,' says Savage, changing the subject. She pulls her notebook from her pocket and looks at her neat blue script. She prefers to do things the old-fashioned way and doesn't trust electronic devices. 'Miriam Kovac, thirty-nine. No fixed abode but picks up her post at the hostel in Vauxhall. I thought I was going to come apart.'

Billy nods. The last few hours have overflowed with grief and pain. The homeless community that gathers around the food banks and shelters is a close-knit one. The men who died were well liked. They were loved. Each had drifted to London after losing their way.

'You're ringing,' says Savage, nodding at Billy's pocket.

'DS Dean,' he says, answering the unfamiliar number.

'It's me,' says Fran, her voice low. She clears her throat. He can hear her frowning, trying to find the right tone. 'Let's pretend this isn't going to be horribly awkward, okay? Leave our personal troubles at the door? I need to brief the divisional commander. Graeme Argyll tells me you're talking to the witnesses. Can you give me a precis so he's got something to throw up to the politicians when they ask?'

Billy sucks his cheeks. Everything tastes of acid and emptiness. He loves hearing her voice. Loves talking to her. Loves being able to help her impress the bosses, even while part of him would love nothing more than to give her duff information and let her make a tit of herself in front of the top brass.

'Bedlam,' he says, his voice softer than Savage is used to hearing it. He sticks a finger in his ear. Talks to her with his eyes closed. 'Bloody madness, to be honest. There's barely anybody here who doesn't have three nicknames. It's all "I think Tiger saw Jock going to talk to the Professor" and whatnot. I'm trying to disentangle it. But the names you've got – they match what Helen and I have managed to piece together down at the scene. It would break your heart, I swear. They're just milling around, lost. It's like a zombie movie.'

'Witnesses who will give a statement and actually appear at a hearing?' asks Fran hopefully. 'I don't suppose they could give you the name and home address of the killer, could they?'

Billy lets himself smile. She sounds, briefly, like herself. 'I spoke with a guy called Mikel Klein. He's got a mobile and has given me the number and swore blind he'll stay in touch. He was close with both victims. He's still shaking at the thought that it was nearly him who ended up dead. He's verified the names and backgrounds of the two victims from the park. Couldn't be sure whether he'd met the other victim before.'

'Jethro Cadjou, yes?'

'I showed him the photograph the digital forensics team found online – the one from the local paper. It's too grainy so the fact that he didn't recognise it might not be relevant.'

'And he saw what happened?'

'Yes and no,' says Billy, with a sigh that is more apology than exasperation. 'Our two were very close. Best of friends, according to Klein. Watched out for one another. They hung about in the park most days. Took it in turns getting off the booze – one helping the other. They always fell off the wagon but they both wanted to be better versions of themselves. Those are Klein's words, not mine. Anyway, Klein and a lady that Helen spoke to, they were on a bench, staying dry under a blanket, waiting for a few other known faces to start appearing so they could all head up to the church for a feed together.

'About half an hour before it all started, Klein heard the two victims having a bit of an argument with somebody. Now, it was chucking it down and I get the impression Klein was a bit out of it on his drug of choice, but he said that the two victims were thick as thieves with a third chap. Knows him by the name of Enoch, but hasn't really had anything to do with him and couldn't offer a description that didn't sound like he was making it up on the spot. He said he couldn't tell who they were arguing with, but he presumed it was Enoch because he was somebody who had caused trouble in the past. Not popular, apparently. Bit of a headcase, according to Klein. He was one of the people who would disappear for days and weeks at a time and then turn up again without a word. Off on the "pilgrimage", or so he said. Some sort of barefoot trek out into the back of beyond, but whether it's real or a cover story or just imagined, well, that's anybody's guess.

'Anyway, Klein saw these two – Andrew and Gwyndaf – looking all upset and arguing with one another. Next thing, the lady is shrieking and grabbing him by the arm because somebody in a mask and dark clothes was sticking a knife into Gwyndaf. Andy tried to help him, then to run, and he just put the blade right through him. Slit his throat right there, blood spraying like they'd just stuck a harpoon in a whale.'

'You said the description sounded made up?' asks Steadman, and her voice goes muffled for a moment as she presses the phone between shoulder and chin. He imagines the scent of her. Remembers the feel of her skin upon his lips. Shivers and closes his eyes.

'Same as the uniforms got from the office workers overhead. Couldn't tell if it was a mask or just so much dirt and blood. Looked like something ripped from an old book, or so he said, which might mean bloody anything. Average height, average build. Speaking in a foreign language they didn't recognise. Didn't run – just walked off calm as you like. There are some neat footprints in the blood that got forensics very excited. Military boots, by the looks of things. Size nine.'

'This "Enoch",' she says, thoughtfully. 'Anybody else able to point you in their direction? The church is very involved with that little group of people. Maybe they can give you a steer...'

'Helen and I are standing here right now,' says Billy, trying not to sound as though he's showing off. 'I might look like a drowned rat, but Helen's still managing to present the warm, approachable face of the Metropolitan Police.'

He hears her give the smallest of laughs. Feels his heart break.

'You should have taken your coat,' she says, with a hint of warmth in her voice.

Billy can't think of what to say in reply. 'Bloody stupid shoes leak like a colander,' he grumbles, and immediately curses himself. They'd been a gift, an attempt to remake him into something that she could consider growing old with.

'Well, you can go back to your steel toecaps now,' says his wife.

'Sorry,' he mumbles, feeling stupid. 'Actually, Fran…'

She's already rung off. For a moment the world spins. He pictures himself crashing into the wet tiles at the doorway of the church, breaking his face, leaking blood all over the floor. Wonders if she would visit him in hospital. Whether she would nurse him to the end if he found out he had an inoperable brain tumour and that was why he was thinking such mad thoughts and feeling so unlike himself, why the world kept spinning and he couldn't keep his food down.

He reaches out, supporting his weight on the little noticeboard outside the wooden double doors to the church. The glass is wet and dirt-streaked and shows posters advertising service times and communion. A colourful card from an orphanage in Haiti is pinned up in the top corner, a childish hand thanking their many friends in the local parish for their generosity. There's a little flier pinned up beneath it. It advertises a talk delivered by an author and theologian who is, according to the publicity material, a controversial religious commentator and well-known contributor to

Radio 4. The event was last night at seven p.m. Billy takes a picture of the flier on his phone.

'Anything?' asks Savage, behind him.

'Food is served between five and six p.m.,' mutters Billy. 'This was meant to be right after. Maybe they sold tickets through a website, which means there'll be a record of who was coming. Potential witnesses. Job for a DC, somewhere down the line.'

'I've heard him, I think,' says Savage, nodding at the name. 'How do you pronounce that?'

'Struan,' reads Billy. 'Reverend Struan Talbot. I think I've read something of his. Maybe not.'

'Shall we go see if the vestry has a kettle?' asks Savage, pulling her arms in tight and miming an extravagant shiver.

Billy nods. He closes an eye, feeling the headache start to thrum inside his head. He knows the name; he's sure of it. He's read so many books this past couple of years, has fought so hard to keep up with his wife as she has become so much more than him. He looks again at the poster. There's a picture of a book cover in the centre of the cheaply made flyer. *The Devil's Breath: Psychotropics and the Rise of Christianity*. He remembers a podcast he tried to listen to at Fran's insistence. A chat between three different religious experts, all trying to work out the nature of the Holy Trinity. He'd dozed off, bamboozled by the whole affair.

'Me this time,' mutters Savage, retrieving her phone. 'Sure thing,' she says, a moment later, and hangs up. She pulls a face at Billy.

'Vestry will have to wait. They need us at the British Library.'

Billy takes a moment. Swallows something foul. 'We're busy,' he says.

'There was an incident there yesterday afternoon. Homeless man trying to smash his way into a display case housing some old Anglo-Saxon document. Security walked him out, but he left his bag behind. His name was written on the inside and when their security people googled it, well...'

'Third victim?' he asks. His mind floods with an image of the dead man's sister. Sees her so damn pretty and perfect, changing into her dress without a care in the world just four hours after watching her brother be filleted. 'We're going to have a lot to ask the sister.'

'She's not answering the FLO, actually,' says Savage. 'And yes, it was Jethro Cadjou's bag. Forensics are on their way, but Jim wants us there to provide – in his words – some bloody idea about what matters and what doesn't.'

Billy feels his thoughts nagging at him. He can't leave it. Needs to know why Talbot's name seems so familiar. He punches the name into Google and finds a large banner headline on the *Evening Standard*: Struan Talbot paying an emotional tribute to his 'saintly' friend.

'What's that face for?' asks Savage, eyeing him. 'What are you thinking?'

Billy puts his hands in his pockets. Steps back out into the rain and trudges back towards the car. Savage follows after.

From an upstairs window, Enoch watches them leave. He's sore. There's a hole in his shoulder and an ugly graze on his hip. But Enoch is used to pain. He deserves pain. Pain brings him closer to God.

God stands beside him. Puts his hand upon his injured shoulder and Enoch feels himself healing.

God looks upon His work. And sees that it is good.

13

I dream.

I see you, Esmerelda. I see you as you should have been. Two years old now, dark-eyed and chubby-thighed, oak-brown curls and the same fierce frown of concentration as your mum; stern and focused. You wear the rag-doll dresses I would have chosen for you. You have butterfly clips in your hair. You prefer to be barefoot. You walk early, impress strangers with your vocabulary. You love music. When you fall asleep it is with a suddenness and simplicity; a sudden cessation of energy as you fold yourself into me and slumber warmly, damply, against my chest. I feel myself smiling within the dream. Feel the softness of your moist curls between the comb of my fingertips.

Only when I feel truly at peace does the vision become nightmare. Your hair turns to cobwebs against my knuckles. I stroke the skin from your brittle bones. You become cold as the grave within my embrace, depleting, diminishing with each caress; turning to dust and ash as surely as if you were a burnt log plucked from the hearth. I try and piece you back together. I feel the confetti of your disintegrating matter, scoop up handfuls of you as the chill air swirls you into nothingness and black, black snow.

Now the beasts come. Only now, as I sob and wail and squeeze my fists, the walls writhe with the presence of the damned: snouts and tusks; fur and tail; teeth and twisting, coiling tongues. I can't move. I'm pinned to the bed, blood upon my tongue; some unyielding force pushing me flat against the mattress.

And I know that I am no longer asleep. My eyes are open, my heart slamming into my ribcage, and yet the creatures from the nightmare remain. The ceiling is a wriggling mass of adders and intertwining limbs; a frogspawn-slimed tapestry of reptilian flesh, knotted with dismembered arms and legs. For an instant I see the thing that squats, toad-like, upon my sternum. For an instant there is a figure in a dirty white robe kneeling astride me; a sensation of cold, spoiled meat against my feverish, sweat-soaked skin. And in the darkness, I see him peel back the cloth of his cloak. He is naked beneath, skin the yellowy-white of a harvest moon.

He stares down, eyes becoming beetle backs amid the hair and tallow of his implacable face. He places gnarled, old-man hands at his own throat and slides his nails beneath the flesh as easily as if it were silk. He takes a handful of his own skin and pulls down, unpeeling himself, tugging at his suit of rotten skin to expose the rank redness of sinew and meat; stark flashes of bone; the ugly pulsing orb of a heart that squirts a black bile to spatter down upon my upturned face as…

I jerk upright as if yanked by angelic hands. Suddenly I am sitting up in bed, frozen to the bone, coiled in a tangle of sodden sheets. I cup my face in my hands. Smell blood. I fumble for the light, squinting in the sudden brightness at the half-moon shapes scored in my palm. One of the wounds is deeper than the others: a horseshoe shape stamped right into the centre of my palm. I touch it with my index finger and feel the shape within. Sick, shaking, I probe at the edge of the wound, shuddering as I slowly ease out the fingernail that I had plucked from the wood and fallen asleep gripping in my fist.

I throw it away into the furthest corner of the room. I try to slow my heart but I'm still trembling. I try to hold on to you, to the brief vision of what would have been had I just been able to give you life. *I can't find you.* All I can see in the fading echo of the dream is the figure atop my chest – the old man in the dirty robe, flaying himself as if his flesh were an offering.

I reach for the water at my bedside. Force myself to drink. I realise that the bed is soaked through. I'm lying in a pool of my own sweat and tears and drool and... a smell assails my nostrils. I screw up my eyes, fighting the urge to cry, disgusted and ashamed. I've wet myself. Wet myself in a stranger's bed.

I drain the water. Climb out of the sodden tangle of sheets. I pull off the soaking shirt and begin stripping the sheets and blankets from the bed. I cry a little, face twisting into a series of grimaces as I bundle up the evidence of my shame. There's a thick towel hanging over the radiator and I wrap it around myself as I gather up all of the dripping material. I pull open the latch on the door and move silently into the corridor, gripping my bundle of sheets. I move as softly as I can, stepping sparingly upon the bare wood of the hallway, moving like shadow down the corridor and into the lingering warmth of the hall.

I peer into the living room as I make my way to the

kitchen. Everitt is sitting in an armchair, a book open in his lap. He's fast asleep, mouth slightly open, head tilted back to expose his throat. I hurry on to the kitchen and into the little room beyond. I find the light and in the sudden glare of the bare bulb I set about finding washing powder and softener, fumbling around with the unfamiliar dials of the washing machine. I breathe a sigh of relief when it starts to click and whirr, filling with blue water and rinsing away evidence of my unforgivable shame. I have an overwhelming urge to have a hot shower, to rinse myself clean of the last lingering traces of the nightmare, but I don't want to wake my host. Instead I fill the deep old Belfast sink and scrub myself with handfuls of icy water, shivering nakedly as I splash and scour at every inch of myself. Only when I feel as though I'm something close to clean do I wrap myself back in the towel and switch off the light.

I retrace my steps, stopping in the kitchen to fill another glass with water and drain it in one long gulp. My head is pounding suddenly. I need to eat and yet there's a tight feeling of sickness in my throat. I feel so lost. Feel so far from home. Feel so lonely I can barely breathe.

Everitt's no longer there when I pass the living room. I didn't hear him go to bed, but I wasn't paying attention. The book he was reading is still lying out on the chair he was sitting in. There's still a little warmth coming from the fire. I don't want to go back to my bedroom. Don't want to face the bare mattress or run my hand over the trunk of my dead brother's pitiful few possessions.

I move silently into the living room, scooping up a few pine cones from the basket and dropping them one by one into the smouldering ashes. I pick up the book from the armchair and pull a multi-coloured crocheted blanket from the blanket box beneath the window. Wrapped in its folds, legs drawn up beneath me, I wait for the fire to offer up enough light to see by. Slowly, by the flickering red-gold flame, I inspect the book. It's thick and heavy, bound in a soft leather the colour of an old French wine. The lettering is picked out in gold. *De Materia Medica* by Pedanius Dioscorides.

The name is familiar. I close my eyes for a second, trying to trace the feeling of connection back to its source. Suddenly I'm a child again, sitting at the kitchen table in the cottage down the lane. Mum has her back to me, stirring something on the cooker top. There's music drifting out of a little radio on the windowsill. It's dark outside but the cottage is warm and smells of fresh-cut herbs. And Jethro, my big brother, is sitting at the table beside me, his pencil moving at speed over the lined pages of his notebook, a weighty old textbook open in front of him. He'd seen me staring. Looked up and smiled and stopped what he was doing so he could tell his little sister about Dioscorides.

'He's the father of modern botany and pharmacology, alive at the same time that the gospels were being written. Can you imagine? There would be no such thing as medicine without his discoveries. Every drug, every poison – every hidden capability buried away within the petals and stems and roots – this is the book that categorised and catalogued them. Other physicians – that's the old word for doctors and scientists – added their own discoveries. It passed hand in hand through some of the greatest and most enquiring minds the world has ever known. There are answers here, Moineau. If I keep looking, I'll find what I'm looking for.'

I pull myself out of the memory before it overwhelms me. Feel a dryness in my mouth and see my pulse beating, thudding, against the fragile prison of my wrist. It was only days later that he tried to kill himself. Only a matter of hours until his mania would dissipate and the sorrow would claim him.

I open the book and run my fingers over the old, thick paper. It's older than our family Bible; the pages feeling more like cloth than paper. There's an extravagant woodcut on the opening page: a watery sketch of some unfamiliar climbing ivy and a faded inscription, promising the reader that the contents provide: '*all manner of strange trees, herbes, rootes, plants, floures and other such rare things*'. Underneath, handwritten, is a name I can barely make out: great curled lettering and a date: February 1546. I peer again at the name. Could it be Matteus? Perhaps Matioli? Over the page are more names, handwritten in the margins of a great swathe of introductory text. I see the name *Gerarde*, and the date 1597. I rub my hands on the towel, aware of the value of the tome I hold in my hands.

I turn the page. It's a beautiful book, richly illustrated with pictures of plants, flowers, herbs, spices. I see names I recognise: aconite, colocynth, hellebore, henbane, hemlock, myrrh. I stop on one page, illustrated with an exquisite sketch of a purple-headed plant rising from a pastoral scene – a bonneted maid picking wildflowers in front of a humble country cottage. I turn the page. There's spidery writing in the margins – little notes and improvements and additions to the words on the page. It's only when I reach a section entitled *Solanum Somniferum* that I see a handwriting I recognise. It's Jethro's – three lines, scribbled beneath a picture so unnerving that I feel gooseflesh rise on my arms. It shows a brown root transformed into a crude drawing of a child: arms, legs, some approximation of a face, topped off with a crown of sprouting green leaves. It reads: '*What with loathsome smells, And shrieks like mandrakes torn out of the earth, That living mortals, hearing them, run mad.*'

I close the book. Hold it like a child. Hold it like I would hold you.

When sleep comes, there is only the dark.

14

'It's not just me, is it?'

'What?'

'The sculpture?'

Billy scowls up at the colossal figure, bare-chested and bearded, seated on a great rectangular plinth and leaning forward, bright-eyed, expertly walking a pair of compasses across an astral chart. It's Sir Isaac Newton and represents man's endless search for knowledge. It does, he has to admit, look a lot like a bearded giant sitting on a Portaloo.

'You're a child,' grunts Billy, but he permits himself a tiny smile that pleases Savage as much as a belly laugh. The rain has eased off a little but there's an ugly wind slicing across the courtyard outside the British Library, keeping the tourists at bay and giving the pigeons a plumped-up, pissed-off expression that, to Billy at least, marks them down as proper locals.

'I'm just saying,' giggles Savage, as they walk briskly up the stairs towards the big glass double doors. 'When I brought our Joseph here, he wanted to know why there was a big beardy fella eating a Chinese takeaway while having a shit.'

'Takeaway?' asks Billy, despite himself. 'What's the takeaway bit?'

'He thought the compasses were those training chopsticks you get in the Fiery Panda,' she explains, pulling off her hat and trying to make her hair look slightly less insane. They pass through the glass doors and Billy is delighted to feel a great waft of warm air wrap around him. 'Haven't been here for years,' she adds, looking up at the distant roof and the two flights of high, steep stairs. 'Bet it's still all books and whatnot.'

'I pop in now and again,' says Billy, running his hand under his collar and wringing out the tails of his jacket onto the woefully inadequate welcome mat. 'Twelve million books, I think.'

'I've managed to finish six this year,' says Savage, taking off her coat and straightening herself out. She loops her lanyard over her neck. Billy leaves his in his pocket.

'Six what?'

'Six books. Front to back. Reread *Twilight*, if that counts.'

Billy pulls a face. 'No, it doesn't.'

'You're a reader?' she asks, sounding mildly surprised.

'It shouldn't be something that necessitates a label,' he says, disappointed in her. 'That's like asking somebody if they're a breather.'

'Get you, Dickens,' says Savage, her mood growing warmer the longer she stands beneath the huge radiator overhead. Her hair starts to puff up before his eyes, great tendrils of frizzy brown rising into the air like charmed snakes. 'Ah, here we go...'

A slim young woman with round spectacles and long, straight brown hair, is hurrying down the steps towards them. She wears cream-coloured jeans and a green T-shirt displaying an image of a kitten holding a gun. She has an electronic tablet under her arm and is raising her eyebrows at them both in a manner that suggests she's been sent to help them and isn't hugely comfortable in social situations.

'Are you the police?' she asks, making a face that suggests she thinks it's a silly question. 'We have the science ones. Apparently you're the detective ones. I'm not really a police aficionado, if I'm honest. My stepdad always had a fantasy about fire-bombing one of those speed-camera vans. But he was a bit odd. Anyways. Erm.'

Billy looks to Helen Savage for guidance. The woman is in her mid-twenties at the most. Her fingernails are bitten down to nothing at all and she wears no make-up, jewellery or perfume. The badge on her T-shirt names her as Dr Jasmine-Rose Keighley. She follows Billy's gaze and realises she hasn't introduced herself.

'I'm, well, I'm JR, actually,' she says, flustered. 'Erm, yeah. The Treasure Room. I'm really, well, I suppose I'm like the Anglo-Saxon expert, or something. Maybe. They asked me to talk to you. So I'm talking. Erm…'

Billy takes a little step back. Savage steps forward, all smiles. 'I'm Helen,' she says, brightly. 'Detective Constable. This is my Sergeant. Billy, if you can believe it. Jasmine-Rose? That's gorgeous. My youngest, Cicely – she nearly got Jasmine.'

The young woman relaxes. Manages something like a smile. 'Can I show you?' she asks. 'Where it happened, like.'

She leads them up the stairs. It's not as quiet in the great space as either of them might have expected. Scholars, academics, people trying to stay out of the rain: they mill around, drifting in and out of great cavernous rooms, sitting plugged in at laptops or drinking hot froth in the coffee shops on the first floor. There's a low murmur of chat, voices lowered, but still plainly audible. Last time Billy was here was for a book launch. There were security guards all around to ensure nobody spilled a drop of the publisher's fiver-a-bottle red wine. Apparently, the tiled floor is irreplaceable.

'Treasure Room,' says Dr Keighley, leading them into a dark space. 'Eighty miles of shelving, twelve million books. The jewel in the crown is this exceptional space. It showcases early gospels on papyrus, the first complete New Testament, some of the finest art from Europe's Middle Ages, and the Gutenberg Bible from 1455. It has original works by Shakespeare, song lyrics written by the Beatles, the notebooks of Beethoven and the Brontës...'

Billy tunes the words out. Looks back as he makes his way up the stairs. The steps feel slippy. Treacherous. He could see himself tripping and falling, coming apart like a sack of old bones. He arrives at the top of the stairs out of breath and cold again, the heat seeming to dissipate the deeper into the old building they go. He glances up and sees the academic pointing out something interesting to Savage, who nods along, pretending to listen, while absorbing every single detail of the space around them. A security guard stands at the door, big and broad. A science officer in a white suit is bent over a glass case in the centre of the room, lit by gaudy yellow bulbs. He waves a hand, idly, at the newcomers. Savage waves back.

'I've been in here before,' says Billy, more to himself than to anybody else. It's a good place to kill an hour or two while waiting for a train at the bustling stations nearby. He's seen more than his fair share of guest lectures and interesting talks on subjects that Fran has told him he will be interested in. She's invariably been right. He likes learning new things. Likes thinking in different ways. That's what drives him so crazy about Fran's assertion that he's incapable of change. It's simply not bloody true.

'Bag's been photographed,' says the science officer, as Billy wanders over, shielding his eyes from the glare of the bulb. 'Give me a second to finish up and you can have a look at the photographs.'

'Cheers,' grunts Billy, looking around in something like wonder. It's an extraordinary environment: a true treasure trove of humanity's great works. He finds himself smiling slightly as he glances at the little notebook, bearing the original handwritten score for Handel's *Messiah*. He finds it wondrous that such marvels would be his to touch, to venerate, if not for a pane of toughened glass.

'The St Guthlac Roll,' says Savage, appearing at his side. She gestures at the artefact in front of them: a series of circular drawings showing robed figures in a series of colourful tableaus. 'I've never heard of it,' she says, under her breath. 'Anyway, Jethro was trying to get into the case. Or at least, trying to get at what was inside. Sobbing his eyes out, apparently. Talking nonsense, according to security staff. Told them he needed to touch it, to test it, to...'

'Absolutely crack-a-lacking, isn't it,' asks Dr Keighley, from the other side of the case. 'The roll, I mean. One of my favourites, actually. You'll know the origins, of course.'

Billy does. Savage doesn't. Both reply with: 'Remind me.'

'Well, I mean, where do I start?' she muses, chewing

on her non-existent thumbnail. 'Essentially, what you're looking at is a long, thin strip of parchment covered in eighteen roundels, depicting key moments from the life of St Guthlac. Is that enough?'

Savage pulls a face. 'Not really,' she says, apologetically.

'St Guthlac,' mutters Billy, roiling his shoulders inside his wet jacket. 'Warrior monk?'

'And so much more,' says Dr Keighley, excitedly. 'I'm by no means the expert on this particular artefact, though the era is supposedly my particular specialism.'

'Get you,' says Savage, to her colleague. 'How did you know that?'

'I said – I've been here before. I've stood here. Read this. Remembered it. I doubt it'll catch on.'

'Who was this St Guthlac then?' asks Savage. 'I'm presuming we'll be asked, and it would be nice not to just stand there looking dense.'

Billy angles his head and reads the information attached to the display case. 'Guthlac (674–715)... a saint from the Anglo-Saxon kingdom of Mercia... soldier in the Mercian borderlands... lived the life of a warrior... a religious conversion and became a hermit in Crowland, in Lincolnshire... lived in solitude on an island in the middle of a marsh...'

'Fought devils and demons, if you believe that sort of thing,' adds Dr Keighley. 'The roll itself was completed in the twelfth century but the stories we know about him come from Felix's *Vita Sancti Guthlaci*, which was written only a few years after Guthlac died, when his cult was still very popular.'

'Cult?' asks Savage, suddenly interested.

'Very popular, in his lifetime and not long after,' explains Dr Keighley. 'Very much set the tone for what a Christian life should be. Piety and suffering, really. He spent fifteen years living in not much more than a swamp. Drank a cup of muddy water and a piece of mouldy rye bread every day. Wore nothing more comfortable than raggedy animal skins. All but withered away until there wasn't much left of him but still found the strength to pray and fight demons and found a church that pilgrims came to from far and wide to worship.'

'Tell me about the demons,' says Billy, staring into the case. He studies one of the scenes; it shows the saint beset by horrific monsters, assailed by beasts with fangs and claws and cloven hooves.

'Well, modern thinkers would tell you that the mouldy rye bread wasn't a great idea,' says Dr Keighley, with a shrug. 'Ergot, if you've heard of it. The spores contain what we now think of as LSD? Am I saying that right? It's something my mum told me about, but I don't know if people still take it. Anyway, the theory is that he hallucinated the horrors that he saw. Other people think he may have been schizophrenic or suffering a breakdown as a result of being so malnourished. And then there are people who believe that he really was fighting off the imps of Satan, which is a sentence that feels very strange in my mouth.'

Billy smothers his grimace with his hand. He feels very old. 'What did people think at the time?'

'They thought he was a true holy warrior,' she says. 'Apparently he could talk to the animals, could predict the future, had visions that provided him with the wisdom to counsel a future king. It's a marvellous story. Several miracles have been ascribed to him, both before and after his death. And the death itself was very Hollywood. The smell of ambrosia emanated from his body and when his body was dug up to be transferred to the new abbey being built in his honour at Crowland, it was entirely uncorrupted. It became a shrine. Very popular, up until the Vikings raided and scattered him and his relics to the four winds. Philistines, the lot of them. Though, of course, not really.'

'Ambrosia the rice pudding?' asks Savage, looking confused.

Billy shakes his head at her.

'What's happening in that one?' asks Savage, pointing at a depiction of the monk thrashing a demon with what looks like a multi-tasselled whip.

'Ah, the scourge of St Bartholomew,' says Dr Keighley, rubbing her hands together as if this were her favourite part of the story. 'When Guthlac's strength was fading and the creatures that tormented him in his hermitage were starting to sap his faith, St Bartholomew appeared to him. Guthlac had been dragged to the very lip of Hell by these horrible creatures, but he gave one final prayer and, suddenly, there was the flayed apostle, right in front of him.'

'Flayed apostle?'

'St Bartholomew was one of Jesus's disciples,' explains Billy, quickly. 'Spread the word for many decades after the crucifixion. Paid for it by being flayed alive. Most of the depictions of Bartholomew in art show him carrying his own skin.'

'Oh that's horrible,' says Savage, wincing. 'Why are all the saints people who suffered horrible deaths? It's hardly an advert for Christianity, is it?'

Billy ignores the question. Looks to Dr Keighley, who carries on the story. 'Bartholomew gave him a scourge. You're basically talking about a really nasty cat-o'-nine-tails. And he presented him with a psalter – a Bible, really, if you're not writing an essay – and bound it in the skin of one of the demons whom they vanquished side by side. The psalter and scourge were in the tomb with Guthlac after his death. Those bloody Vikings took the lot. There's a legend that they ended up with a collector in the seventeenth century, but you'd have to speak to Struan about all that. He's the expert.'

Billy rolls his head on his shoulders, hearing something pop at the top of his neck. He feels Savage looking at him. She recognises the name but knows better than to say anything in front of a witness.

'And Jethro Cadjou was trying to get his hands on it?' asks Billy. He gives a little laugh as something occurs to him. 'Cadjou who lives alone, in the Fens? The middle of a swamp? Keeps to himself? Prays? Maybe old Guthlac here is his role model.'

Dr Keighley considers it. 'He'd need to have followers if he really did see himself in that mould,' she says. 'Guthlac had people who lived by his side. People who followed his example of how to be a true Christian. Give me a second and I'll find the names for you. Two of them are saints as well, I think, though don't quote me on it.'

Savage looks as though she's about to ask a question but is interrupted by the ringing of her phone. She pulls a face and walks away to answer it. Billy is left staring at the artefact. 'Struan?' he asks, at last. 'That would be Struan Talbot?'

'Reverend Struan Talbot,' Keighley corrects him. 'He's very particular about that. He was supposed to be giving a talk about his new book this week. I'd hoped to go but I think it was called off because of all the hoo-ha down at the river. I've heard most of it before, of course. He's a very interesting speaker. Always finds a new way to make you interested in things you've heard before, though he can be quite provocative. His new book sounds fascinating – all about the different drugs and potions that he claims were infused into the communion wine of the early Christians to provoke visions that confirmed their faith. It's making a lot of people angry online, but I think he likes all that. He's the one to speak to if you really want to know about all this. I mean, if the man who tried to break the case really is the one who went on to stab those people... It's horrible, isn't it? I mean, he could have done what he did here. Could have stabbed random people. It's awful. Just so ugly.'

Billy decides he hasn't got the energy to correct her. He turns to see the science officer approaching, holding up an electronic device for his inspection. 'Have a flick,' she says, handing it to Billy. 'Pages and pages of gibberish, from what we can tell.'

Billy takes the tablet and starts examining the images. The first shows the bag that Cadjou left in the locker area when he first entered the British Library. It's a soft leather satchel that ties with a thong rather than a buckle. It has a drawstring neck and one thick strap. It contains a thick wad of papers, all covered in the same barely legible handwriting. Billy flicks forward through the images, squinting at the words. He can't understand it. Most of it looks more like musical notation than actual lettering.

'We've got all sorts of software that will try to make sense of it,' says the SOCO, casually. 'Oh, right, yes – that's a bit odd, isn't it?'

Billy stops scrolling. He's looking at an ultrasound image: high quality. It's full colour and shows a beautiful, slumbering, nearly full-term child.

'That was inside the Bible,' says the science officer, leaning past him and moving the roll of images forward to the next screen. It's small and bound in a pinkish leather. Calfskin, perhaps.

Billy flicks back to the image of the child. There's some information printed on the top. A date and name.

'The sister,' says Billy, mostly to himself. 'This was, what, nearly two years ago? She hasn't got a child, has she? There was nothing in the report...'

The science officer shrugs. 'Not my area,' she says. 'Either way, it was the only thing in the bag that looked like it had been taken care of. Not a crease, not a thumbprint. He treasured it – that's for sure.'

'Here's the name I was looking for,' says Dr Keighley, raising her own tablet to demonstrate that she's been hard at work on some research on his behalf. 'Nicolas Hobekinus,' she reads. 'English herald and antiquary, Whig politician and decorated army officer who was a fellow and president of the Society of Antiquaries.'

'Imagine I don't know what you're talking about,' says Billy.

'The person who might have had the psalter and scourge

after the Vikings sacked Crowland,' she explains, looking a little disappointed in him. 'He owned the roll, you see. This one,' she clarifies, nodding at the priceless artefact. 'We can trace its history back a few centuries, but a lot of the origins are rather murky. We do know that Hobekinus gave a talk on it at the Young Devil Tavern in Fleet Street in 1708. You can see the little holes where it was pinned up. Of course, the real treasure hunters would give their right arm to find the missing roundels. Did I say? Roundels are just circular images, really. We think these ones might have been sketches for a planned stained-glass or a larger painting. I doubt we'll ever know. I've just had a flick through a couple of chat groups and you can see how people get carried away, can't you? Apparently the church where he's buried used to have no end of problems with people trying to dig the poor chap up and see if the scourge or the psalter or the missing roundels are in there with him. Some people really are quite the silly geese.'

Billy grinds his teeth. The headache is horrific. He feels as though there's an icicle being pushed through the top of his head and into his brain. He feels himself sway. Screws up his eyes and imagines what Fran would say about all this. Wonders if this is how Guthlac felt on his diet of mucky water and LSD-soaked bread. Wonders if Jethro Cadjou suffered headaches and visions and called upon God for help in casting out his demons.

'Post-mortem's done,' says Savage, taking his arm and moving him away from the glass case. 'Psilocybin. Wolfsbane. Mandrake…'

'You're just naming weird shit, Helen,' growls Billy.

'In his stomach,' she explains. 'Huge volumes, showing

sustained use of psychotropics. Hadn't been taking his medication either – not for a long time.'

'This is Cadjou, yes?'

'Of course it is,' she says. 'Keep up. It's certainly changing the complexion of how the SIO is viewing him. You've seen the security footage, haven't you? He spoke with the killer before he took the knife to the stomach; no fear on his face, nothing. It was like he knew him, if you ask me. And if he was off his medication, taking God knows what…'

Billy tries to process it. He keeps thinking of the cherished ultrasound image. Had Claudine lost a child?

'That Klein chap's been ringing the incident room asking for you, by the way,' she adds. 'Says you're not answering your mobile. Head's cleared a bit and he's got something he thinks might be important.'

'Are you going to tell me?' grunts Billy.

'He didn't say.' Savage shrugs. 'Do you think we should put our hands up for a trip to this place in the Fens? I mean, it has to be done and it's going to be prioritised, isn't it? Has to be. And we need to speak to the sister again – that much is crystal clear. This Struan chap too. God, it's huge, isn't it? So much to keep in one head—'

Billy stops listening. He pulls out his phone and looks at the list of missed calls. Calls up a blank page and begins to jot down all that Dr Keighley has told him.

'Little Mercy,' shouts Dr Keighley, from the far side of the case. 'The church, I mean. Where he's buried.'

Billy looks up, his eyes bloodshot, head full of fire and ice. 'Sorry?'

'Hobekinus,' she explains. 'The church where he's buried. It's in a place called Little Mercy. What a strange name.'

Billy closes the file on his phone. Calls his senior officer. He's going to make her a deal. She's going to let him run with a hunch, and in return, he'll dip a quill in his heart and sign her blasted divorce papers.

'Fran,' he says, when she answers. Then, for spite: 'Ma'am...'

15

Mikel Klein seems like an entirely different person now that his chemical balance is hovering around his sweet spot. He's the right level of intoxicated and medicated to be able to access most of his memory and find the right sounds to make the pictures in his brain into words. Billy is enjoying his company. Of the two of them, Klein looks the smarter. He's wearing a blue hoodie and a long grey cashmere coat. Billy's still in the same suit. It's been soaked and dried out so many times today that it's starting to look like scrunched-up tracing paper. Billy can't help but feel as though it suits him.

'...stress, innit? Proper stress. You don't know you're self-medicating, you don't realise that the things that get you through are the things that are starting to kill you, trying to kill you, and then there's a point where you're not trying to sustain your life any more, you're trying to sustain your addiction and all your priorities change and next thing you're stealing from your wife... stealing from your wife... and your mam and you're begging outside the offy trying to get the three quid you need to take the edge off the hangover, to soften the day... and then you realise that you're not just taking some time out, you're not just on a bender, you're homeless and… you're homeless and… you've got nowhere to go and if you don't find a blanket… find a blanket, you're going to freeze to death but that isn't too bad because at least the pain will be over…'

Savage has stopped taking notes. Klein has a way of talking that even the finest of secretaries would struggle to transcribe. He's talking while taking bites of a huge glazed doughnut, managing to cram the confection into his mouth without in any way impeding the flow of words. He's got a bottle of ginger wine sticking out of the pocket of his coat. Billy keeps looking at it with envy.

'You said you'd remembered Jethro,' says Billy, trying to nudge him onto the right conversational track. They're leaning against the railings, looking out onto the water, the Tower of London to their rear. It's bitterly cold but the rain has let up long enough for Billy's clothes to stop sticking to him, even if his shoes still squelch with every step. They've had to watch the six p.m. briefing on their phones. They haven't got time to stop what they're doing just to make sure that every bugger else knows exactly what they've been working their backsides off to uncover. The top team know that they're following up something useful and that's just about enough to excuse them the tedium of doing things by the book.

'Picture in the paper, picture in the paper,' says Klein, nodding and spraying crumbs. 'Better picture, more like himself, if you get me. You should have said… should have said. My pal Gordo told me it was Jesus who got done. If you'd said it were Jesus, I'd have known from the off.'

'Jesus?' asks Billy, resisting the urge to look at Savage.

'Just a nickname, eh? Same as my pals got nicknames. Beccelm – like Betch-Elm, but spelled different. Cissa. Not real but they liked it well enough. Doubt Enoch's Enoch, eh? I still get Copperknob.'

'The hair?' queries Savage, looking at his wispy strands of washed-out ginger.

'You'd think.' Klein grins, suddenly energised. Just as quickly his shoulders slump, face falling. 'Can't believe the bastard killed Jesus.'

Billy takes a breath. Squeezes his eyes tight shut and waits for the pain to pass. 'You're telling me that you and your friends knew Jethro Cadjou as Jesus, yes?'

'I did.' Klein nods, sucking his fingers. 'They had another name for him. I called him Jesus because he gave them sanctuary, you know? Stupid name, I suppose, but they all talked about him like he was the Second Coming so it just made sense to me. I never went... never went... though it were tempting, like. They all came back bright-eyed and looking good and off the gear. I was curious to see it for myself, to see him.'

Billy waits for more. Nothing comes. Instead, Klein removes the bottle from his pocket and takes a glug. Billy gets a whiff of something herby and sweet. It's definitely not ginger wine.

'So, you're telling us that Mr Cadjou, the third victim, used to welcome members of the homeless community into his home in Lincolnshire, is that right? And that your two friends were among those who took advantage of his hospitality.'

'Never took advantage,' says Klein, bristling. 'They went like they were on their way to Lourdes. Plenty others did too. It was just one of those things that got whispered about, y'know? This holier-than-thou bloke living in a swamp. He'll give you a roof, a place to get clean, three square meals. He'll talk with you, pray with you if you're into it. Not a bad bone in his body, according to my pals. They were the ones who really got into it. I suppose I was a bit jealous – they had this thing, this place, and I wasn't part of it. That's where all the nicknames came from – the chapel, the sanctuary. The Hermitage…'

'The gentleman you mentioned earlier… Enoch?'

Klein looks down at his feet. 'He was there too. Baptised in the swamp, apparently, though I don't know who would have the balls to do something like that. I mean, was he a vicar or something? Even if he's some prophet or something you probably shouldn't just go baptising people. You can get in bother… get in bother…'

Savage sucks her lower lip. 'Did your friends tell you anything else about Mr Cadjou's home? About what happened when they visited?'

'They always came back with those halfwit smiles, y'know,' says Klein, scowling. 'Big gleaming eyes and looking like they'd just taken a stroll on the road to Damascus. It never lasted long but they always came back to London ready to go to church and spread the word and live good and decent lives. A drink or a smoke later and they were slipping back, but the intention was always there. Not Enoch, though. He wouldn't touch drink or drugs. Eyes kept on shining, which is a hell of a thing to look at. Black as coal, they are, though that face…' He mimes a shudder. 'You still haven't pulled the bugger out of the water yet? Not that I'm saying it was him, or anything. Just asking a question.'

Billy runs his hand through his hair. 'The divers have found nothing. Blood on the bridge has gone to the lab and we have to hope that he's a match. Tell me more about his face.'

'Enoch's face? Fuck, you'd need a special effects team to recreate it. I reckon he was burned. Really shiny skin, all patchy, like the way skin looks when it's grown back after being scabbed over. Same on his hands. I tried not to look at him more than I had to. There was always something about him that just sets my teeth on edge, though my mates said he was as good as gold at the sanctuary. I kind of hope he just walks past me, that he's nowt to do with all this. It's all a bit much, isn't it? I'm going to be seeing it on repeat in my head, I swear it. That knife... that knife...'

'You weren't able to specify what kind of blade it was when we spoke earlier,' says Savage.

'I thought it was the poison in my brain making me remember things wrong,' says Klein, apologetic. 'I swear though, the handle of it – I can see it clear as day. It wasn't any modern knife. The handle looked more like something from a movie, like it was all leather and bone. I only saw it for a second...'

'And yet you still can't say that it was Enoch holding it?' asks Billy, pulling a face.

'There's gaps in what I see.' Klein shrugs. 'I can remember the shape of somebody and I can see the knife and I can see the blood and my pals... I don't know what else will come back. I've asked around for you. Those who knew your man Jethro – they'd only met him at the Hermitage. It were his first visit to London I think. That's what it said in the paper. You see the picture of his sister? Bloody hell, she's a looker, isn't she?'

Billy turns to Savage. Tries to ignore the allure of the

sticky drink as Klein takes another long pull on the bottle. 'Any of the hostels got anything for you yet?' he asks.

Savage wrinkles her nose. 'A couple know of this scarred, dark-eyed man who they've seen at the shelters and soup kitchens, but he's never given a name or details that lead us anywhere. Digital forensics have tracked the smartphone that was in Gwyndaf's pocket. The phone company has been uncharacteristically helpful, despite it being unregistered. Four trips to South Lincolnshire, each time using the road network, over the past twelve months.'

'Somebody drove them?' asks Billy. 'You're cross-checking ANPR, yeah?'

She nods. 'We might be onto something or it might be absolutely bugger all,' she grumbles. 'How do you tell the difference, eh?'

'You just do your damnedest either way,' says Billy, massaging his temples.

'You do that a lot,' says Savage. 'Migraines, is it? You can get a piercing that helps. Twisty bit of your ear. Daith, it's called. I've a sister who swears by her daith.'

'I bet she fucking does,' grunts Billy, looking at his phone. There's a message from Fran. She really appreciates this. She knows that once it's all officially over, she'll be able to look back on their time together with happiness.

He wants to throw the damn thing in the river.

'Do you reckon I've earned my keep then?' asks Klein, entirely without subtlety. He puts his hand out and nods at it. Billy gives him two notes from his wallet. Looks again at the poor sod and puts another tenner on top.

'Thanks,' Billy says, and means it. He's about to turn away when a thought bubbles up. He plays with his phone for a moment, looking for an image. 'Do you know this chap?' he asks.

Klein squints at the screen. 'Looks like a hypnotist or something, doesn't he?' Klein grimaces. 'Maybe. I think he's been at the soup kitchens a few times – handing out, not receiving. Why? Who is he?'

'A chap I really want to talk to.' Billy broods, looking hard at the photo of Struan Talbot. He feels Klein looking at him. Looks into sympathetic eyes.

'You look like there's a sadness in you,' says Klein, softly. 'That broken look, y'know? I see it... see it a lot on the streets... people whose soul has just sort of fractured, yeah? Do you want to talk? There are some good people to talk to if you're willing to play your part, y'know? They'll help you if you can get sober, if you can start to slay your demons...'

'I am sober,' growls Billy. 'Not a drop for well over a year.'

'I managed eight,' says Klein, gently. 'Then I had a sip. Nine weeks later I'd lost my house.'

'Fuck off with the dramatics,' says Billy, waving a hand. 'Go on now. You've got our numbers; call if you remember anything.'

'And you call me if you want to talk,' says Klein, seemingly reluctant to leave their sides.

'Fuck's sake,' says Billy, and thrusts his hands in his pockets, stomping off in the direction of the bridge. He hears Savage say goodbye and come jogging after him. She catches him by the arm.

'Touch a nerve, did he?' she asks, making a face. 'Hey, we've all got our own way of coping, haven't we?'

Billy scratches at his face. He tries to think of a reply.

None comes. 'Pick me up at seven,' he says, and walks away. He is a dozen steps away before he remembers to shout 'please' over his shoulder.

Twenty minutes later, Billy is buying vodka in the off-licence. He toasts his wife's name before he takes his first sip, sitting on a bench and staring at the water.

Enoch watches. Waits.

He stares at the scruffy policeman as he sobs and drinks and sobs and pukes and staggers, blindly, towards the place where Enoch was forced to shed blood in the Lord's name. Hears him crying into his telephone. He misses her. Needs her. Can't live without her. He's going to the Hermitage tomorrow but when he gets back, he needs her to truly listen to him. And yeah, he's had a drink. What business is it of hers if he's had a fucking drink...

Enoch shivers as a fresh agony digs into the place where the bullets bit him. The pain is constant. It's unbearable. But Enoch has always lived in pain. Pain is his penance for the man he was before he found the true and proper path. He feels Hell's fires licking at his pink, scorched skin. Feels the rapture as each cell in his body disintegrates and is reborn, over and over; a billion tiny agonies exploding within him.

In his fist, a newspaper. It shows the faces of the martyrs. Shows the countenances of those who gave their holy blood in service to the Lord. And it shows her. Dark-eyed. Beautiful. All that he was promised.

'Mother,' he whispers, and his lip brushes the meaty surface of the soft leather wrappings that hang loose at his face. 'Mother, I am coming home...'

PART TWO

16

The air is thick and grey and seems to press down from above. Billy feels as if he's been trapped inside a Tupperware tub. He heaves again. Shudders. Tries not to cry.

'Better?' asks Savage, and for a moment, he fears she's going to rub his back.

'Bad prawns,' he says, wiping his mouth.

'I feel your pain,' she says, though he knows she doesn't believe him.

It's coming up to nine a.m. The sun should be up. He should be able to identify shapes and outlines. But it's all just mist and haze and sleety grey air. It feels like driving into a dissolving world.

'Shall we crack on? Not far off, I don't think, though I might be wrong. It's all a bit far off the map, innit? I think there should be a sign warning: *Here be Dragons.*'

Billy can taste vodka and bile, paracetamol and blood. The air tingles at his lips as if it contains tiny fragments of ground glass. He's trying not to shiver. He slept in the suit again last night, came to on the living room floor with his trousers around his ankles and one hand in an open box of cereal. It transpired that he'd made himself cocktails before he passed out, raiding Fran's old drinks cabinet for the dregs of unwanted gifts and undrunk spirits. He'd made something out of Cointreau, Tia Maria and ginger wine that looked like a terrible hallucination. It's in his pocket now, eating through the metal of his hip flask.

He knows he's definitely going to start drinking again. Knows that he's going to start making very poor decisions. It's quite a liberating feeling. Finding out what happened to those poor buggers in the park might be his last opportunity to do some good. He fancies he'll be living alongside Klein within the year, maybe dead inside two. He's okay with it.

'Put him back on,' says Billy, climbing back into the passenger seat of the Škoda Octavia and grimacing as he catches a glimpse of his reflection. Savage had urged him to change his clothes, to have a quick shave and maybe a bite of toast before they set off. She'd arrived an hour before they'd arranged. She hadn't been able to sleep and had a feeling he'd be up and about. As it was, she had to lean on the doorbell for a good thirty seconds before he was able to drag himself to the door.

'Him?'

'Talbot,' spits Billy.

They've been listening to a series of podcasts and radio interviews that Savage downloaded to her phone before she went to bed last night, as per Billy's drunk request sometime around midnight. Savage hasn't yet asked Billy the exact nature of his suspicions, but the moment can't be far away. Billy isn't even sure what he'll say in reply. He senses that religious passion is at the heart of what happened and is beginning to believe that at least one of the victims was a lot more involved in what occurred than they have previously been led to believe.

He fancies that Talbot might be the kind of wide-eyed God fanatic who would gladly spill the blood of innocent people and call them martyrs. He simply sounds too good to be true. The scale of his hypocrisy is enough to make him feel sick to his stomach. He knows that his agnosticism is really only a temporary label and that in truth he is searching for a belief system, or a God, that he can really believe in. He envies the faith of others. He sometimes yearns for the comfort of a loving God.

'...impossible to tease out the differing strands of what we think of as religion with what we are now acknowledging as a kind of vague, nebulous spirituality – a belief in some kind of formless force that binds us, and which can be moulded into a more satisfactory shape by the sheer force of will. It's both a fascinating and maddening time to be a theologian. Parish priests have long found themselves providing a role that is as much social worker and psychologist as it is to do with matters of godliness. I find myself answerable for the vagaries of so many aspects of life, and I realised in my youth that what most adherents of the Christian doctrine are really in the market for, is moral superiority. Moral certainty, shall we say...'

'Lovely voice,' says Savage, for the third time. 'Soothing. Sort of melodic.'

Billy grunts. The wipers screech across the window and the pain behind his eyes threatens to pull him under. The world keeps spinning. He skips the podcast forward a few minutes.

'...interesting idea, certainly, and not without its parallels in scripture. At its most basic, a "walk-in" is essentially the idea that a person's original soul has departed his or her body and has been replaced with a new, generally more advanced soul. It's mind-blowing and blasphemous and thoroughly intoxicating as an idea, don't you think? It would certainly explain how sometimes a person can be one way for part of their life, and then somebody completely different for the rest of it.

'Really, true believers maintain that it is possible for the original soul of a human to leave a person's body and for another soul to just walk in. That rather reduces the idea of the human body to the status of a rather complex suitcase. But there is no shortage of evidence if you care to look. Souls are said to walk in during a period of personal problems for the departing soul. It's like suicide without the need to experience death, I suppose. It's like parking your car and walking away with the ignition still running and somebody else simply slips in and off they go. The "new" individual retains the memories of the original personality, but the personality and abilities change.

'Some of the more obscure cults that sprouted in medieval times had very similar ideas about resurrection. There's evidence to suggest that adherents believed that any vessel could be inhabited by what I think of as the liquid essence of a departed soul. It's fascinating, isn't it? Imagine if the saints never really leave us, we just decant them from one vessel into the next and the next – a chain stretching back centuries. There's a book to be written about it, even if it strikes most people as the most frightful humbug—'

Savage switches it off. Blows a raspberry at the radio.

Pushes a button on her iPhone and fills the car with the altogether more agreeable sound of Dolly Parton.

'You're not suggesting this chap as a suspect, are you?' asks Savage, glancing over. She's grimacing, staring into the nothingness, the yellow lights of the car disappearing amid the pixels and particles and rain. She's slowed right down, buzzing the window open so she can look out for a left turning that the map promises her is just up ahead. She shoots him a look. She knows from Talbot's publicist that he spent the afternoon preparing for his lecture. He was in the church most of the day, trying to get his laptop to sync with the verger's ancient overhead projector. There's no shortage of witnesses. He didn't find the opportunity to slip away, kill three people, butcher a couple more, get shot, fall into the river and make his way back to the church just in time to cancel the evening lecture. 'I don't understand what it is you're thinking.'

Billy ignores her. He closes one eye and tries to focus on his phone. He's been trying to read up on Nicolas Hobekinus, but the words keep blurring, expanding and contracting. He jabs at the screen. The page turns white and then flicks on to a linked story. He's in the online archive of the local paper where he'd been attempting to read the piece on Hobekinus as part of a series of profiles on famous local sons and daughters. Somehow he's found himself in a 'Bygones' section of the paper, lost in nostalgia, black-and-white photographs and a group of little news items entitled ON THIS DAY.

The words swim in and out of focus but he's able to make out the gist of the lead item. It's an appeal by Rev

Leigh Holborn, vicar of St Wendreth, to 'Let the Dead Rest in Peace'.

The introduction is in bold, a plea from a godly man tired of wasting the church's mediocre resources on repairing the damage done by ghoulish treasure hunters.

'...more problems at the grave of seventeenth-century antiquary Nicolas Hobekinus, rumoured to be buried alongside a treasure trove of ancient documents... the elaborate tomb has long been the subject of myths and legends and successive members of the clergy have tried in vain to stop grave robbers from attempting to dig down into the resting place...'

'What is it you're mumbling?' asks Savage, performing a complicated U-turn and switching off the satnav.

'If there was ever anything buried with the poor fellow then it's long gone,' reads Billy, adopting the mannered intonation of an elderly Anglican who's finding the whole thing rather tiresome. 'The church records are quite clear about the placement of the grave and the contents. Stones, larger tombstones, iron railings – we've even cemented it off. And still we get people sneaking in with a spade and trying to disturb the poor man's eternal rest...'

'That's good,' says Savage, distractedly. 'I didn't know you could do voices.'

Billy rubs at his temples. Focuses on the words on the page and clicks on the vicar's name. It's highlighted in blue and takes him to a page full of different headlines, all linked to news stories featuring St Wendreth's. He scans the banner headlines. It's mostly appeals for funding or celebrating some new and glorious milestone in the history of one of the churches overseen by his diocese. He is about to put the phone away when he spots the little story at the very bottom of the second page.

'*MISSING MAN'S CAR FOUND CLOSE TO HISTORIC CHURCH*'.

Billy checks the date. It's a cutting from thirty years ago, obviously scanned and uploaded when the newspaper was putting its entire archive into a digital format. He squints at the wording.

'The vehicle belongs to missing father-of-two Samuel Parris, 43, whose disappearance last autumn has baffled police. The committed family man is not known to have been a regular attendee at the centuries-old church and police say that the discovery of the vehicle, half submerged in an area of Fenland to the east of the church grounds, raises more questions than it answers. A police spokesman told this publication that officers were not actively investigating the disappearance but urged Mr Parris to make contact with his family.'

'What's all that?' snaps Savage, coming to a halt and shaking her head. 'You ever see that film?' she asks, gulping, theatrically. 'You know, they think the baddies are coming and he ends up having to shoot his kids and the next minute the army are there to save the day…'

'Leave off,' grumbles Billy. 'This church – the one where Jethro took a tumble when he was a young man. A year before it happened, a bloke went missing nearby. Car found in the Fens. You can tell the local coppers reckon he's done a runner.' He scrolls down to the story. Clicks on the dates and enlarges them, doing the maths. 'This bloke goes missing, yeah? A year later, Jethro tries to do himself in at the church. The church is a few miles from this bloody

Hermitage where Jethro has been living the past few years and where the waifs and strays of London have washed up to be blessed by this holy man... Self-same holy man who turned up in London three days ago and tried to smash his way into a priceless artefact honouring the memory of St Guthlac, legendary hermit. The artefacts rumoured to tell the entire story of Guthlac are alleged to be hidden in the tomb of Nicolas Hobekinus, who happens to be buried in Little Mercy.'

He stops, rubbing his hands together. 'If I tell the DCI any of that I'm going to be sectioned. But there are links – you can see that, yeah? And I have a horrible feeling that his sister is busy tidying away a load of stuff that would help us disentangle it all. I mean, what's she doing here? A woman like that, I mean.'

'A woman like what?' asks Savage, sending a text message to the local PCs who are supposed to be meeting them and leading them the rest of the way to Dead End Lane.

'Audrey Hepburn, but with that look on her face that makes you feel like you're shit on her shoe.'

Savage wrinkles her nose. 'You get that off her, do you? I thought she looked shocked and scared and sad, same as anybody else would be who'd just witnessed all that.'

'She went and changed into a grand's worth of designer labels as soon as she got the chance,' says Billy.

Savage shrugs. 'Putting your warpaint on isn't that weird, Sarge. It helps you feel a bit in control when things are getting away from you. Anyway, if she lost a baby a couple of years back, well... she's bound to have perfected the art of hiding her feelings deep. You would, wouldn't you? I mean, who really knows what's going on with anybody else?'

'We fucking should,' says Billy, and without thinking he reaches into his pocket and retrieves the hip flask. He takes a sip. Feels the sickly sweet burn. Closes his eyes and sits back as Savage starts grumbling into her phone and telling the locals that she's driven off the map and thinks she might be able to see dragons.

He glares at his screen and jumps a little in surprise as it buzzes in his hand. It's a voicemail, finally coming through after however long it may have been in this godforsaken no-signal zone. He plays it back. Experiences the eerie feeling of hearing the same voice that he has been listening to on the stereo suddenly bleed into his ear.

'Detective Sergeant Dean, this is the Reverend Struan Talbot. So terribly sorry to have missed your call in the wee hours but it sounds terribly important and I would, of course, be only too glad to assist the police in any way I can. Jethro's death... well, it has quite undone me. I find myself at the next pit-stop pub on the publicity tour and damnably far from London. Might we speak on the telephone? I'm currently conducting a little research and have a speaking engagement tomorrow evening at a tiny little place very dear to Jethro's heart. I'm in Ely at present and can certainly tarry here for a spell should you wish to catch up with me sooner rather than later...'

Billy sits back in his chair. For a moment the headache seems to lift, the pain in his shoulders receding as he busies his mind with nothing but connections. Then there's a crunch and the slipping of tyres and he's thrown forward with a start, his neck snapping forward and back as the seat belt stops his momentum.

'I'm so sorry,' mutters Savage, trying to find reverse. She cranes her neck forward. 'There's a bloody river about three feet below us and I can't see a bloody thing. I can push if you want to get in the driving seat.'

Billy glares at her. Unbuckles his seat belt. Sees the first proper blobs of rain start to spatter against the window screen and takes no comfort from Savage's rueful smile. Steps out into the downpour and feels his shoe disappear into four inches of cloying mud.

'God give me strength,' he mutters, and puts his palms on the bonnet of the car.

Wrapped in the grey ribbons of mist, Enoch wonders whether God will hear the sinner's prayer. He doubts it. God has little time for such trivialities. He told him as much Himself, that little smile at the corner of his mouth. *The man who prays is the one who thinks that God has arranged matters all wrong, but who also thinks that he can instruct God how to put them right.* Enoch has remembered every single word that God has ever spoken to him. He has written much of it down. One day, before the end, he will have the new gospel bound and disseminated among those hungry for the word of the Father. He wonders if he, like Guthlac, will be presented with the flesh of a saint and the tongue of a serpent with which to bind his Holy Book.

Enoch shivers. Bleeds. Cries. Smiles. Thinks upon the sinner and rejoices. His own prayers went unanswered for a very long time. It was only when he started to help himself that God interceded and showed him the way. He grips the flesh-and-bone handle of the knife. It still thrills him to know that the blade he holds in his own unworthy hand was a gift from one of the first true followers of Christ, a weapon forged in Heaven and given to a living saint to smite the enemies of God. That it rests upon Enoch's own scarred palm is enough to make him catch his breath. He scrapes his thumbnail along the blade and peels the dried blood of the martyrs from the ancient metal. Raises it to his mouth and sucks, deeply, on its tinny, animal flavours. He feels himself grow strong. Feels himself growing ever more excited as he breathes in the familiar air.

He has almost reached sanctuary.

Almost reached the chapel beneath the earth.

He has almost come home.

Home to her.

To *Mother*.

17

I feel fingers against my cheek, rough skin moving gently against the smoothness of my jaw. I wake up to see Peg leaning over me, smiling softly. I feel as if I'm waking from an operation. Feel like I did when I came around after the anaesthesia and the nurse had to tell me, again, that you had died without drawing breath.

She takes a step back, peering at me as if expecting me to do something remarkable, to disassemble or levitate or spin my head around like an owl. She seems almost disappointed when I just snuggle back into the blanket. She wrinkles her nose and shakes her head. 'Don't get comfy,' she says, ruefully. 'They're here.'

I make sense of myself. I'm in the living room, scrunched up in the chair by the dead fire. There's a heavy book at my side. I feel clammy and cold. There was a nightmare, wasn't there? And, oh God, I wet the bed...

'Who?' I ask, becoming aware of the sound of banging on the front door. I pinch the bridge of my nose, glancing back towards the window. It's a grey, gloomy day beyond the glass, a spiteful rain pummelling the windows. I push my hair back from my face. Smell myself. Run my tongue over my teeth and grimace. I feel disconnected, detached:

some part of me floating above all this like a kite on a string. Memories return the way that hearing goes after a long flight: a sudden popping and clearing of the tubes. I suddenly understand that the police are at the door. 'God,' I mutter, breathing deeply. 'God, I feel awful. I'm so sorry, I'm all over the place...'

Peg puts the backs of her knuckles on my forehead. Pulls my eyelids down without a word. 'Peaky,' she says, expertly. 'Bit anaemic too, by the looks of your reds.' She nods, having a little conversation with herself and taking charge. She helps me out of the chair, rough hands around my smooth fingers, yanking me upwards with the strength of somebody used to hard work. 'Run upstairs and get something on. Have a spritz of something fruity. Take a breath. Take that book with you, eh? Maybe under your pillow for safekeeping.'

I feel lost, childlike. 'I don't understand what's happening,' I say, glancing in the direction of the door. 'I feel like I'm hiding something – like I'm looking for something...'

'Just be honest,' she says. 'As honest as you can.'

'I had the worst dreams,' I whisper, feeling an uncommon desire to be held, comforted, cosseted. 'I saw things that...'

'We'll talk when they're gone,' she coos, holding my gaze. Her eyes are extraordinary up close, seamed with gold threads that sparkle in the light. She reaches behind her and hands me a mug of black coffee. I can smell the sugar in it. The rim *tinks* against my teeth as I take a sip, the sweet sting of hot liquid scorching my top lip. 'Get it down you. It's strong enough to melt the spoon.'

She hurries me out of the room and to the stairs. I look back as I reach the top step and see her check her reflection in the mirror by the door. I feel as though we're complicit in a deception. I just don't know what either of us is hiding.

I give myself nearly fifteen minutes to get ready. I pull on the dungarees and baggy jumper and find a scarf in one of the drawers, which I use to tie my hair back from my face. I rub a little lipstick into my cheeks but haven't time to do anything about the dark circles beneath my eyes. I try three times to leave the room. Each time I stop and retreat to the bare bed, staring out at the hazy, rain-lashed reeds and the distant smudge of trees beyond. I can't seem to control my breathing. I find myself probing at the wound on my palm, testing the edges of the cut and feeling a strange floaty numbness as the pain prompts a flood of endorphins.

I give my attention back to Jethro's chest. I've already let him down. I should have looked through it last night. Should have got myself back on the road and headed home to London having done my sisterly duty. Instead I'm here, embarrassing myself in front of strangers, preparing to humiliate myself in front of authority figures well used to spotting liars.

They're waiting in the living room when I finally find the courage to descend. I don't know either officer. There's a pleasant-faced woman with big brown fuzzy hair and a sensible outdoor jacket. She gives a nice smile and introduces herself as Detective Constable Helen Savage. Her colleague is crouching down by the fire, probing at the embers with a black metal poker. He's dripping water from the hem of a threadbare, sodden suit. He's in his mid-forties. His dark hair is plastered across his head and his face has a soapy, wind-slapped look that suggests he's been wincing into a storm. He doesn't smile. Just jerks his head at me like we're mates from the pub who've spotted each other in the park. 'Do I say *enchanté*?'

I give the kind of nervous little laugh that none of my colleagues would ever expect from me. I bite down on it quickly, reminding myself who I spend my days pretending to be. I'm cool, intelligent, efficient and ambitious. I'm a professional communicator. I've counselled ministers and millionaires. I can handle this. 'You can,' I say, watching as he puts a log on the fire and scrapes the tip of the poker through the cold ash. 'There's nothing stopping you.'

'You don't sound French,' he grunts, eyes focused on the fire.

'No?' I ask, turning to his colleague as she gives me a look of apology and settles herself down on the armchair. 'Should I try harder? I can light a cigarette and give you looks of disdain over the top of my sunglasses, if you prefer.'

'You'll have to forgive Detective Sergeant Dean,' she says, taking care not to rest her damp back against the fabric. 'Early start and bad weather. And he thinks he's funny. He's a bit peeved that you slipped away when we'd have been glad of a chance to chat.'

I sit down too, settling into the rocking chair. I don't know what to do with my hands, folding them in my lap and then letting them dangle at my sides. I don't know where Peg is. Don't know if I can keep myself from falling. The dream seems close; the echoes of last night's delusions crowding me, probing my defences, nipping at my soft places with cruel little claws. 'I didn't know I was supposed to be anywhere specific. I had things to sort out here.'

DS Dean stands up, pushing his hands into the small of his back. His grey suit looks as though it might have been expensive before the rain soaked and crumpled his well-pressed trousers and neatly buttoned waistcoat. He has nice-looking brown brogues, with dark water bubbling out of the holes every time he shifts his weight. 'Here?' he asks, with a little twitch of his nose. I sense a nastiness about him, a barely concealed temper, like he's the kind of man who would love to be slapped by a woman so he has a chance to prove he's not sexist by breaking her jaw.

DC Savage reaches into her bag and retrieves a file. She gives me that same smile: mumsy and nervous and sorry to be a bother. 'By here you don't mean this house, I presume? You mean the little ruin down the track. Jethro's place. The Hermitage.'

'Why are you calling it that?' I ask, bristling. 'It's Glavers Cottage. He was happy there.'

DC Savage puts her head on one side, radiating compassion. At the fireplace, DS Dean barks a sharp laugh. 'You don't have to convince us, Ms Cadjou,' he says, lacing every word with sarcasm. 'We have nothing but sympathy for what you must be feeling right now. I can only imagine the pain you're suffering, not knowing what to think, unsure whether to mourn his loss or be absolutely disgusted at what he was a party to.'

I look from one to the other. My tongue feels dry and swollen, my pulse points prickling, sweat trickling down my back. 'That's a repulsive thing to say,' I protest. 'Jethro was a victim. Wrong place, wrong time. The police even said that he was a hero, that maybe he saved my life…'

DS Dean sits down on the sofa, throwing himself back against the fabric and giving an elaborate shrug. 'We're getting new information in all the time, you see. Things that can put a new complexion on the narrative, as it were. Jethro may have left no imprint, may have wanted nothing to do with technology, but you can't come up to London and not get picked up on a hundred cameras. We've put together quite the timeline of his little jaunt to the capital. Quite the unusual gentleman, your brother.'

'He was ill,' I protest. 'I've told you this. He handled it, did his best, controlled it as best he could. He just wanted his life to be safe and quiet and small. Something made him shoot up to London and I hope to God it wasn't just because he missed me. I don't know if I could live with that.'

DC Savage leans in, her pen hovering over a page of her notepad. 'I understand there was an incident when he was a young man?'

'He was twenty-three,' I mumble, throwing up my hands. They both stare at me, saying nothing. I hear the drop of rainwater on the hard floor, the crunch and squeal of a vehicle moving down the track at the end of the drive. I sigh, petulant and pissed off. I've no choice but to go through it again. 'He was in the last year of his degree – already thinking about his PhD. He'd been suffering with manic depression for some time. We didn't know it was full-blown paranoid schizophrenia until after it had happened. The college had tried to get him help. So had we. Mum and I even moved here so he had a safety net under him. We changed our lives to be here for him. It still wasn't enough.'

'Mum and I,' says DS Dean, parroting my accent. 'What a lovely way to speak.'

'We heard he fell from such a height that he ended up more underground than overground,' murmurs DC Savage.

She gives a little smile, amused by something. 'Do you remember *The Wombles*?'

'It wasn't a fall,' I say, my lips thin as a paper cut. 'He jumped. It was a religious ecstasy. He saw angels sometimes. He'd worked so hard, exhausted himself. His tutor gave him more time, tried to be there for him, but Jethro's mind just broke. He was in hospital for months. When he woke up his mind was scrambled. He remembered me and Mum and his brain was still this incredible library full of facts and philosophies, but he couldn't get it to work right. He couldn't take care of himself. Mum couldn't stand to see him as he was, and I was off at boarding school. He stayed in a private facility for years. He was happy, or as happy as he could be.'

DS Dean sifts through his pockets and pulls out a paper tissue. He uncrumples it, wipes his nose, then reaches over to throw it into the dead fire. 'And next thing he was back in the family home, eh? Isn't medicine marvellous? And you, well, you were climbing the greasy pole and paying for his care, is that right? What a little trouper you are. And he was… actually, tell me again.'

'He did what made him happy,' I say, trying not to rise to the provocation. 'He read. Wrote. Conducted little experiments. Astrology, botany, translating books into one language and back again. Sketched. Made things. Walked. Wrote to me. He looked after animals. Worked at the cattery for a bit – the soup kitchen in Peterborough when he could get there. He drove when the roads were quiet, but motorways scared him. He liked his own company, but he was chatty with anybody who wanted to talk with him.'

He wipes a hand over his face. Rubs it on the baggy gold cushion at his side. Gives a nod of his head. 'We have it on good authority that your Jethro occasionally provided shelter for members of London's homeless community. They spoke of him like he was a bloody saint. Half of what you sent for him ended up in their pockets; you know that, yes? And there was no shortage of hard-luck cases who took him up on his offer of a place to bed down and get well. Those who needed fresh air, different skies – they'd come and stay here for a time. Cold Turkey Farm, according to one ex-junkie who got clean under Jethro's roof. He offered a sanctuary of sorts. One of them called the place "The Hermitage". It sort of stuck. Bloody lonely place, isn't it? End of the pissing world.'

I don't know what to say. Don't know what to feel. I could almost cry with relief when Peg bustles in from the kitchen and places another coffee in my hand. She offers nothing to the two police offers. 'He was always kind-hearted,' says Peg, and I follow her lead, grateful to be steered.

'Cared too much,' I mutter. 'That's what Father always said.'

'I'm told they weren't close,' says DS Dean, pulling his phone from an inside pocket and scowling at the screen.

'You've been told a lot, haven't you?' says Peg, standing beside me with her hand on my shoulder. I can't believe I barely knew her yesterday morning. Suddenly I feel as if I'd come apart without her nearness.

'Did you know about the down-and-outs who came to stay?' asks DS Dean, still fascinated by the missive on his phone. 'Did you care?'

'Peg told me there were visitors,' I say, and feel her

squeeze me, gently. 'Hippy types, I guess. That must be the same people.'

DS Dean puts his phone away. Looks at the pair of us and shakes his head as if we're here for his amusement. I find myself hating him. 'The first two victims were homeless men,' he says, quietly. 'Andrew Calvert, forty-one, originally from Aberdeen. Gwyndaf Clements, fifty-three. Left the family home in Colwyn Bay in 2011 and was living rough for the last ten years. He was wrapped in a sleeping bag when the attacker pulled out his knife and stuck it in him. Andrew tried to stop him. He took four stabs to the chest for his trouble. He's still clinging to life. It happened right in front of at least a dozen other members of the homeless community. You'll know this, of course – I shouldn't wonder that you know as much as we do.'

I take a moment to digest it all. Look, for a moment, at the injury to my palm. It's bleeding again. 'That's a strange thing to say,' I mumble.

Dean shrugs. 'You're a journalist, aren't you?'

'Not even remotely,' I protest, finally feeling as if I'm on safer ground. 'I'm a communications executive.'

'You mean PR?'

'Among other things.'

He wrinkles his nose as if there's shit on his top lip. 'On a nice wage, so I'm told. Certainly brought in enough to pay for Jethro's care without having to really do anything of significance. Must be lovely, having money. Must really lift the weight of responsibility. Go on, be honest with me – must be a bloody weight off your mind now the daft sod's not your problem any more.'

I let out a low, cat-like hiss, unable to stop myself. 'You really are a horrible man,' I spit, teeth clenched.

DC Savage sits on the lip of the chair and pulls a face that is all apology. 'You have to understand how hard we're all working to try and make people feel safe again. There's no explanation for any of this. We have to follow up every possibility.'

I feel my temper rising. Shake my head. Jiggle my feet and bite my lip and go through the whole elaborate dance of somebody whose temper is about to erupt. 'You can't just talk to people like this. You're the police. You're meant to at least pretend that you think we're all equal. Jesus, how dare you talk about "down-and-outs". How dare you! I haven't done anything wrong. Jethro died in front of me. He was a victim.'

Dean waves a hand as if trying to waft away smoke. Looks at me with a cruel smile on his face. When he talks, his back teeth are clenched together, and I can see the bulge at his jawline. He glares a hole in me, looking like he's trying to keep his temper in the face of extreme provocation. I know I can be hard to like, but I don't deserve this. He looks like he wants to ball up his fist and slam it into my cheek. It's a look I know. A look that makes me combative and scared all at once.

'Your brother's toxicology report shows more than just trace levels of henbane. He was a psychiatric patient who was off his tits on psychotropic drugs. We've got more footage of him trying to smash his way into a glass case at the British Library, no more than forty minutes before he came to your office and started talking gibberish. I think he and our attacker planned this together and your brother lost his nerve. He came to warn you and ended up dead for his trouble.'

'You don't think that,' I say, sounding pitiful. 'You can't think that. He was a good, kind, sweet man.'

'And you still say you can't properly describe the man who killed him?' asks DC Savage.

'I'm not being awkward,' I snap. 'I can't make the picture any clearer, can I?'

'Anything at all, Ms Cadjou,' she says, all sweetness. 'Any help at all could be the difference.'

I start to pull myself out of the chair, but Peg's hand stiffens at my shoulder and I feel the strength of her again as she pushes me back down. 'You still don't know who did it, do you? Who he was? You haven't found a body? The knife? A motive? You know none of those things, but you know that my brother was a bit eccentric and you're setting things up so that if you don't find who really did it, you've got a perfectly good suspect you can hang it on. I know how these things work. It's good PR.'

The officers exchange a look. I see the corner of DC Savage's mouth give a faint, less-pleasant smile. 'We aren't all deviants in the Met, love. Some of us joined up to keep people safe and to catch villains.'

'You're not doing very well then, are you?'

'I need to hear it again,' snaps DS Dean. 'Every single word he said when he turned up at the office and started—'

He gives a low growl as his phone chirrups into life, and he glares at the screen as if it's personally wronged him. He answers without a word and his expression darkens as he listens to whomever is speaking. I look up at Peg and she gives a tiny shake of her head. I focus on my breathing. Look to the fire and see the balled-up tissue suddenly flare into a rose of flame.

'Problem?' asks Savage, as he hangs up.

'The Hermitage,' he mutters, knitting his brows together and glaring at the fire. 'Round back. The barn with the red tiles. They've found something.'

Savage winces, all apologies. She looks like a mum who's turned up late for a parent-teacher conference. 'Would you excuse us?' she asks, standing up. She twirls a finger in the air, looking distracted and slightly dotty. 'I understand your brother's things are being stored here, yes? We'll need everything. If you could just sort of linger here and I'll pop back as soon as—'

I don't get a chance to answer. In a moment DS Dean is in front of me, both hands gripping the arms of the rocker. He's got his face so close to mine that I can smell aniseed and toothpaste and see the tiny smudge of ketchup at the corner of his mouth. The tip of his nose touches mine and I push back against Peg as she moves forward and puts her hand on his arm. At his side DC Savage does the same, squeezing his bicep as if to say that he's gone far enough and she won't cover for him again.

He pushes away from me. Stamps towards the door then turns back. He looks at me with real disgust, with a hatred I don't know what I've done to deserve.

'You know he was involved, love,' he snarls. 'You know he was dangerous. I've seen you in the CCTV, glancing back at the security guard over and over, hugging your arms like you were freezing to death while he was standing there. You were petrified of him. You knew what he was capable of. His mate stabbed him because he tried to back out. And you know it, don't you. I can see it in your bloody eyes.'

I lower my head. I've got nothing left to say.

18

I'm still sitting here when Everitt drifts into the living room, still dressed in his dusty cords and ragged sweater. He gives a little nod of his head. I follow his gaze. The fire lit by DS Dean has died in the grate.

'Hopeless,' mutters Everitt, his voice so raspy it makes me think of a file drawn across metal. 'I'll get to it. You sort yourself out.'

'You're being very kind to me,' I say, managing a smile. 'This is such an intrusion. You did so much for him – so much more than I ever did...'

He screws up his face. Shakes his head. 'We could have been better friends to him. Could have been better people, I reckon. Mercy isn't supposed to be a finite resource. I used to think that compassion fatigue was something that the psychologists made up to get themselves a grant. How could somebody with a decent heart and soul get tired of doing the right thing? Sounded like madness to me. But the buggers were right, by the end. We'd started thinking of him as more trouble than he was worth. I feel like the worst kind of sinner saying that out loud but as God is my witness, we'd had enough of him. His friends too. They took advantage something proper. Peg's not somebody to let people take advantage but she let them pull the wool over her eyes. We're all paying for it now. You most of all.'

I don't reply at first. It occurs to me that this is the first conversation we've actually had.

'The police are suspicious,' I say, eyes brimming over again. 'They think he was a part of it somehow. And I'm wondering that too.'

'Jethro would never hurt anybody,' says Everitt. 'It's not in his nature.'

'But his nature could change,' I say, lowering my voice. 'Before the accident, when we were living together in the cottage, when he was getting ill – there was this mania about him, this nastiness that overtook him. I don't think I've properly thought about this in years, but before it all got too much I think I was afraid of him. I think Mum was too. I don't know, it all feels like somebody else's memories – I just wish I'd talked to him, given him some proper time. I mean, what was he doing in London? What was he thinking turning up at my office like that?'

'He was looking for somewhere to feel safe,' says Everitt, not unkindly. 'It's a primal instinct, isn't it? Atavistic. Antediluvian, even. We run to the person who makes us feel better by holding our hand.'

'And I didn't hold his hand,' I say, looking down at the floor. 'Didn't even smile until I forced myself to.'

I think back to those fleeting moments before the attack. Think of the look on his face: bewildered, hyper; an urgency in his manner. He'd wanted to talk to me. Wanted to tell me something. I'd only just started to find a space for him in the madness of my day when the man with the knife pushed through the glass doors and the bloodshed began. I flinch as if slapped, my mind filling with pictures that I haven't dared to look too closely at. It's all a blur: muffled sounds and ripped-up photographs. I see Jethro turning to face the attacker and for an instant I'm able to look closely at the vision. He's average height. Bulky. There's dampness on his dark clothes.

I peer closer into the memory. The back of Jethro's head is blocking my view but there's a moment when the fog lifts and I'm looking directly into the eyes of the man who stabbed my brother to death. I'd thought that it was blood on his face: a great miasma of redness and gore. But here, in the clutch of the recollection, I realise that his face is covered with some crumpled, ragged swatch of cloth. He's featureless save for two dark eye-slits. He looks like a risen mummy: a B-movie monster bound in bloodied rags. I open my eyes to tell Everitt that I've remembered something important, but he's already drifted away into some other part of the house. I think I heard the door bang a few moments ago. I've no doubt Peg has followed the police officers down to the cottage, keen to find out what prompted them to make such a hasty exit.

I'm alone. I have time.

I pull myself out of the chair and dash upstairs. The chest remains dark and uninviting: the scrolls and curlicues upon its lid seeming to move as the weak light from the window moves across its surface, stirred by the falling rain.

Stay with me, Esme. Please. Help me do this. I want you to be proud of me. I want you to know that I'd have been strong enough to be the best mum you could have wished for.

I expect the hinge to creak. I'm disappointed. I lift the lid without a sound, the weight of the old wood even heavier than I'd expected. I feel like I'm opening a coffin. I expect something to sit up and lunge for me, some creature born of secrets and hidden truths.

I peer inside. There's a smell of mothballs and lavender; the faintest trace of meat and leather, the old paper that they use to wrap purchases in Knightsbridge delicatessens.

It's all but empty. This great antique specimen that we lugged from France as if carrying the Ark of the Covenant contains nothing more than some musty bedlinens and some bags of scented purple crystals. I hold the lid up and rummage around inside the folds. The material is soft and luxurious: an expensive cotton. I touch something papery and grasp for it with the tips of my fingers. I pull it out of the twists of fabric and close the lid. I hold the paper up to the light. It's creamy, old-fashioned. It has the roughened edges that suggests it's been pulped and recycled. I think of the expensive journals that they sell in the bookbinding shops. It's no more than a quarter of a page; the perforations at its edges suggest that it was torn instead of cut. On its surface, Jethro's handwriting: the extravagant copperplate that I could never decipher as a child but which always looked unfathomably beautiful. I hold it to the light.

'...*pedes vermes, vermitudo interet...*'

I say the words under my breath. A memory rises, just like the hairs upon my forearms. They were the words Jethro spoke: his final utterance in life, a prayer and invocation.

I sit down on the edge of the bare mattress, reaching over to grab my laptop from my bag. There are emails from work, messages from new clients, a couple of old friends reaching out having heard about my misfortune and eager to offer a listening ear. I ignore them all and pull up a web page.

Carefully, typing with one finger, I copy the strange words into a search engine. I click on the first web page. It's a list of curses found on old Roman tablets: hate-filled missives imploring the gods to smite whichever enemy they chisel into stone.

'...curse tablets, known to researchers as *defixiones*, were a popular form of expression in the Roman Empire from the 5th century BCE to the 5th century CE... these savage mementoes of centuries-old vengeance call upon the gods to 'bind' someone else's body; to strip them of their power. Others addressed retribution, theft, love and sought to outdo one another in the levels of retribution they were willing to wish upon their enemy...'

My eyes flick over streams of horrid, putrid invective: tablets calling upon the gods to commit unspeakable atrocities upon those who have wronged the writer.

I find Jethro's handwritten words halfway down the page. '...*ut illius manus, caput, pedes vermes, cancer, vermitudo interet, membra medullas illius interet...*'

The translation is beneath. '*May the worms, cancer, and maggots penetrate his hands, head, feet, as well as his limbs and marrows.*'

I sit still for a moment, trying to work out what I think. Peg had told me she had Jethro's possessions in the chest that she'd brought him from his house. She'd volunteered to go through it with me. But the chest contains only some old fabrics. But the paper in my hand suggests that it did contain Jethro's writings. And those very writings echo perfectly what Jethro said as he faced his attacker. And yet Jethro hadn't said it vengefully. He hadn't called upon the ancient gods to smite the man who stood before him holding a blade. He spoke softly, almost with love. Spoke as if they were known to one another and the words carried a deeper meaning.

I stare into space for a moment. I feel so terribly lost. The nasty police officer had spoken about some incident at the British Library, hadn't he? Something involving Jethro. A disturbance, of sorts. He'd said that he expected me to know about it all already.

Should I, Esmerelda? I know how to play this game. I know how to find things out. I've never been what you'd call a journalist, but I've been in and around politics for years and I know who to ask and how to ask them.

I call up the list of the trustees at the British Library and work my way down the list. I see three familiar faces and pick the one who has the fewest letters after their name. No OBE, no CBE, no knighthood. He's an academic, based at Durham and has been on the Board of Trustees for three years. His name is Professor Graeme Hutton and I'm about to talk him into a breach of confidentiality that will do his future prospects no favours whatsoever.

Don't judge me, Esmerelda. I'm good at this bit. It's a silly job at times but it's helped me understand people. Everybody's ambitious. Everybody's out to feather their own nest. Everybody with a little bit of power wants more.

I take a sip of water. Gather myself. There're no contact details for him on the British Library website but I find him at the college where he's emeritus professor of something so obscure that it makes me feel stupid. I log in to the email account I used to use when I was still part of the Westminster machine: the letterhead showing the House of Commons logo and carefully designed to look official without overtly claiming to be government-affiliated. I keep the missive brief. I need information. I need help. I don't mention Jethro, but if he's got any sense he'll google me before he does anything in response. Or maybe he won't. People are so unpredictable.

I sit back, sweat at my temples, a tremble running from my elbows to the tips of my fingers.

I look again at Jethro's words. It doesn't make sense. For the best part of thirty years the only person he was ever a danger to was himself. He was endlessly kind; almost saintly in how much of himself he would give away to those who needed it more than him. He cared for injured animals; offered words of kindness to those suffering from melancholy, madness. And then suddenly he took a train to London, caused a ruckus at the British Library and got himself stabbed to death in the atrium of Mount Carmel House.

I lie back. Breathe through pursed lips. I can hear the rumble of more vehicles arriving; blue lights, yellow lights, casting eerie lava-lamp patterns on the wall. For a moment it almost feels as if he's near me; as if I could reach out and close my hands around his cold, dirty fingers and tug him back into the real world.

I'd do it better next time, Esmerelda. If I were to be given a second chance, I'd do everything so very differently. You know that, don't you? You know that I'd listen to the doctors when they told me to rest. I'd be better, I swear. A better daughter. Better mother. Better sister.

On the bed beside me, my mobile phone chirrups into life.

I told you, Esmerelda. There is no greater motivator than greed.

19

B illy is scowling. He's always scowling, but this time it feels entirely justified.

'You called us over. You said we could go in…'

'Almost ready,' says the big man in the blue coveralls. He's endlessly patient. Infuriatingly well-mannered. 'Do please put your goggles on, Detective.'

'They steam up.' Billy tugs at the zip of his own one-piece protective suit like a child in an itchy jumper.

'Here, let me,' says Savage, at his side. She takes the goggles from his hand and lengthens the elasticated strap. She hands them back with the look of an exasperated mum.

'Stupid things,' grumbles Billy, making fists. His fingers squeak against one another inside the prison of their blue latex gloves.

'The feed is live, Ted,' says another anonymous science officer, light and camera mounted on a sleek, expensive-looking piece of apparatus that encircles their chest.

'I'll try not to fucking swear,' Billy protests. He wonders if Fran's watching. Wonders whether she's feeling proud or panicking that he's going to let her down. He'd like nothing more than to pull his pants down and moon the lot of them. Go out with a fucking bang.

The big man leads the way inside the red-brick building. He narrates, talking into a microphone clipped to his chest and addressing the watching audience back at HQ. Billy and Savage follow like children.

'Hello there, ladies and gentlemen. Theodore Banner, crime scene manager. The time is now 1.18 p.m. I hope the light is okay for you. We've endeavoured to erect a few spotlights outside the property and they're providing sufficient illumination thanks to the missing tiles in the roof. As you can see, we're entering a derelict outbuilding to the rear of Glavers Cottage, home of one Jethro Cadjou. You'll see that the centre of the structure is given over to what I'm told is a "coracle", a circular raft that has been intertwined with reeds and sticks to craft what looks at first glance like a nest. There are blankets and clothing at the bottom of the structure along with several hunks of rotten bread, some empty tins of food and some rain-damaged paperback books. All of this will be bagged and sent for examination...'

Billy looks through the steamy plastic. Considers the boat. Imagines Jethro seated within, a bird in his nest. Thinks upon St Guthlac: the hermit who lived a life of perfect, pure suffering and won the favour of his God. Wonders, for a moment, if Jethro maybe had it right. Wonders if he should turn his back on everything and go live in a bog like a fucking nutter.

'You'll see that this wall here has been crudely painted over,' continues Banner, directing the camera at the rear wall. The bricks have been daubed with emulsion, haphazardly rolled. Rivulets of dried paint run down to the lip of the huge chimney breast and its precariously balanced columns of bare brick.

'Ultraviolet inspection has revealed a more elaborate picture beneath the paintwork,' says Banner, theatrically, and waves a hand. The lights flick off and Billy finds himself in darkness. Beside him, Savage mutters an expletive as she stumbles off one of the plastic stepping stones laid out to safeguard the scene.

'Not quite Michelangelo, but certainly a shame to have covered it up,' says Banner, conversationally, as he raises a pocket UV light and illuminates the elaborate fresco on the wall.

Billy stares, transfixed. It's a spectacular piece of work, pre-Renaissance in its style. It takes him a moment to make sense of the image.

'Biblical, clearly,' continues Banner. 'I'm no art scholar but the gentleman in the robes here is clearly some form of saintly figure, as you can see from the halo and robe. At his feet are three figures, each with their heads bowed in prayer. The names are hard to make out, but this word appears to be *Cissa*. As you can see, it's the background that really does require further inspection. A true tapestry of the demonic: serpents, beasts, devilish little creatures who, as you can see, are conducting what can only be described as horrific tortures upon this poor screaming infant. This particular part of the image appears to be the gates of Hell. Which, I presume, means that this chap here with the skin hanging around his waist is St Bartholomew. He's presenting our sainted figure with a whip, and what appears to be a Bible bound in the skin of this slayed demon. It's hard to tell. There's writing beneath but my Latin isn't what it was. Clearly some considerable time has been spent on this, but the overpainting was done in a hurry.'

Billy stays quiet. Beside him, Savage follows his lead. If there's some credit to be had for making the connection to St Guthlac, they'd rather have it when there's time to be properly appreciated.

'As you can see, this colossal metal range blocked up the fireplace, but we've been able to move it and gain access to the subterranean chamber. Please, do watch your step.'

Billy slithers into the gap beneath the metal range and the bare brick. Even through the face mask and suit he can smell mould. Can smell earth and blood.

'Fucking hell,' whispers Savage, beside him.

'We rather fancy this may have been a priest hole,' says Banner. 'Pure guesswork, but these old properties often had hidden spaces where Catholic masses could be held during the persecution of the Papists.' He directs his assistant to switch on a brighter torch and to point the camera at the furthest wall. There's a simple altar. It's covered in tiny bare bones.

'Birds. Frogs. A few rodents,' says Banner, simply. 'And you'll see that there's a big rectangular gap right in the middle where it's conceivable that a Bible might be.'

Banner presses his finger to his ear, listening to a question. He nods, agreeing with some piece of wisdom. Does as instructed and angles the camera to the far corner of the room where somebody has noticed a twist of what might be rope.

'Good eyes,' says Banner, chattily. 'Yes, this appears to be a thong – excuse me, not the thong you're thinking of, more a lengthy piece of leather. We're unsure what it's made of but with your permission...'

Banner crouches down and picks up the length of leather.

Unravels it, carefully. 'Cat-of-nine-tails,' he says, separating out the lengths of skin. 'I imagine this end was attached to a handle of some sort, but it's clearly been rather crudely excised from the shaft. The leather feels rather like frog skin...'

'St Bartholomew's scourge,' says Billy, to himself, and is grateful nobody hears him. He is beginning to feel like he is going mad. Wishes, despite himself, that he hadn't found his way here. Although their devotions led to bloodshed, there's something pure and otherworldly about this cosy, sanctified space. He imagines he, too, might have known a kind of peace here, a place of prayer and reflection and where talking to God might, somehow, be enough to garner a miracle to restore life to the dead or to bring back a soul taken before its time.

'I can't fucking breathe,' he growls, and pushes past Savage and up the little sloping path, squeezing out into the body of the barn and stomping over the stepping stones. He emerges into the grey, wraith-like mist; the claustrophobic silence of the air that hangs above the ancient Fen. Just beyond the perimeter he sees the old woman who has been looking after Claudine. She's chatting to one of the local coppers: two neighbours exchanging gossip over the garden gate.

'Fucking yokels,' grunts Billy. He trudges towards the pair and is gratified to see the woman turn her back and head off down the path. The copper gives him a bright smile. He's a young lad. Fresh-faced and blue-eyed.

'Any secrets left, Constable?' demands Billy. 'Give her chapter and verse, did you?'

The PC seems oblivious to the sarcasm. Gives a big,

wide-eyed smile. 'She knew my dad,' he says, all friendly. 'Sorry, my dad was a copper here too. Friends in common, sort of thing. We were just chatting about old times, y'know. Lovely lady, offered to bring me a tea. Her husband gave a talk at my school when I was young. Quite a nice chat, really.'

Billy looks through him. Wonders if he's simple. Forces himself to stay calm. 'Did you tell her what we've found?'

'She already knew,' says the PC. 'Asked if we'd found "the chapel". Worth talking to her, I reckon. No, to be honest we were chatting about the man who lived here. Jethro. Such a lovely man. Took in animals nobody wanted. Awful what happened to him. The man was a saint according to my dad, and he'd know. Found him when he had that accident at the church in Little Mercy. Said he never thought he'd live. Proper miracle that he pulled through. Always had a smile for you, did Jethro. It's the eccentrics that make this country great, don't you think?'

Billy realises that if he stands here any longer he's going to punch the simpleton. He just scowls through the mask. Stomps back to where Savage is emerging from the barn.

Banner's still talking to somebody in his ear. Billy isn't privy to what the top team are saying to the man in charge through his earpiece. He's not important enough. It was just him that led them here, just him who followed this lead and changed the whole complexion of the fucking case.

He feels hot suddenly. Caged. Watched. Pulls the coverall off as if it were covered in toxic radiation. Rips it at the zip. Pulls the goggles off and tosses them down. Grabs for the hip flask in his pocket and drinks deep.

He turns back, a pressure on his arm. Savage is holding

her camera phone. The screen shows a table of high-ranking officers. They're waiting to pass on their thanks and a few words of admiration to Detective Sergeant Dean.

He sees Fran. Elegant and polished and a smile on her face that says she's proud of him.

She flashes a look at the flask in his hand. Sees her lip curl. Sees the last of the love drain out of her.

He turns away.

Stomps off towards the Fen, cheeks burning with shame.

Enoch, hidden in the Fen, talks to God. He asks, humbly, for the pain to stop. The bullet wounds are starting to smell. The holy pages, pressed to the suppurating wounds, are not healing him as He had promised. God is not replying to his calls. God seems, of late, a little distracted.

He watches the policeman. Hopes that God will tell him to kill him. He doesn't like him. He reminds him of the bullies who were mean to him before he learned how to live well, to follow a righteous path, to do God's work and to give himself over to the Lord's holy purpose. He is surprised to find that he still feels like Enoch. He had imagined that after the killings, after making space within himself for the returned soul of the child, he would feel reborn, clean, new.

He wonders whether, perhaps, he is being punished for shedding the blood of the man on the bridge. Whether he exceeded his instructions when he slashed at the security guard in the lobby of the big office block where he helped St Guthlac ascend into the waiting arms of Bartholomew. He'd been surprised that God had wanted him to commit such violence. Had been saddened to see his brother supplicants fight so hard for their lives. Perhaps he was the only true believer. God had told him as much. And he is a man of faith.

He slithers back into the reeds. Squirms into the water like a reptile. Feels the icy-cold kiss of the ancient waters bathe his wounds. Slips beneath the surface and into the black darkness of his own quiet thoughts.

He searches inside himself for the spirit of the child. It saddens him that Jethro had lost faith towards the end. It was he, after all, whom God had picked out. He who had first volunteered to become a chalice for the child. But the bad man had interfered. The dull, grey-faced man had told him that it was not God's voice that he heard but the voice of an illness, the voice of a condition that he could overcome if he just took his pills and ate right and tried with all his might to remember what happened that night in the church all those years before. Jethro did as he was bid. Submitted to the other man's teachings. Remembered the thing that he had witnessed, and which had plagued him so unmercifully that he had tried to kill himself. God spared him. Chose him. Directed him to follow Guthlac's example and promised that if he did so, he could restore the smile of the one person he loved above God.

Enoch permits himself a moment's doubt. From what he's witnessed, there isn't very much about the woman to suggest she is worth all the fuss. He hopes that when she sees him and stares into his eyes and sees her returned daughter, she will have the good grace to say a prayer of thanks. Her brother died for this, after all. They all died for this.

Enoch carves another cross on his skin. Blood rises into the black water. Creatures feed gently upon him in the shallows. He is so scarred that his skin shimmers.

For an instant, Enoch wonders whether he may, somehow, be on the side of the demons rather than the angels. Wonders whether he has somehow fallen victim to the work of the Devil instead of God.

The thought is repulsive. Sinful. He knows he must be punished.

He takes the blade in his hand and begins to carve at his skin.

In his blessed agony, he hopes to be redeemed. Hopes to hear God.

There is only the pain, the cold, and the dark.

He sounds intense, excited: honoured to be able to help. He tells me this in his opening salvo, stumbling over his words as he says how much he's had to do today; how it's not always a blessing to be thought of as a safe pair of hands; how students these days need to be breastfed. 'Sorry, is that rude, probably terribly politically incorrect; forget I said it; crikey, I'm really making a mess of this, and...'

I let him gabble until he's absolutely desperate to be put out of his misery.

'...of course, all academics now live with the mortal terror of saying the wrong thing or making a joke that has some new connotation and I genuinely don't know a single colleague who hasn't had a few sleepless nights trying to remember whether they complimented somebody for a fetching blouse they wore one day in 1996 and...'

'Really, Professor Hutton, think of this conversation as being akin to the confessional booth,' I say, smooth as silk and radiating trustworthiness. 'I'm no stranger to the worst excesses of the "woke" brigade. It feels strange to think of myself as very much left of centre politically and yet the rules change so often that I'm sure I'll be getting called a Nazi before the week is out.'

He laughs as if I've just cracked a world-class punchline. I hear him relax a little. He's in a safe place. He's chatting with one of the better class of feminists – a pragmatist, a realist – someone who actually understands how the world works. He can be himself. I hear the change in his voice, the equivalent of unbuttoning his trousers or kicking off his shoes. I've been witness to this kind of performance so often that it no longer surprises me. I've yet to meet a man of influence or power who can't be completely unravelled by a woman telling them that they understand the pressure they are under to stay on best behaviour.

'As I said in the email, it's just to spare our minister any blushes at a sub-committee meeting scheduled for the back end of the week. You know how the Opposition can be, lobbing in the occasional spin-bowl just for the fun of watching us squirm and slither about. It's probably nothing but we were very keen to get ahead of the curve, as it were, and it did strike me that you'd be the, well… no disrespect to your colleagues but you seem to be the most press-savvy of the board; somebody with actual real-life experience, an ability to know which way the wind's blowing…'

He hums sagely, as I move through my list of flattering clichés. God, men are easy to manipulate.

He clears his throat, unsure whether to appear modest or proud. He aims for a little of both and manages to hit neither. 'Of course, well, yes… and yes, it's most flattering to think that anybody at Westminster is even aware of a fusty old professor busy white-gloving his way through old documents that even my students can't find the enthusiasm to pick up.'

'Oh, my minister is quite the judge of character,' I say,

sitting back against the headboard and making myself comfortable. I expand the picture of him on my screen. He's fiftyish and lean: a neat goatee beard and slicked-back grey-black hair. He has features that don't quite manage to be handsome. There's a marked asymmetry to the shape of his face, a wonkiness that makes his features hard to read.

'So how precisely can I be of use?' he asks, and there's a squeak as he settles back into what I imagine to be a leather recliner.

'You'll have been briefed regarding the incident at the library three days ago, I presume,' I say, still keeping my voice ultra-professional. 'My understanding is that the police have questioned security staff and requested surveillance footage. Is that correct?'

'Dreadful business,' he says, sounding genuinely forlorn about the state of the world. 'I'm told he was a little, well, I don't quite know what the correct term for it is, but he certainly wasn't playing with a full deck of cards, if you'll catch my drift.'

'Would you perhaps be able to run through me events as you understand them?' I ask, guilelessly. 'It's so much easier if I work on the presumption that you know more than me about the whole affair.'

'Delighted,' he says, and sounds it. 'And, well, yes, it's the sort of thing one might have thought of as a storm in a teacup, if you'll forgive such a ghastly phrase, but the involvement of the Metropolitan Police does rather make it seem like something, well, one might say, erm…'

'Significant?' I proffer.

'Precisely,' he says, gratefully. 'It's the cause and effect that concerns me. Just because one thing happens and then another thing happens, there's no causal line from one to the other, is there? And yet people do draw that inference. He'll have family, I've no doubt, so one really must watch one's words about such things. No doubt there'll be compensation at some point, though if they're looking for that to come from our coffers, they may find themselves disappointed.'

'Sorry, Professor,' I say, halting his tirade and trying to get him back on track. 'Who'll have family?'

'Sorry?'

'You said "he'll have family". Who will?'

'The poor gentleman who was murdered down by the bridge,' he says, sounding a little impatient. 'That's the matter you're referring to, isn't it? We're not in the midst of some dreadful French farce and coming at this from opposite ends, are we?'

'Sorry, yes, I think we may have actually lost connection for a moment,' I say, trying to gloss over the miscommunication.

'This is a safe line, isn't it?' he asks, playing out some absurd espionage drama in his mind. He strikes me as the sort of man who knows what his preferred code name would be if ever called upon to serve his country. I imagine he'd like to be named after a Russian chess master or some sly, slinking big cat.

'Perfectly safe, Professor,' I say, and the leather creaks again. 'Sorry, do continue.'

'Well, I only know this because we're lucky enough to receive internal communications regarding any matter that may be bumped up to trustee level before our next meeting. Usually these little outbursts are dealt with quietly and without need for consideration at a senior level, but because of what came after, well...'

'The incident at the bridge,' I say, solemnly.

'Indeed. A terrible thing. Truly, those poor people. Began in that pretty little park where the grey squirrels will eat from your hand, if I have my geography correct. And Mount Carmel House, too, so I'm told. One would have thought such places might be off-limits to these people. I had a meeting with a publisher there once, three or four years ago. Came to nought but a lovely lunch.'

'These people, Professor Hutton?'

'Well, whoever's behind it, I mean. I did read that there was some religious overtone but whether or not one can really believe that is hard to say. When does religion become zealotry? When does an ideology become something with murderous intent? I've published four textbooks on theology and I've yet to see a single line in an ancient manuscript that encourages the slaying of one's enemies. I give a lecture on just that point, actually. Always well attended.'

'And the police are linking the murders with the incident at the library, yes?' I ask, keeping my voice even.

'Indeed. Quite a tragic fellow, from what the security guard relayed back to his team leader. Dressed like a down-and-out, smelled like a midden. I mean, between you and I it can often be difficult to discern the vagrants from the well-remunerated eccentric. Sometimes one will ask a security guard to move along a chap who's sleeping in front of a fourteenth-century grimoire and when they raise their head you realise they're the vice chancellor of some half-decent university. Even so, the gentleman who caused the rumpus, well, he did have a very particular air about him. The security guard in question said he seemed rather manic, certainly very upset. People are welcome to be as upset as they choose – you'll understand that – but we do like to keep an eye on people in case their upset starts to become contagious, as it were.'

'The gentleman in question – we're talking about one of the victims of the Embankment Killer, yes?'

'That's the name they're giving him, is it?' asks the professor, tasting the word and giving a little sigh of disappointment. 'Can't see that catching on. But yes, the man who caused the disturbance was the same chap who was stabbed to death in the lobby of the big glass-fronted building. The security guard recognised the picture and we instituted our security protocols to ensure that information was preserved, footage was kept safely stored and everything was neatly documented. I believe the police officers in question were able to confirm the man's identity from fingerprints left on the glass of the Guthlac Roll…'

I jerk my head up. The rest of the world turns to damp sand and slowly falls away. My hands hover over the keys of the laptop and, as I stare at my knuckles, I see my fingertips start to tremble. I press my fingertips to my neck and try to slow my breathing. There's a sense of rising panic in my chest. I can hear the rushing of my own blood inside my skull.

'The Guthlac Roll?' I say, barely able to get the words out. I cough and apologise. Say it again, but in the tone of somebody who has never heard of such a thing.

'Fascinating artefact,' he says, and I sense he is excited at the prospect of sharing the story with somebody who's never had the good fortune of hearing it before.

'And this is the exhibit that attracted the attentions of the gentleman in question, yes?' I ask, feeling the room reel and spin.

'The footage left no room for doubt,' he says, sadly. 'Tried to get through the glass case as if the answers to the universe's big questions were trapped inside. Threw himself at it bodily, sobbing, yelling, crying. The security guard told his line manager that he wasn't sure whether the gentleman was speaking English or something that had a more Eastern European lilt, but it was certainly unintelligible to his ears. So too the poor tourists and students who were milling along in that particular gallery at the moment it happened. I'm only grateful that we instituted the bag-search policy when we did, or I fear he'd have brought something along that could have caused real danger to passers-by.'

'He was attacking the exhibit?' I ask, again. I picture the dark, high-ceilinged room; the case after case of priceless artefacts; scribblings in the hand of great painters, artists, philosophers, theologians. Jethro would have had no interest in any of the other curiosities. He'd only have had eyes for the centuries-old text that had fascinated and entranced him in those last weeks before he tried to take his own life.

'With gusto,' he says, sighing, as if the world is full of horrors he doesn't attempt to understand.

'How long did the disturbance continue?' I ask, quietly.

'Moments,' he says. 'No more than that. He walked in, checked his bag at the cloakroom and went straight to the gallery. He walked past the more, shall we say, high-profile items on display and went straight to the case containing the rondels.'

'Rondels?' I ask, automatically, and for a moment I'm a kid and I'm sitting at the kitchen table and I'm asking my big brother the very same thing. And he's telling me. Telling me about the saint he's studying and the life he lived out in the wild murk of the Fen. Remembering how he'd smile when she understood him. When she listened. When she cared. 'And he tried to get at them?'

'That's very much the impression that is given on the recording,' says Professor Hutton. 'The police seemed similarly disinclined to accept this version of events, according to the head of security. Thankfully we had the video to show precisely what occurred. A little underwhelming, I fear, though tantalising, certainly. I mean, I know nothing about the gentleman who lost his life but it's clear that he experienced some profound feeling when he gazed upon the roll. It's a rather marvellous artefact, of course, but it's not one that I would have associated with religious ecstasy or some kind of rapturous loosening of one's faculties. He was actually very personable when our security guards stopped him in his task. It was clear to them that he was in the grip of some delusion and that it was a matter for a health professional rather than the police. Of course, had we known what would happen soon after…'

'Indeed,' I say, my voice catching. 'That's why you let him go.'

'It wasn't so much a decision, as an absence of a suitable alternative,' says Professor Hutton, sounding like a politician trying to find a creative way to lie. 'No damage was caused, save some scratches on the glass. And yes, he gave the other people a scare but they could all tell he was suffering from some kind of malady. The poor man had tears streaming down his cheeks. Our guards were trying to work out how best to take care of him when he succeeded in, well… At some point, that's to say…'

'He gave them the slip,' I say, quietly.

'If one were to use such language, I wouldn't be able to contradict you,' he says, sounding guilty and relieved at once. 'It really would have been the most inconsequential of events if not for what followed, and I do think it would be unspeakably unfair if any future inquiry were to muddy the good name of this noble institution...'

'He left his bag,' I say, replaying his words.

'We gave that to the police untouched,' he says, proud to have been a part of such swift and competent practice. 'Obviously the cloakroom attendant had felt duty-bound to sift through the contents when she realised that the gentleman had left without coming back for it but from what she relayed to the head of security, the contents are only likely to cause more confusion. A thick notebook, I believe; um, a Thermos; some old jam jars with some kind of soil within; pens, pencils; a pouch of tobacco; some letters, though it would have been beyond the bounds of propriety for any of our staff to have read the contents. I only tell you now because I happened to be familiar with the gentleman whose name was on the envelope. He's very much the expert when it comes to these medieval manuscripts, though some of his theories are so wildly speculative that one does hesitate to think of him as an actual academic or theologian.'

'Who?' I ask, and it comes out harder than I want it to.

'Reverend Struan Talbot,' he says, with a touch of disapproval in his voice. 'I can't in good conscience recommend your minister try and talk to him in confidence. Very much a self-publicist is Struan. A fine mind, of that there's no doubt, but the man's arrogance is astounding. Quite the reach, too – all those adoring fans only too happy to feed him information for no other reason than the image he's cultivated as this maverick man of God. Honestly, in a different age he'd have been selling snake oil, though that's just between you and me and the gatepost, I hope. He was on the phone to the senior archivist not long after we contacted the police, desperate to know whether there had been any damage inflicted on the roll. Volunteered to analyse it and ensure there had been no exposure to any infra-red radiation or, Heaven forbid, some form of toxin that might lead to the slow disintegration of the artefact.

'Honestly, the man's a fantasist. He's never afraid to put a tragedy to personal use. We've had countless requests over the years for him to be able to take a sample of the scroll and subject it to some new battery of tests. The answer remains a resounding "no" but clearly he saw an opportunity to insert a crowbar into an area of perceived weakness.'

I hear the door slam downstairs. Peg yells my name and starts talking, loudly, as she shakes the rain from her coat and hat and tugs off her boots.

'...*have to prepare yourself, love. They've found something in the red barn that's getting them so bloody excited, and I can't honestly say that things aren't looking a bit bleak... coffee might do it, or something stronger – then we can have a look in that chest and see what...*'

I press the phone close to my face but there's no doubt he's heard the incongruous stream-of-consciousness drifting down the phone. I sense a tension in his voice when he speaks again.

'I've probably said enough,' he says, tightly. 'Just for my own records, do you think you might give me a direct line at the Commons so I can go through switchboard? One does rather worry about cybersecurity and such and while you sound absolutely delightful I think perhaps propriety would dictate that…'

I end the call. Switch off the phone. Close the laptop. Lie back and stare up at the ceiling, mouth dry.

Jethro had begun to remember.

21

'You look like you've seen a ghost.'

Peg's in the doorway, holding two mugs. Her face is blotchy from her walk through the rain and there's a glassy redness to her eyes that suggests recent tears. She came up the stairs without making a sound. I wonder how many years she lived here before she knew which floorboards creaked.

'I think I've done something rather rash,' I say, grimacing at the inadequacy of the statement. 'I've probably just made matters so much worse.'

'Now's the time for it,' says Peg, with a little smile. 'I think we're both in for a few dark days.'

I try and clear my thoughts. I need to focus. She's been to Jethro's place. She might have answers. If nothing else, I need her to explain the absence of papers in the storage chest. 'They've found something?' I ask, cautiously.

She sits down on the bed beside me. She smells of outdoors: damp hay and stirred silt. She's got nice skin, up close. I doubt she's ever used a moisturiser but her complexion is fresher than mine.

'They wouldn't let me past your car,' she says, inserting one finger into her ear and slowly turning it as if chalking a snooker cue. 'I saw enough, though. It's a gift being a batty old lady – you should try it. People always think you're harmless. Saw a load of people in those big white suits carrying equipment into the main house and the outbuildings. Your DS Dean was standing there with his hands in his pockets, rain pouring down and soaking him to the skin. He was just staring at the house like he could burn it down with his eyes. Nasty man, that one, wasn't he? Anyways, they shuffled me off soon enough, but it wasn't a wasted trip. That daft sod from the radio is parked up just beyond our forecourt and I lingered near enough to hear him tell his bosses what was going on.'

I wait for a moment as she sips her tea and licks her lips. She gives a little nod of satisfaction. Closes her eyes as she speaks.

'They've found a little chamber inside the red barn. Hidden away under mounds of this and that. Underground. The radio chap said it was a crypt and a bunker in the same conversation but by the end he'd settled on "chapel". Whatever it was, I didn't know it was there and I thought I knew everything about Jethro's life.'

I try and keep my breathing steady. I don't want to betray what I know and what I don't. She stares into me for a moment, and I can't hold her gaze.

'You knew there was something down there,' she says, as if my every secret were sketched on my eyeballs. She offers it as a statement, not an enquiry.

I look away. I notice that I'm biting the skin off my lip and make a conscious effort to stop. I've started picking at the skin around my fingernails too; begun plucking at my eyebrows. Wetting the bed. All of my childhood habits are returning. I'll be crying in my sleep next. I'll be seeing things that aren't there.

'The barn wasn't always a barn,' I say, quietly, dropping my hands to my lap. 'I thought you'd remember that, as a local. It was living accommodation when the place was first built. Servants' quarters, wasn't it? It was stuffed full of old farming machinery and tonnes of rotting hay when we moved in. Jethro set himself the task of emptying it out. I think he liked the idea of having a little place of his own – near us but with his own space. Mum just let him get on with it. I helped now and again. It was nice. He'd talk to me while we were digging out all the old rubbish. He'd tell me things. I think they're my best memories of being here, really.

'When he got down to floor level, he found this area in the brickwork on the floor that didn't match anything else. It was like there had been a tiny little chamber built into the furthest corner. The floor was mostly mud and loose rock by then, but he dug down another couple of feet and found a whole different floor. His spade hit metal and stone. I only know about it because he told Mum and Mum mentioned it in a letter to me. I'd already gone to boarding school by then. When I asked about it again, Mum said it was "something and nothing", which was an English phrase she really took to. But the second that horrible detective said they'd found something...'

'Well, they'll be grilling you about it I'm sure,' says Peg, sipping her tea. I notice that she's placed the other mug on the side table, and I take a sip of something strong and sweet and herbal.

'Burdock,' she says, in answer to my puzzled expression. 'Bit of this and that. Always a favourite with your brother.'

We sit in silence for a moment. I realise I'm going to ask the question just as it tumbles out of my mouth.

'Where are his things, Peg? I've looked in the chest and there's just some linens. He wrote all his life. Journals, thoughts, diaries, letters – anything and everything that occurred to him. They're the only reason I came back. I know things were lost in the flood, but…'

She pats my hand, reassuringly. 'You can blame Everitt for that,' she says, shaking her head. 'When you're married long enough you sometimes think that the person you're with is a mind reader. I was sure all the stuff that survived the flood was in that chest yonder. I told you as much, didn't I? Well, His Majesty informs me that he passed it all on to one of your brother's pals a few days ago. Jethro had said it was okay, apparently, and Everitt's so mild-mannered he'll go along with just about anything. I feel a right ninny for not having known. I just hope that policeman doesn't read anything into it when he comes over for a rummage. It might be as well making the robes scarce too.'

I can feel the headache creeping in at my temples. I sip again at the herbal tea and enjoy a brief moment of dissociation, a deadening of the senses – a dizzy kind of high that makes everything Peg's saying more tolerable, less upsetting.

'Robes?' I ask, tired to my bones.

'When he and the apostles walked into the Fen, they got muddy and I said I'd get them back to white. I kept hold of them in case they were needed again.'

'Why were they in the Fen?'

Peg looks at me with pity in her eyes. She lets her eyes drift past me to the window where the rain pummels the reeds and the ancient water. 'They were playing at religion,' she says, lowering her voice. 'I don't even know if they had any real idea what they were doing. It was a mishmash of different bits of scripture. Bits of this religion, bits of that, but they were all into the idea of rebirth. Goodness knows where they got the robes. I only knew what was going on because I was out walking and saw this procession of hippies wading into the water up to their necks.

'Jethro just stood there on the bank. He wasn't really a part of it. He was barefoot but he looked more like a vagrant than a disciple. I swear, I think he was wearing something made out of coffee sacks! But that was Jethro, wasn't it? I mean, we all know he wasn't well. People took advantage. He was just such a good person and there's a certain type of person who really knows how to take advantage of that.'

I can feel my eyelids fluttering. I can feel the soft wings of questions brushing the inside of my mouth, but my tongue seems too thick and furred to let them out.

'Guthlac,' I say, plucking the word at random. 'Did he talk about St Guthlac?'

Peg's mouth creases into a sharp smile. She rolls her eyes theatrically. 'Last few weeks it was all he could talk about. Believe me, I'm nigh on as encyclopaedic on the subject as his pal Struan.'

I force myself back from the brink of sleep. 'Struan Talbot.'

'Yes, we spoke about him before, didn't we? I hope he can make some sense out of Jethro's writings – it would be a lovely tribute if he got a credit in whatever book he's working on.'

I take a moment to reassemble all of the information I've

been served in the past few minutes. 'Struan Talbot has his writings?'

'As I say, blame Everitt. He turned up when I was in the village and Everitt didn't think to tell me until the police were at the door.'

'And Struan Talbot's been here before?'

'We've had this conversation, haven't we?' she asks, draining her tea. 'He visited your brother from time to time. I can't say I know the man particularly, but he seemed a very agreeable fellow and clearly cared deeply about your brother.'

'I'd like to see Jethro's things,' I say, as clearly as I can. 'How can I get in touch with Struan?'

She smiles at that, a little flustered. 'I'd have said if I knew how,' she says, looking away. 'I wasn't sure if it was insensitive, you see. But, well, you're a grown-up, so...'

'It's okay, just tell me.'

She pulls a face. 'The church where your brother was found – back when he wasn't well. Struan... he's giving a talk there tomorrow evening. He's promoting that book that's got all of the great and the good kicking up a fuss. I wasn't sure if I was still going to go. It would seem a little ghoulish without Jethro. I mean, they're his tickets – I just said I'd go...'

I finish my drink. Raise my hands to my mouth and start chewing on my thumbnail. Peg reaches out and gently lowers my hand. I feel tears prick my eyes again at the intimacy of the act, the simple gesture of something approximating motherly care and attention. *I swear, Esme, I'd have made you feel loved. Truly, every day, you'd have been adored.*

'I'll go with you,' I say. 'I'd like to talk to him. I want

to know about the Jethro I never really got to know – the Jethro he was before.'

Peg looks pleased. She pats my hand as if I've passed a test. 'He'd have been glad to see you there. He went back a lot. It was a place that brought him some kind of peace, I think.'

I don't understand at first. 'He visited the church where he tried to kill himself?'

Peg nods. Shrugs. 'He never hid from what he'd tried to do. He thought of that night with fondness, if you can believe that. He told Everitt that even though it cost him his mind and most of his memories, he was rewarded with something far greater.'

I wait for more. Eventually she gives in.

'He saw God,' she says, simply. 'Saw Heaven. All His angels, all His blessed saints. They welcomed him into their number and wept when he was pulled back to his earthly life. I've never known what I believe about much, but I know that as far as Jethro was concerned, he'd been safe and warm in Heaven, and somebody dragged him away. Maybe that's why he always lived so simply, eh? I mean, in a different age he'd have been one of the hermits – some kind of reclusive wild man living out in the wilderness and searching for God.'

I look out through the glass. Somewhere down the track, the police are searching through my brother's hidden chapel. Beyond is the water where he watched the apostles be born again. In London, he lies on a slab of cold steel; puncture wounds to his mortal flesh having died whispering words in a forgotten tongue. I have to fight to keep my breathing steady. Have to force myself not to betray my feelings. Suddenly, I begin to share the suspicions of the detective. Suddenly, I can no longer think of Jethro as an innocent victim of a random attacker. I think of a religious zealot – a fantasist and fanatic. I see martyrs, giving themselves to the blade in an act of true faith.

Oh, Jethro, I whisper, deep inside myself. *What did you do?*

22

Billy pushes his way through a snarl of reeds and grass. Tufts and twists grab at his ankles, adhere to the damp legs of his trousers, tug at his shins and shoelaces. He feels as though he is walking across a bridge made of the dead and dying; as if each desperate clutch at his clothing were designed to pull him down, to envelop him, to pull him under. He hates it here. The land doesn't seem real. The land sits atop the water like ice, every patch of earth seeming somehow temporary and insubstantial. He's trying to imagine how it felt for Jethro Cadjou to live here. He's trying to climb inside his mind.

The discoveries beneath the barn have unsettled him. If he's honest with himself, he hadn't really expected his line of inquiry to yield results – all he'd wanted was to be able to show some degree of innovation and insight, and to demonstrate to Fran and her senior managers that there's room on an inquiry for an old-fashioned plodder like him. And yet his discoveries are now being treated as the prime line of inquiry. Back at HQ, the people in the good suits have moved Jethro Cadjou and the two homeless men from the status of innocent victims to an altogether less sympathetic footing. They may have been complicit in their own deaths. They may have been willing martyrs. They may, perhaps, have driven themselves mad at this place of sanctuary; absorbing the teachings of a hyper-intelligent but horribly damaged man. And they may have brought bloodshed to London's streets as a consequence.

The reeds thin out as he pushes his way forward. He can smell the water; deep and ancient and black. The mist still twists about him like rope, and he can hear the eerie, dying-man croak of something amphibian. He should probably turn back. Should go back to Savage and try to enjoy the feeling of being briefly admired.

The top brass are happy. They've got something they can tell the press and the politicians. It might all just come down to the work of a group of half-mad zealots. The public can get on board with that idea. It's nobody's fault. Nobody in authority could be held accountable for the actions of the insane. He's sure that top-level strategy meetings are taking place within pressure groups and think tanks at this very moment; special advisers to government officials already trying to mine the situation for political advantage.

He hears a sound somewhere off to his left: a squelch, like a foot being pulled from thick mud. The reeds are too high for him to make anything out but the primal part of him stiffens at once, poised to fight or flee. The headache has lifted a little since he walked away from the crime scene and plodded off into the marshy wilderness of the Fen, and he feels like he's thinking clearly. The drink is helping too. He's topping himself up from time to time, taking medicinal pulls on the ghastly cocktail in his hip flask. He fancies that it's helping him be a better version of himself, lending him insights and seeing connections that would be invisible to him in sobriety. He wonders whether this is how Jethro and his disciples felt when they began to hear the voice of God, wonders when sanity left them.

'Oh, Detective…'

It's her. Claudine. Impossibly beautiful; dark-eyed and fragile. She's a broken bird, a magpie with shattered wings. He watches as she parts the reeds and picks her way onto a little patch of slightly drier land. He stares at her without a word. He realises that it's raining slightly, the air a haze of raindrops. She's soaked to the skin, her dark hair clinging to her fine cheekbones, dripping water down the collar of her ill-fitting coat.

'You can call me Billy,' he says, and surprises himself. His voice sounds like his own.

She narrows her eyes. 'We're on first-name terms now, are we? Is that normal when you suspect somebody of involvement in mass murder?'

Billy finds himself smiling, an unfamiliar twisting of his lip. He shows his teeth. 'That's what you think is it? That I have you down as being involved in all this?'

Claudine pushes her hair back from her face. Shakes her head. She looks angelic. Timeless. 'I think you don't like me very much,' she says, tiredly. 'I think you believe Jethro was a part of what happened and not just a victim. I suppose I can't really blame you for that. You didn't know him.' She looks down at the tangle of reeds. Blinks back tears. 'Neither did I.'

Billy feels the two sides of himself warring in his chest. He wants to punish her sudden vulnerability, to squeeze admissions from her as she stands here so fragile and lost. But he also wants to wrap his arm around her. To tell her that she's been through hell these past days and that he understands; that he's here for her, willing to listen; that he, too, knows how it feels to push down your feelings of heartbreak and pretend to be somebody else.

'We've found his chapel,' says Billy. 'Under the outbuilding, behind the chimney. It's hard to look at that and not see the victims of the attack in a new light. We have a suspect too. Another man who used to come here…'

'Lots of people used to come here, according to Peg,' says Claudine, quietly. 'They wore robes. Waded in the waters. I think for most of them it was all rather beautiful. Jethro would have been happy to see people smiling. He wasn't capable of violence; I promise you that. He'd weep for hours if one of the dormice he tried to revive didn't quite make it. If he found a dead animal, it was like he'd witnessed a tragedy that there was no way back from. He was so gentle…'

'A regular saint,' says Billy before he can stop himself.

She looks disappointed in him. 'You're talking about the Guthlac fascination,' she says, chewing her lip. 'Well, go on – what's wrong with that? The saints are supposed to be examples of how to live a good life, aren't they? Isn't that their sole purpose? After his accident he couldn't remember very much about anything, but he remembered the saints as if they were his classmates at school. And Guthlac was there in the centre of his being – this ancient warrior who heard the voice of God and lived a life of quiet goodness in a wild, uninhabited place. Jethro yearned for that the same way his idol did. Wanted to come to a place far away from everybody else and just be at peace. He found what he was looking for. And yes, he tried to share it with other people and some of them might have taken that message and done something terrible as a consequence. But isn't that the history of religion? Hasn't the history of humanity been one long list of people getting the message wrong?'

Billy smiles. There are two points of colour on her cheeks. When her passions are roused, she seems almost sublime.

'You lost a baby,' says Billy, and he hadn't known he was going to say it until the words were already on the air.

Claudine recoils as if he's punched her in the stomach. Her eyes fill with tears for a moment. He hates himself in his entirety. Hates her, suddenly, for making him feel so bad. Hates Fran and everybody like her.

'You horrible man,' says Claudine, quietly, her accent wavering for a moment so that she sounds considerably more French. 'How dare you... how dare you throw that at me like it were... like it mattered, like it was relevant...'

'Jethro had a photograph of your ultrasound picture in the bag he left at the British Library. He cherished it. Not a crease, not a blemish. He was looking forward to being an uncle.'

Claudine's face seems to crease in on itself as she holds back her tears. Her hands creep to her stomach and she holds herself, cradles the place where her child used to be.

'She never even took a breath,' whispers Claudine. 'Esmerelda.'

Billy moves towards her. Tries to soften his features. 'I'm sorry.'

She looks up, anger in her eyes. 'You don't get to be sorry. She's not anything to do with you.'

'Jethro must have been devastated,' says Billy, angling himself so she has to keep looking at him. He gives a nasty little laugh. 'Bet he'd have been quite the uncle, eh? Would you have trusted him to babysit? Would you have let her come here and play Hermits with Crazy Uncle J?'

Claudine looks like she wants to slap him. The temper flares and then fades in an instant. Her shoulders sag. When she talks she's looking past him, staring into memories only she can see.

'He was so happy when I told him I was pregnant,' she says, and a tiny smile twitches her lip. 'I swear, so many of the things I'd tell him would just seem to fall out of his head, but he never let go of his memory that I was pregnant; that he was going to be an uncle. I couldn't even tell him myself when I lost her. I think I went a little mad with grief for a time. There was a funeral for her, but I didn't tell anybody. I had to tell my partners at work that I'd lost her, and they were very good at spreading the word. I came back and it wasn't to a load of sad eyes and hugs. I'm not that sort of person. Not to them. So it was like it never happened. They all just kind of came to the conclusion that it was best not to mention it. They don't really know me.'

'Who told Jethro?'

'I don't know,' she says, chewing on the inside of her cheek. 'He sent flowers to the funeral. I must have rung him when I was taking the medicine the doctor gave me. I don't remember. He kept writing to me about her. Kept telling me to pray. He said there was always hope. I couldn't even read what he wrote. I was a bad sister – I know that. I couldn't connect with him, couldn't bring myself to wade in to all the mad platitudes and religious *merde* that he kept trying to tell me about. I swear it was like trying to crack a code. I'd leave his letters unopened for days and it was mostly bloody gibberish when I did try and read them – all psalms and bits of Latin and quotes from forgotten saints. I should have just come to see him. Hugged him. I should have done so many things. But I didn't.'

Billy wipes the rain from his face. Looks down. A large dragonfly is buzzing around his knees. He doesn't know whether to hold out his hand for it to alight upon his finger, or swat the damn thing away.

'Where's she buried?' asks Billy. 'Esmerelda, I mean.'

'In France,' says Claudine, wiping her eyes with the back of her hand. 'With Mum.'

Billy looks her up and down. Purses his lips. Licks them. 'Who was the daddy?'

Claudine glares at him, twin points of flame upon her dark, dark eyes. 'I don't think that's any of your business.'

Billy shrugs. 'Might be, might not.' He cocks his head, looking at her fine jawline and wanting to stroke it with the back of his hand. 'Doubt it was immaculate, love. A few candidates, were there?'

Claudine licks her lips. Looks at him with pure scorn. He can feel her reading him, assessing him, weighing him up. Can see her knowing the truth of him – the failed marriage, the endless battle with his temper, the failure to please a woman he loves – all the way to his bones.

'What a horrible little man you are,' she says, shaking her head. 'Good judge of character though. Yes, you're right. An unexpected pregnancy, shall we say. And no, I never did quite whittle it down. That make you feel better, does it?'

Billy shakes his head. There's a part of him, deep inside, that feels nought but disgust for the way he's behaving. He doesn't even know why he so desperately wants to make this poor woman cry. He just can't seem to help it. She's so poised and elegant and beautiful, so untouchably elevated. She's all that Fran has worked so hard to emulate. She's a symbol of everything that he's not. And for that, he wants to hold her head beneath the water until she's no better than he is.

'I think your brother did all this as a sacrifice,' says Billy, rubbing his jaw. 'I think in his messed-up head he decided that there was a way for his Almighty God to put things right. And like a million other nutters before him, he thought sacrifice was the way. The blood of the martyrs, yeah? Blood sacrifice? Willing disciples with nothing to live for...'

Claudine turns away from him, scorn dripping from every pore. He grabs her by the arm. Squeezes.

'I think he did this for you. Made this all happen. I think he loved you far more than you could ever have loved him, and he did all he could to give you the happiness he thought you deserved. Gave his own life so that God would undo the pain he'd caused you. I think this is all tied up in saints and apostles and the fucking Almighty. But more than anything, I think this is all to do with you and your dead baby...'

He sees the slap coming. Catches her by the wrist. Can't really help what happens next. Hits her before he has a chance to stop himself. It's in the belly, where the bruises don't show: a good gut punch. She doubles over and falls to the ground. He feels bad immediately, just like he always did when Fran wound him up past the point of no return. He crouches over her. Strokes her shoulder. She curls up in a ball. He wishes he hadn't done it. Wishes he'd done it harder. He spits and walks away.

★

Enoch stays long enough to watch her get back to her feet. She's a little unsteady. There is dirt and tears on her cheeks. She rubs at her stomach, trying to get her breathing under control. A dragonfly flits around her. It's joined by another. A third. From where he squats, crouched in the reeds where he was baptised and reborn, he watches as the sainted woman extends her arms. Watches, mouth open, eyes blazing with righteous fervour, as the dragonflies settle upon her – a great shimmering mass of iridescent wings. For a moment, through the haze of his own years and the mist of the holy waters of the Fen, she is an angel.

He crosses himself. Scores another crucifix into his unworthy skin with the tip of the sacred blade. His blood rises. Pools. Drops into the black water of the Fen. For a moment he hears the voice of God. He hears the Almighty telling him that the moment has come, that the martyrs must make good upon what they promised to do in His name. That he is a vessel into which a new life will soon be poured.

Enoch looks upon the woman as she walks, slowly, back into the reeds.

Breathes one word.

'*Mother.*'

23

We don't talk much on the drive. Peg looks too little to be at the wheel of the big old farm vehicle, sitting forward in the driving seat to peer through the dorsal fin screeched onto the muddy glass by the ancient windscreen wipers. It's been a cold, bleak day and the fleeting contact with DS Dean only served to make me feel less connected to myself. I feel ethereal, vague. I think of a child's drawing in crayon: waxy blurs overspilling my outline.

'Bad crash there a few years back,' mutters Peg, nodding in the general direction of the darkness. She glances at her watch. 'How are we running late? How?'

I don't offer a reply. I'm not sure if she means it as a rebuke. She was pacing the living room for an hour while she waited for me, closing cupboard doors loudly and shouting up the stairs to remind me of the time. I lay in the deep, cold bath. Looked at the windblown sand of my belly, shimmering stretch marks my daily reminder of all that I lost.

I couldn't make myself move any quicker. I felt as though my batteries had run down, my every action treacly and furred. I did my make-up with fingers that felt rubbery: numb. I couldn't hold my arms up for long enough to blow-dry my hair so it hangs, lank and black, dripping rainwater and bathwater onto the collar of my borrowed coat. Peg tells me she used to wear this purply Afghan jacket when she was a young woman. It's coarse and tickly and smells of old tobacco and spilled beer. I'm wearing a pair of shabby jeans, the knees faded and threadbare. I think they might be Everitt's. I know the trainers are: white Golas, size seven. They just about fit though I'm having to wear hiking socks.

'You're doing okay, yes?' she asks, glancing over at me. 'I know he rattled you, but you've got to remember that you've done nothing wrong. You're a victim. Jethro was a victim.'

I lean my head against the passenger window. I want a drink. Vodka and orange would be nice, served with lots of ice in an upstairs bar in Southwark. I try and imagine what my colleagues would make of me here and now. I've been ignoring their messages, hiding away from the plaintive emails and tentative enquiries about whether I'll be able to pop back in for a debrief in the next few days. They're missing me. The clients are missing me. I've made myself indispensable and they hate me for it.

'I'm not a victim,' I mutter. 'A witness, maybe.'

'Same thing,' she tuts, as the bright lights of a passing car throw orbs of dirty light onto the dark, tree-lined country road. 'What you saw – nobody should have to see that. And then to make you feel bad about it; well, I don't know how he can justify it to himself.'

I smile, tiredly. If I'm honest I've got some sympathy for DS Dean's position. He's hunting a very high-profile killer and evidence is mounting that at least one of the victims may have been somehow complicit. I've no doubt he's being pressured from above. I don't like the way he glares at me, but I get the impression that it comes from a place of actual outrage rather than a desire to assert his dominance over me. I've been up close and personal with plenty of ambitious people, and they rarely go purple in the face about issues and ethics. They respond with rage only when their authority or ability is questioned, when their lies start to unravel and their contradictions are exposed. Billy wants to catch a very bad person and if he has to lean on me to do it, I'm sure he'll see it as a price worth paying. But I'll never forgive that punch. Never.

'Up yonder,' says Peg, glancing over at me. 'You sure you'll be okay? Oh bugger, we're already five minutes late…'

The little church materialises out of the darkness like the prow of a ship. It's not a pretty building. It's built of a joyless grey-black stone and the narrow window slits contain shards of mullioned glass. They gleam with a dark iridescence that they make me think of insect eyes. The tower has the look of a crooked thumb, a gnarly digit pointing skywards and encircled with rusted black railings. They were put in place nearly thirty years ago when a local student managed to break into the church and climb the spiral stairs, leaping into the darkness while in the grip of some unfathomable madness. He struck his head on a tombstone. Died for a time. Not much of him came back but, for a time, I did my damnedest to love what remained. I wonder if I should bury him here. Wonder whether they would allow it. Would it be perverse? I don't know the rules.

'Not a bad turn-out,' mutters Peg as she pulls the truck into a muddy parking space fifty yards or so from the wall of the church. There are half a dozen other cars parked nearby. We're on the outskirts of Little Mercy, somewhere between Wisbech and Crowland. It's a flat, featureless landscape; trees and fields and wetlands. There's a general sense of dampness to the place, as if I were being painted into a watercolour awash with grey-green paint.

The cold air hits me like a slap. I huddle inside my coat while Peg fiddles in her pockets for tickets, purse, distance glasses and reading spectacles. She links her arm through mine and nods us down the path. We pull faces into the driving rain as we hurry to the church. Headstones rise from the long, wet grass like so many shark teeth.

'I hate being late,' I mutter, as a security light flicks on overhead and throws a great beam of gaudy yellow light onto the footpath. I glance up and see the leering faces of goblins and ghouls – leering stone eyes and twisted mouths – a gallery of nightmarish faces staring down from beneath the overflowing gutters.

Peg crosses herself as we duck inside the entranceway, catching our breaths and wiping the water from our faces. I can hear the sound of a muffled voice from beyond the closed door: a ripple of laughter, a smattering of applause. I can smell wood polish and lilies.

Peg gives my arm a squeeze and we silently make our way into the body of the church. It's small and bare: flagged floors and half a dozen rows of cushioned pews directed towards a simple altar and a golden cross. There are chocolate brown timbers in the plastered roof. From their joists hang garlands, bound in faded silks and ribbons, dead flowers and dried herbs. The air is cold as stone and the handful of enthusiasts who sit haphazardly around the church are all still wrapped up in scarfs and coats.

On the raised area in front of the altar is Reverend Struan Talbot. He stops mid-sentence as he spots us shuffling in at the back. He raises a hand as if there's a harsh light obscuring his vision. He seems to lose his train of thought for a moment as his gaze falls upon the both of us. Peg mouths her apologies. He purses his lips, his mouth forming a strange little embouchure, as if he's sampling a wine and isn't sure whether to swallow or spit.

'Come in, come in,' he says, recovering himself and turning the raised hand into a welcoming wave. Heads turns. A few of the other guests mouth hello to Peg. An elderly gentleman pretends to deliver a slap to his wrist, chiding us for our poor timekeeping. I settle onto the pew, Peg pushed up so close to me that I can barely lift my arm. She crosses herself again as she makes herself comfortable. I give apologetic smiles as she knocks the Bible from the shelf in front of us and it clatters to the stone floor with a bang.

'We were just killing time until you arrived,' says Talbot, with a full smile. He's a slim chap with a curiously unlined face, a canvas stretched tight over a frame. He wears a neat goatee, and his grey-black hair is neatly razored at the back and sides, parted in the centre and gelled flat. He and the professor emeritus could be twins. With his tweedy three-piece suit and purple scarf, he has the air of a 1920s gangster trying to hide his roots. His voice is cultured and marbled with the soft vowels of a cultured Midlothian education.

He lets his gaze linger on me for a moment and I can sense him putting the pieces together. He gives a little nod as he realises who I must be. Memories rise. The last time we spoke I was still a child and he was telling me not to worry – he had friends within an old church charity that would ensure Jethro was looked after. He was as good as his word until I turned eighteen. Then the financial burden fell to me. We hadn't spoken since.

'So, so… yes,' he says, clapping his hands. 'As you can see, I really know how to fill a venue. I think the days of the lecture tours in auditoriums are a thing of the past, are they not? Still, I prefer a more intimate venue and I certainly enjoy a more discerning audience. It's extraordinary to me but somehow there's an overlap between the people who are interested in my work, and the cultured, good-looking people in every region where I give a talk.'

There's a ripple of laughter from the assorted pensioners in front. They're enjoying this man. He has a twinkle in his eye, and he's got a slightly fruity way of talking that suggests they might get the opportunity to be pleasantly offended before the evening is out.

'Congratulations, I suppose,' he continues, with another clap of his hands. 'You are clearly the people who will survive the revolution. It takes a serious effort of will to come along to a cold little church on a wet weekday evening and listen to some crusty old theologian talk about saints. So give yourself some hearty pats on the back. Not too rough, mind – none of us are as young as we were.'

There's a titter of laughs. Some wag in the second row shouts 'speak for yourself' and the audience relax into comfortable chuckles as his wife tells him to behave himself.

'Ah, it's good to be back.' Talbot smiles, hands on his hips. 'Always one, isn't there? Thankfully we're in a house of God so I have one or two reminders of the importance of forgiveness.' He stops, looking around at the old stone walls and the dangling garlands. He glances at an empty seat in the front pew. Wipes his nose with the back of his hand. A wistful look passes across his features: the shadow of a bird upon a pond. 'My friend Jethro should be sitting there,' he says, not looking at Peg or me. 'You'll all know Jethro, yes? One of the last great eccentrics and somebody very dear to me. It was at his insistence that I included Little Mercy in the publicity tour. I can see him sitting there now. He'd probably have carrier bags covering his sandals and I've no doubt that halfway through my lecture I'd notice a hedgehog in his pocket or a bird nesting in the hood of his coat. We've all lost somebody whose soul was genuinely untainted. In another age he would have been labelled a martyr, though I suppose we shall not know what he died defending until we learn the motivations of his attacker. All I know is that I have lost a great friend. Might we perhaps bow our heads for a moment.'

I feel Peg's hand on mine. I look down and see that I'm gripping the hem of my trousers, my knuckles pressing against my flesh like skulls pushing their way through the earth.

There are mutterings of 'gone too soon' and 'such a lovely man' from the assorted faithful and one or two heads turn to look at us. I don't bow my head. I keep my eyes fixed on Struan Talbot. He looks up at me over the bowed crowns and for a moment our eyes find one another. He gives a tiny twitch of a smile.

'Well then,' he says, clapping his hands again. 'That rather leads me on to the book. That's what you're here for; yes, I have copies to sell and I'd be glad to sign any that you've already snapped up and brought along. If you have any of my earlier work, I'd be glad to sign those too. But for now, I want to talk to you about the concept behind my new study. Now, I warn you, there's a small chance that you'll be briefly offended by some of what I have to say. All I would ask is that you keep an open mind. I am, after all, a man of faith. I'm a believer. I'm a Christian, though perhaps I'm the sort who watches documentaries about dinosaurs and who is willing to accept that some of what we know about Noah's Ark might not be entirely dependable. But I love God. I feel His love and closeness. And I believe to my very core that He would not be offended by the idea that psychedelic drugs may have played a major part in the instances of religious ecstasy experienced by the early followers of Christ.'

I look at Peg. She's got a rapt expression on her face, staring at Talbot as if he were a televangelist promising to heal the sick. I feel a cold kind of disgust unwinding in my stomach; an emptiness where you should be, Esmerelda. I have to fight to stop myself from sneering. How dare he talk of God's love and mercy when he took you from me without allowing you to draw breath. No being who witnessed your tiny, fragile, pink-blue body could think of the creator as anything but a monster. *He took you from me, Esmerelda. Took you for His own and left me with nothing but emptiness, sorrow and hate.*

'So, psychedelia,' he says, with a little flash of teeth. 'I'm sure you're thinking of tie-dye T-shirts and Woodstock, yes? Well, you're not far out, man. But take the T-shirts away and put some dirty robes on the picture in your mind and you might just see something close to the reality. The bottom line is this, my friends – over the past few years I've found what I consider to be absolute proof that the early adopters of Christianity may very well have been gloriously out of their minds on powerful psychedelics. Yes, it does rather create a picture, doesn't it? Imagine Sunday Mass if everybody were tripping out on LSD. It might liven things up – that's for sure.'

The audience are listening intently. He's a good speaker. He's witty and charming and there's a clear enthusiasm for his subject.

'It will soon be recognised as an incontrovertible fact that some early Greek-speaking Christians – the so-called *Mystery* sects – had hallucinogens in their ritual wines,' says Talbot, with an apologetic shrug. 'My new book has been an intense labour of love. It's the result of a decade of intense investigation that has seen me delve into Vatican archives, Greco-Roman texts, near-mystical medieval records and to work with some of the finest minds in the field of archaeochemistry. What's archaeochemistry? I hear you ask. I asked it too. Essentially it's a new discipline that can isolate the exact chemical make-up of ancestral food and drink. We can, in essence, work out whether the communion wine was "spiked". Now, stay with me as I know that this could drift into the realm of the dull, but for a moment I need to talk to you about language. You see, for a period of well over a thousand years – centuries before the time of Christ and for some four hundred years after – wine is consistently referred to as a *pharmakon*, which translates as "drug". Their "wine" and our cabernet sauvignon would barely recognise one another. The wine of the ancient Greek sects were made with plants, herbs and toxins, making it highly intoxicating but more than that, a true hallucinogenic.

'Book V of Dioscorides' *Materia Medica*, an ancient pharmacopoeia, is devoted to the different recipes for these fortified brews. Archaeologists given access to wine vessels recovered from a farmhouse in Pompeii have identified a veritable witch's brew of different ingredients, drugs and poisons within the preserved remains of the liquid in their base. Alongside remnants of willow walnut, they found a cornucopia of opium, cannabis, and two members of the nightshade family: white henbane and black nightshade. These plants contain tropane alkaloids known for their hallucinogenic effects, including scopolamine. This drug has been known for centuries as the Devil's Breath.

'That's all quite a long way from the ceremonial sipping of a mouthful of Christ's blood at Eucharist, wouldn't you agree? But the symbolism is inarguable. And for me, the most exciting discovery of the whole experience is one that has a particular relevance to this lovely part of the world. You'll all know the venerable St Guthlac, of course: esteemed hermit of this parish. Indeed, where would your tourism industry be without it?

'The question I now must put to you, however, is whether the terrible beasts and demons with which Guthlac did righteous battle were not perhaps the results of hallucinations brought about by eating mouldy bread. Ergot poisoning. You might know it as St Anthony's fire. You might not know it as a drug very similar to LSD. But our humble hermit so famously consumed nothing but dirty water and stale bread. Is it not possible that what he saw was more akin to a nightmare than a true battle against the forces of darkness? Or, and I make this case quite forcefully, might not the partaking of these compounds have been a deliberate act that permitted imbibers to see beyond the veil: to open their eyes to the nearness of angels and demons, to saints and the damned? To tune themselves in to a frequency where God's majesty became as real and as terrifying as their own intimate realities?'

Talbot pauses. Looks up at the sound of a creak from behind me. I turn and see DS Dean slipping into the back of the church. He's got a scowl on his face. It deepens when he spots me and Peg.

'The more the merrier,' says Talbot, waving at the newcomer, who sits down at the pew behind me. I catch the smell of him: sweat and cologne. Something chemical, too. Something deep and rank and earthy: buried meat.

'I think it might be time for a reading,' says Talbot, cheerfully. He reaches for a hardback book from a little pile hidden away behind the lectern. Opens the book and begins to read. I stop listening. I feel DS Dean shifting about in his seat. A moment later his head is close to mine, his damp face and hair so near my cheek that I can smell the strong mints and tobacco on his breath.

'You didn't tell me you were coming,' he whispers, his lip at my ear. 'We could have done a car-share – saved the planet a little bit.'

'You didn't tell me either,' I say, more a hiss than a whisper.

'I don't have to,' he says. 'That's how this works, yeah? I'm a policeman. A detective. I'm looking for a killer.'

'And I'm the sister of a victim,' I say, holding my head so still that I begin to feel a tightness in my neck.

'A victim with a chapel under his barn,' replies Dean, with a dry laugh. 'An altar. A cross and a psalter and enough religious iconography to fill a cathedral. A victim who just happened to come to London and kick up a stink at the British Library and who we've got on CCTV chatting with our chief suspect.'

'Maybe you should arrest him then,' I say, coldly. 'Do you think he'll go to jail for it or is his death enough of a punishment?'

'We want the truth,' he says, stubbornly.

'So do I. That's what I came here for. I don't understand why he was there, what he wanted, why he came to see me. But I do know I let him down and...'

'Please be quiet; some of us are trying to listen.'

Dean and I both throw angry glances at the elderly, white-haired woman who has turned in her seat to give us a telling-off.

'I can't face all this chummy little England shit,' says Dean, snarling. 'Can I buy you a drink?'

I think I've misheard him at first. It sounds so incongruous after his previous tone that I wonder if I've imagined it. I glance at him, still up close, and he's waiting, eyebrows raised.

I look past him. Peg is still lost in Talbot's words. I can't face any more of this either. I can't stand the feeling of cold, desperate absence in my stomach. I nod and he gives a grunt of acknowledgement.

I follow him outside. I'd rather wait for Talbot while looking at the stars.

24

The Church of St Wendreth, Little Mercy

*M*e. Claudine Cadjou. Orphan. Loveless. Sister to a dead man and mother to a stillborn child. *Me*, standing on the lip of the graveyard and thinking of bones.

Seeing, feeling, tasting...

The rain and the dark and the cold, cold air.

A ragged flag flapping overhead, somewhere above the whine of the electric wire.

Flurries of wind honed upon headstones into saw-toothed points.

Trees bending low, topmost branches brushing wet grass.

Briskly whispering leaves.

And him. The man who hit me. The man who looks like he wants to hold me down and make himself feel better between my legs.

DS Dean.

He's doing something peculiar with his shoulders, rolling one, then the other, then twisting his neck as far as it will go, palm under his chin. He's manhandling his jaw, too, wrenching it from side to side, eyes wide and staring. There's a sudden crack, gunshot loud. It sounds as if he's snapped his neck.

I think of leering skeletons. Think of the shape of his bones beneath the soft membrane of skin and blood.

'Better,' he grunts, rubbing at the place where the hinge of his jaw meets the rest of his skull. He puts his fingers under his tongue and yanks downwards. There's another terrible crunching sound. 'Bastards,' he spits, and screws up his eyes.

I lean in the little porchway of the church. I think of Jethro: his maddening exactitude with words when I was small. *It's not a porch, Claudine – it's a parvis…*

I shake the memory away, flashing another glance at the silhouette of DS Dean. He stopped walking the second we were outside. He lingers now on the top step, testing the darkness; a cat reluctant to step into snow. The light of the church extends only a few feet into the gloom before the night air becomes an impenetrable wall of rain-slashed black. There are magpies somewhere.

He jerks his head sideways again. This time there's no sound. Instead, he starts cracking the knuckles in his left hand, tugging on the top knuckle as if trying to get the top off a pen.

'That can't be good for you,' I say, keeping my voice low in case it carries back into the church. I can still hear Talbot's murmur, the titter of genteel laughter, the smattering of applause. 'Doesn't it hurt?'

'I don't fit together right,' he says, dourly. 'Made up of scrag-end and bollock-skin, me.' He looks back and scowls at me, his expression suddenly fierce, brows meeting like ram heads. 'Broke my jaw when I was a teenager. Never sat right since. I'm all of a twist.'

I say nothing for a moment. I listen to the rain. Breathe

in the cold, damp air. I don't know what he wants. I don't know what I want either. Jethro tried to kill himself here when I was a girl. Threw himself from the roof and crashed off a tomb into a freshly dug grave. Killed a piece of himself and became somebody else. And now I'm being picked on by the police officer who believes he may have martyred himself in the attack that cost him his life. I can't deal with any of it, so I shrink it all down. I try and focus on him. On his words and his manner and this moment, this *now*.

'I have a friend who's a physiotherapist,' I say, thinking of a lady who occasionally comes into the office to give staff workstation massages and undo the problems caused by hours spent leaning over keyboards. 'She can teach you the right way to sit – how to unclench a bit. I had a problem with my pelvis and she did some manipulations that…'

'I bet you bloody did,' he says, and snatches his gaze away, glaring out into the rain-veiled darkness of the graveyard. 'Pelvic manipulations,' he repeats, shaking his head. 'Fuck's sake.'

Hot tears prickle at my eyes. I feel scolded. Chastened. I don't even recognise the person I've become.

'You bet I do what?' I ask, hating the meekness in my voice.

'Have friends who are physiotherapists. Bet you've got mates who play the cello and eat tapenade and collect art prints by struggling urban artists. Bet you listen to Dido at dinner parties.'

'Dido?' I ask, scrumpling up my face. 'I haven't thought of Dido in about fifteen years.'

'Yeah, whatever.'

He falls to silence, leaning against the damp stone. After a while he pulls out a flask from a pocket. It's small and old and silver. The lower half is wrapped in some kind of leather. He unscrews the lid and takes a swig. Grunts. Offers it to me. 'Go on then,' he mutters.

I don't know whether to take it to spite his nastiness or to turn and walk back into the church. When he'd mentioned a drink, I'd imagined a country pub with a cosy open fire. 'What is it?'

'Bit of this, bit of that. Good for you. It'll put hairs on your chest.'

I give a twitch of a smile. Take a swig without wiping the lip. He grunts his approval while I swill the mixture around my mouth. It's sweet and syrupy: some sort of whisky liqueur. I swallow it down and feel it warming me from the inside out.

'You're not driving then?' I ask.

'I don't know what I'm doing,' breathes Dean. 'Depends, doesn't it?' He closes his eyes. He looks tired to his bones. The skin under his eyes looks thin and dark, like bruised fruit. There's a yellowness to his eyes and sore skin around his nostrils and beneath his lower lip. He looks like he's been breathing in chemicals and smoke.

'Why did you come tonight?' I ask, and shiver as the biting wind blows in a swirling ghost of chill rain. 'Are you following me now?'

He shakes his head. Twitches his nostrils. Looks at me properly for what seems like the first time. 'You look frozen through,' he says, staring into me in that same intense way. 'I'd give you my coat, but it's soaked.'

I can't help but laugh. It's such an unexpected and

fumbled attempt at gallantry that it strikes me as genuinely funny. He looks momentarily hurt. It quickly returns to sullenness, his face hardening.

'Fuck you then,' he says, shrugging again. 'That's your trouble, isn't it? Can't let anybody put the past behind them, can you? Always got to hold on to the image of the person you used to be. One slip-up, one fucking slip-up and suddenly all the work you've done on yourself is for absolutely bloody nothing.'

He raises his hand to his face so quickly I think for a moment he's about to punch himself. Instead he snatches away the wetness on his cheek. I realise that the redness, the yellow eyes, the ache in the shoulders and neck, are all familiar side effects of somebody who lives their life on the verge of tears. I can't help but feel a sudden surge of pity for him, a desire to better know him – perhaps to start again. We both want the same thing, after all. We want to know what happened, and why, and whether my brother was the victim or villain.

'Forgive me for saying this, Detective – you seem as though you've really got it in for me. Or maybe not just me, but people you think I'm like. You don't know me, not really, just like I don't know the first thing about you. But you seem like you need to talk to somebody.'

He sneers at that. Licks rainwater from his dry lips and swallows. It looks like it pains him to do so.

'Fran,' he mumbles, and his bottom lip trembles for a moment. 'She were a Fran when we met. She's a Cesca now. High-flyer, see. Detective superintendent. We were both constables at the same time but we both knew where we wanted to be. I didn't settle for staying at my rank, I chose it. I didn't want the politics. She loved all that. Understood how to play the game. We used to laugh about it in bed – her joining the right organisations and clubs and taking up golf and shaking the right hands. Going to the big nights out with the movers and shakers. Sparkly ball gowns and little flutes of champagne. She'd come home and change into her joggers and we'd have a curry on the sofa and I'd massage her feet and we'd laugh about all the wankers she had to pretend to be impressed by. I never saw it change. Never saw the moment when she stopped finding it pitiful and started to think and be like them; started to think of people like me as cavemen, the grunts who needed leadership; saw people like me as the sorts who needed to be led by people like her.

'Fuck's sake, I did try. Went to the pissing opera, read the right books. I mean, Jesus, I even tried golf! Still for nowt in the end. One mistake, one little mistake, and we're not compatible. She's outgrown me. She loves me but she's not in love with me, and thanks, it's over, all those years of marriage down the tube, and...'

He stops. Takes a bite of the air. He looks as if he's screaming. The tendons in his neck are sticking out. He looks insane.

'I'm sorry,' I say, and it comes out so pitifully weak that I repeat it.

'Come on, we'll go look,' he mutters, shaking his head. He puts his hand out as if he's wanting me to take it. I don't know what's happening, but I feel too weak and insubstantial to be able to muster any objection. He closes his rough hands around my fingers as if I'm a child who needs help crossing the road and he pulls me out of the doorway of the church and into the dark. He stamps his way down the path, his hand gripping mine, and takes a sharp right, stepping onto the damp grass and tugging me after him, picking a path between the headstones. There's absolutely no light and I can barely make out the shape of him. I blunder forward, my trousers soaked through and sticking to my skin. I can hear him muttering. He's fumbling around in his pockets, cursing as he bangs his knee on something hard. I glance back towards the church. It's almost lost in the darkness.

'Fuck's sake,' mutters Dean and yanks me forward. I bump against his back. Something snags at my ankles. There's a sharp stinging sensation. I can feel my heart beating; can smell Dean's sweat and damp clothes; can smell the frog skin and mildew of the air above the Fen, the dank green breath of the distant water. 'Ah, that'll do it.'

I wince as he turns back to me, the light on his mobile phone suddenly harsh in my face. He swings it back towards himself, illuminating the hollows and soreness of his face. I suddenly feel afraid of him. There's a lunacy to him: a lustre to his eyes that speaks of zealotry and madness.

'Yonder,' he says, and waves the torch in the direction of a small outbuilding. He shakes his head, seeming to come to a decision. He knows something. There's new information. It's changed him – changed the dynamic between us. 'You would, wouldn't you? Cold night, up for a bit of how's-your-father – you pop in there and have yourself a belter of a time. But you hear something, see?'

He swings the torch in the direction of an ancient-looking headstone: the lettering weathered but the skull and crossbones motif at its top still visible. I shudder, cold and afraid.

'I reckon they were pratting about with this poor bastard,' he says, as if I know what he's talking about. 'The last verger says they've reburied that poor sod so many times you can still see the spade marks on his skull. Treasure hunters, you see, though no doubt they made it seem more impressive than that when they were planning it. Elevated thinkers, of course. Intellectuals. Philosophers. But they'll have had a shock, won't they? Despite the best of intentions, some bloke with his trousers down comes out of the hut and they react like little kids caught with their hands down their pants. One swipe with the spade, that would do it. And where do you stick him when you're done, eh? Same hole you've just dug up. But what of her, eh? That's what I want to know. She there too? We'll know soon enough.'

I pull my fingers from his grip. 'What are you talking about?' I whisper, glancing down at the overgrown grass. By the light of the phone I can see the snarl of brambles caught around my ankles. I look up again and see that Billy has started off in the direction of the grave. He's kicking out at the wildflowers around him, aiming savage hacks at the heads of cow parsley and a stand of gaudy yellow ragwort.

'I'm going back,' I say, to the patch of darkness that has swallowed him. 'Peg will be worrying. I need to talk to the speaker... Jethro's things – he has some of Jethro's things...'

'I know, you silly girl. I know all about Talbot.'

I glare at him, not understanding. My brain hurts like a toothache. I feel a sharp pain, like cat claws in my shins. I try and pull myself free of the brambles but only succeed in entangling myself further; sharp little thorns scratching across my cold, damp skin.

'Are you coming?' shouts Billy, his disembodied voice snatched away by the wind. 'Pound to a penny he's in there. If they'd listen… if they'd just bloody listen…'

The words cut off abruptly, as if a phone call has been unexpectedly terminated. From ahead there's a soft, serpentine kind of a sound: sludgy water gurgling in a blocked drain.

'DS Dean?'

I yank myself free and stumble backwards, clattering against the side of a headstone. I start to rummage in my pockets, looking for my phone, desperate for light. I tuck my arms in at my sides, trying to make myself smaller. The wind is whipping at me like a scourge, my eyes watering, hair plastering itself to my bare cheeks. I glance up. No stars. No moon. There's just a haze of dark nothingness that stretches all the way down to the grass.

'I can't see you,' I shout, weakly. 'I'm going back. I'm cold.'

I turn back towards the church just as I sense the presence behind me. I breathe a little fluttering gasp of relief. I'm afraid of DS Dean but I'm far more afraid of being on my own.

'I thought you'd left me,' I say, a little laugh in my voice as I twist my feet free of a thicket of grass and turn back to him, eager for the light.

There's a figure in front of me. Taller than me. Broader than me. His shape is only slightly darker than the raven blackness around him. He's faceless. Still. There's no way of making out his features but at once I know this is the man who killed Jethro. This is the man who brought bloodshed into my life.

Time slows. I see him raise his hand just as the clouds part like curtains on a stage. For an instant there is a perfect spear of moonlight, bright as fire. I see the blade in his gloved hand; see the thick blood smeared over the leather upon his knuckles and wrist. I see the ruination of his face: tattered scraps of putrefying flesh and ripped leather. I see beetle-black eyes and rubbery lips and the yellow stumps of teeth curving out of tar-black, rotted-fruit gums.

He holds the knife before me, laid upon his palm like a fish. The blade is old metal; the handle yellow bone and black, mottled skin. He holds it out as if it were an offering, as if he were waiting for me to place a communion wafer into the bowl of his cupped palms.

He speaks one word: the voice splitting, splintering, dividing into a choir of discordant sounds. I hear something reptilian, hear the reverential tones of a minister delivering a sermon, hear the croaking rasp of an old woman strangling at the end of a rope. I hear a frightened child.

'Mother.'

I take the knife from his hand. The voices buzz in my head as if my skull were full of so many angry wasps. I hold the weapon up to my face. This is the blade that killed my brother. It split him from neck to navel and across the chest. It carved a cross into his fragile, unwashed skin.

'Why?' I beg, my voice a whisper. 'What do you want? Why did you hurt those people?'

He doesn't speak. Lowers his head. He slowly sinks to one knee. I feel like a priest unable to offer a blessing. Suddenly, as if a gust of wind had blown onto the embers of a dying fire, I feel rage. I feel an absolute fury: a thirst for retribution, a desperate desire to do bloody violence and revenge myself and Jethro upon this tattered creature at my feet.

I change my grip upon the knife. He looks up. Tips his head back, exposing the shredded mess of skin at his throat.

I can picture the blade slashing across his skin. Can already feel the warm spray of spilled blood upon my cold skin. Can see the blood pulsing into the wet grass and slipping down through the flesh-fed earth to anoint the ancient, sacred ground.

There is a sudden, sickening thud. There is a grunt of pain and surprise and then he is slumping sideways, the outline of his skull subtly changed: an apple with a bite out of its flesh.

DS Dean is on his knees. One hand holds in the bloodied mess of flesh and viscera that spills from his open stomach. The other holds a chunk of headstone, the gritty dark of its sharpest point tarred with thick black blood.

He gives me a little nod. Manages something like a smile. Then he pitches forward onto the man whose skull he has smashed. I catch a whiff of bad blood: offal and putrid meat, the iron tang of blood and disturbed earth.

I don't remember the knife until I'm turning away from the horror and dragging myself, desperately, towards the church; brambles and weeds tugging at my legs like the hands of the risen dead.

Only when I'm near enough to the church to be heard do I let myself start shouting for help. I stumble. Fall. Haul myself up again, thrusting the blade into my inside pocket as if that were where it belongs.

Out of the door of the church bursts Struan Talbot. He grimaces into the cold and the dark and starts forward as I emerge from the gloom. I can suddenly taste blood on my lips, can feel the grit of pulverised bone against my cheek.

Talbot sees me. There's a moment when he can't quite make out who is stumbling forward in the dark. He moves forward, arms open.

When he sees that it is me, his features change. For an instant he lowers his arms. And then there are other people spilling out of the church, pushing behind him, and he is hurried forward, running towards me, raising his arms again as if to offer sanctuary.

I feel his arms wrap around me. Hear him tell me that everything will be okay. *What has happened, child? What has happened...?*

I don't answer him. I feel the crowd press around me, see figures scurrying forward into the graveyard, torches flashing like swords.

Then Peg's hand is in mine and she's holding me and stroking my hair and telling me not to worry, I'm safe, I'm safe.

25

St Mary's Hospital, Paddington

'Forensics, Sarge,' says Helen, chattily. 'Lots of lovely photos of Enoch's smashed-in head, if you fancy taking a squiz.'

She's grateful for the distraction. Grateful for something to look at other than old copies of *Heat* and *Hello*. She's been reading him articles from the piss-poor collection of magazines for the past couple of hours. It's either that or subject herself to one of his intellectual podcasts: God and existentialism, Marxist theory and neo-Agnostics. She feels on firmer ground with the Nolan sisters and a Kardashian.

Even with most of his body in bandages and the tube coming out of his mouth, the unconscious Billy manages to look thoroughly unimpressed.

Helen will have to go soon. Three days she's been at his bedside, only popping home now and again for a shower and a change of clothes and the chance to feed the kids or help them with their homework. She doesn't really have any duty to Billy. Can't claim friendship. But in his way, he's taught her a lot during their brief time together. And his wife won't be coming; that much is for certain. She's busy getting claps on the back and her picture in the paper, part of the team that caught one Enoch Westall, Embankment Killer. He's being written off as a lone nutter. He's an ex-paratrooper. Saw terrible things on active duty in Iraq. Went AWOL in '07 and drifted from place to place until washing up in London, traumatised and angry and desperate to be somebody else.

A succession of churches tried to help him. Somewhere along the line he decided that he wanted to do good in God's name. And when his demons overcame him, he spilled blood. Slashed and stabbed and rejoiced in the screams, convinced he had won the favour of his Holy Father. That's the story being fed to the press. Savage will pretend to believe it. In the end, it will no longer be a pretence.

'Letter in the inside lining of Jethro's bag,' she says. 'Wrote it on the train down to London. I think he was on his way to see Struan Talbot. Andrew, Gwyndaf. Enoch…'

She realises how cold and bare and joyless the little room feels. How very like a monastic cell. She'd like to bring flowers. Balloons, maybe. She'd like there to be some colour to look at when he wakes up. And he will wake up. He's too angry to die.

She reads in silence. Absorbs it all. And then she reads aloud. By the end, her eyes are full of tears. And DS Dean's are fully open.

Chère Moineau,

I am writing this very slowly, concentrating on precisely what I want to tell you. I know that my mind does not work like those of other people. I know that I was damaged when I hurt myself. Perhaps I was damaged before that. I cannot truly say. Memories have emerged like fish rising to feed. Everitt has helped me. We have used a metronome and a mirror, and his gentle voice has helped me to see things that for so long were not there.

I have begun to believe that I have been misled. What I took to be gifts from God were in fact manipulations. I have fought demons so many times, sister. I have woken bloodied and scarred, my flesh torn, my scourge thick with gore. And I have believed myself to be an agent of God, a warrior of the blessed St Bartholomew.

But my new memories shake my faith. Could I really have been so ill-used? Could someone I believed to be my friend really have tampered with the delicate balance of chemicals in my head? Might they have laced our communion wine and wafer while claiming to do God's duty? Might all that I saw these many years have been no more than hallucination? If so, how much else is a lie?

Is the psalter that I have cherished like a newborn really no more than a crude facsimile of something long lost? The bindings do feel as skin, sister, but when I begin to speak aloud, to form the words that might explain my confusion, I realise how insane my accusations.

I do not tell you any of this to advance any cause, Moineau. I simply have nobody else to tell. I fear I have been astray all of my life. There is no righteous path. God watches and waits. Our prayers are echoes. The creator who would put a tumour in the eyes of a child is not one who would answer even the most passionate entreaty. I know this now. Everitt has helped me to remember.

We did terrible things, my teacher and I. We sought to dig up relics from the earth and instead we placed a body in the ground. I know that my heart broke that night and my mind fragmented in the days that followed. I am told that I tried to take my own life. I have no recollection of embarking upon such a path. The night that I sustained my injuries is a blank. My teacher remembers. He has told me what I did and all that he in turn did for me in the years since. But my teacher is wont to lie. He has made promises that only God could make.

My own faith has wavered the more I have remembered. My doubts have grown. So too poor Cissa and Beccelm: the two good men who have tried so hard to slay their own demons and who have broken bread with me in front of our Lord's altar time upon time. We are all reluctant to do that which Enoch is so set upon. It shames me, now, to think that I was so convinced of my righteousness, my godliness, that I believed the poison dropped in my ear. How could I be a reborn Guthlac? How could the scarred man who has supported me in my battles with the demons, truly be St Bartholomew? The more I write, the more I try and make my words make sense, the more I realise how ungodly our actions have been.

Enoch would do anything for my teacher, and my teacher would do anything to further his own glory. We have been profane. Our sermons have been sacrilege. My prayers are become blasphemies. How can the pages of the roll; pages that we did not find in the grave of the antiquary – how can they be, even now, wrapped about the face of poor angry Enoch; the scourge's handle now rammed into the hilt of a sacred blade? How can any of it be real? It cannot, sister. And yet how I long for my own madness to be mistaken and for this nobler insanity to be true.

And so I come to London, sister. So I come to seek proof of who I am, of the true nature of my calling, of what is real and what is not. I do not know what he will tell me, but I know that I will not permit this great sin to continue. If my suspicions are correct, he will order his apostle to shed my blood. He will slaughter all those who knew of how he has manipulated the minds of so many broken, tortured men, women and children. He will seek to preserve his reputation and he will see that his own unholy warrior damns his soul. I take that risk, sister. Please, I beg you, feel no guilt. Just know that of all the things I doubt, my love for you and yours for me is not among them.

I must halt now, sister – we are approaching London and…

Billy can't speak for the tube in his airway. He doesn't need to.

Savage is already on the phone, trying to get through to Claudine Cadjou. They have to warn her. Have to keep her safe from the terrible vengeance of God.

26

Thursday, October 13

Rain again. Grey-green air and a sogginess to every breath. Melancholy skies and the whiff of stagnant water.

I've dressed the part, at last. Bought myself some walking boots, waterproof trousers and a puffy raincoat. There's probably no need for the cerise beret or the garnet-and-gold earrings but I'm only willing to look like a tourist from the neck down. I need to at least recognise a little bit of my reflection.

I've borrowed a car. The police still have Jethro's. They will for a while, apparently. I'm never leaving London so I've no need to buy a vehicle of my own. I was willing to take the train and ask Peg to pick me up from the station but one of the directors dropped by with a bunch of flowers and some files from work and in the process of making stilted chit-chat, I mentioned I would be heading back *North*. He gave me the loan of his weekend runabout, a nippy VW T-Roc Cabriolet that roared up the motorway like a beast released from a cage.

I found myself smiling while I drove: my playlist on shuffle, tapping the steering wheel with freshly painted nails and giggling when I got the words wrong. *You'd have been mortified, Esme, but I think you'd have laughed at me. Do you think I'd have become one of those embarrassing mums? Silly? Brash and daft and dropping you off at school with a coat over my pyjamas? I hope so. I think I might have got some of my imaginings wrong in the past. I'm not sure you'd have wanted brisk efficiency from me. I think you might have craved fun.*

The rain thickens into fog as I trundle over the little bridge. I pause midway across and buzz down the window. I can hear the reeds whispering against one another, can smell mulched herbs and the hazy green wildness of the mist above the mere.

I move forward, the tyres slithering over the mess of ruts and tracks. Lots of vehicles have been here in past days. Lots of police officers and forensic staff have pored over every stick and cobweb in Jethro's home. They have done so with a curious reverence. I wasn't sure at first whether the narrative would leave room for doubt about his innocence, but the newspapers have all co-operated with the agreed version of events. As far as the general public are concerned, he tried to stop the bloodshed. He saved lives and lost his own. The man responsible for the brutality was a religious zealot and a madman. It's all been tied up neatly, complete with an honourable mention for Billy – the brave police officer who nearly lost his life apprehending a killer.

I pull up in the forecourt. Check my make-up in the mirror. I feel a strange little fluttering of excitement, as if I'm calling on an old friend with whom I can share a couple of bottles of wine and gossip until the dawn. Perhaps I am. I can't help thinking of Peg as something more than a friend, now. We've shared few confidences, but we're connected by something that will forever bind us together and when I think of her it makes me feel secure and safe. She'd be a nice mum, I think. I'm a grown woman, of course, but I've always liked the idea of having somebody in my life who makes me feel a little better – somebody to call after a crappy day; somebody to lie up against beneath a blanket and talk about this and that and nothing.

Her car's not here. I wonder if the police have it. I can't imagine why they would. Other than giving a simple statement about what she witnessed in the churchyard, she's not involved in the investigation or its aftermath. She's just Jethro's nice, kindly neighbour. She's made teas for the police officers, brought out biscuits and packets of crisps for the science officers like they were children playing football on her lawn.

I've brought posh biscuits and two bottles of good wine. They're in a basket on the passenger seat and I feel like Little Red Riding Hood as I pick it up and step into the cold air and pick my way through the mud and shingle to the door.

I knock in a friendly way: an old friend, a little comedy paradiddle with warm knuckles on wet wood.

No answer. I try again. Not a sound. I feel my spirits fade. It was meant to be a surprise. I'm meant to be wrapped up in a big hug now, being looked after, coddled, cared for. And nobody's home.

I take a step back and look up at the dark windows. For a moment I'm sure I see movement: a flash of pale skin behind the parted drapes.

'Everitt,' I shout, waving with my free hand. 'Everitt, it's Claudine.'

There's no reply. But he's home – I'm sure of it. I try

the handle. It opens smoothly and I find myself grinning as the warm air of the friendly house welcomes me into its embrace.

I step inside and close the door behind me. Peg's coat is missing from the rack, her boots too. There's a long velvety coat hanging up among the rumpled anoraks and mud-smudged hats and scarves. I take my own coat off and hang it on the first peg. It falls off at once and I find myself grinning, happy that I don't care.

'Everitt!' I yell, again. 'Just me!'

I feel giddy. Silly and high. I don't know why he didn't answer the door, but it doesn't matter, does it? Not really. Maybe he was just out of the shower or using the toilet. He'll be down in a moment, I'm sure.

I head into the living room. It's as messy as before, strewn with newspapers, unopened bills; laundry in various stages of dampness drying on the backs of the sunken sofas like mismatched antimacassars. The fire's flaming yellow and glorious in the grate. I place the basket on the coffee table and bend down to pike the fire. I stare into the glowing coals.

For a moment I wonder whether you're still here, Esme. I permit myself to consider true madness. It would be easy, wouldn't it? Easy to allow you to stay; to convince myself that you are really there, listening to me, growing older beyond the veil. I have a good imagination. I could add Jethro to the pictures in my head. I could talk to him as I talk to you. I could convince myself that I believe.

I wonder if that's what they all did; those poor lost souls who saw a chance for sanctuary, for comfort, for meaning, and who played along with a zealot's delusion as it was better than the cold reality of exclusion.

I turn as I sense somebody behind me.

'Bad penny, aren't I?' I say, grinning, as I turn from the grate. Everitt's standing there. His face is grey. Cold. Unwelcoming.

'I brought you something,' I say, feeling awkward, feeling unwanted. I thought he liked me. I thought I'd be welcome. 'Sorry, sorry, presumptuous of me. I shouldn't have let myself in. It's no problem, just tell Peg I called and...'

He turns away. My temper prickles. I don't like people turning their backs on me. I don't like being dismissed. I know he's a quiet man and these past days with the police at his door must have been hard work but it's not my fault, not really.

'Everitt, wait a moment. I came to see Peg and...'

An ember from the fire spits from a crackling log and there's a sudden pain in my calf as it lands upon my leg and eats quickly through the material. I flick my eyes down, patting at my calf, and when I look up again he's already walked away.

'Hey, is she coming back? Everitt, I can wait in the car if you're going to be funny about it...'

I barge into the kitchen and see his back disappearing through the little wooden door into the utility room. My cheeks are flushed with temper. How unspeakably rude! I stomp after him, determined to get him to look at me, if only so I can make use of my pre-prepared little speech, thanking him for his kindness, his hospitality.

I pull open the door and stomp into the cold half-light of the little stone room. The washing machine has been pulled out from beneath the workbench and sits in the middle of the flagged floor. Where it sat before is a perfect square of empty black air. I look to my right and see a rectangular hatch leaning up against the back door; an iron ring nailed to its centre.

I feel myself grow cold. There's an eerie white vapour hanging in the air above the open trapdoor. For an instant I hear Everitt clearing his throat. The sound rises from the open hatch.

I can't help myself. I squat down and snuffle under the workbench. I touch the edges and waggle my fingertips into the cold black air. I peer forward, squinting into the dead air. The smell hits me like a fist: rotting meat and ammonia, chemicals and iron.

I realise I've left my phone in the pocket of my coat. I've nothing to light my way. And yet I can't help myself. I need to see what's beneath the ground. Everitt has led me here. He wanted me to see.

I sit on the edge of the hole and lower my feet into the darkness. My boots touch stone. I find a secure footing and slowly lower myself down. I touch another hard surface with my boots. There are stone steps. I duck under the lip of the hole and feel for the next step. I touch damp stone, moss-slimed earth. I squint, trying to get a sense of space. My eyes are watering with the smell of the ammonia. I can feel the fear rising in me, can feel the sense of creeping dread steel over my skin, gooseflesh rising on my arms and legs.

My feet slip on the stone and I clatter forward, banging my shins on something hard. There's the sound of something soft clattering onto hard ground. I reach out in the darkness and my hand closes on something leathery and wet. I jerk it away and let out a little hiss of fright. I step backwards and feel skin against the back of my neck. I yelp and spin around again, losing my footing and stumbling blindly forward. Something tugs the beret from my head. Cold flesh brushes my cheek. I bump against something bulky and foul, and my mind fills with images of slaughtered oxen hanging from butcher's hooks.

I wrap my hands around my head, spiders in my hair, eel skin tickling my wrists, the nape of my neck; cold glass knocking against the backs of my knuckles as I spin and fall and lose myself in the dark.

A match flares. For a moment there is an explosion of red and gold and vermillion; fox fur and dragonflies coalescing around the flower of flame.

I'm on the floor in an underground chamber. One wall is piled high with loose pages, sheaves of paper, inks and paints and glass jars full of metal styluses. Hanging from clips like photographs developing in a darkroom, are the skins. Patterned flesh. Frogs. Lizards. Eels.

And Everitt. He hangs next to his own perfectly excised skin: a horrific mannequin dangling wetly, redly, bound at the wrists from a hook in the roof. His skin dangles beside him. It has been removed in one perfect piece. He has been dead for weeks.

I raise my hands to my face to block out the horror.

I hear the sound of the trapdoor slam shut.

On the stairs is Struan Talbot.

Behind him is Peg.

They're dressed in white robes and they're holding hands.

27

Peg smiles. It's the grin of a skull. There's a gleam to her eyes, the lenses white as a winter moon. The pupils are huge, the black so dilated that her irises are entirely absent.

She frees her hand from Talbot's and reaches up to retrieve an oil lamp from a hook by the wall. She raises the match and ignites the wick, her eyes never leaving mine. Behind her, Talbot has a little contented smirk on his face, as if he's watching a film he's seen before and knows that he'll enjoy what happens next.

I hear myself breathing. Feel my teeth chatter as a sudden surge of cold fear runs over every part of me.

'Everitt,' I say, and it comes out as a gasp. I jerk away from the hanging carcass, tucking my arms in at my sides. 'No, Everitt is alive. He led me…'

Peg turns her head towards Talbot. 'She has the gift,' she says, awe in her voice. 'It is as you foretold.'

Talbot grins. He puts his hand on Peg's head and strokes her hair like she's a good little dog. She moves herself against him. I can see the shape of her through the white shift. Can see her skin pucker, her nipples rise.

'Don't use words like "foretold",' he says, cupping her

chin and turning her gaze towards him. 'It makes you sound insane.'

He lets go of her face. Moves her to his side and takes the lamp from her hand. He steps towards me. Despite the robes he looks no different than he did at the lectern in the church. He has the appearance of somebody who knows more than everybody else in the room. He could just as easily be dressed in his tweeds. When he speaks, his manner is one colossal shrug: a vague sense of apology for all the unavoidable unpleasantness and silly theatricality.

'Awkward, really.' Talbot points at the rolls of skin. 'You probably think it's a mean trick to play on the true believers. But they do like their little miracles. They do like something tangible to venerate. It would be easier if I could just conjure up a real psalter and scourge but it's not easy to snap your fingers and create these things. Bartholomew is very precious about his flesh and serpent tongues are a lot harder to come by than toad skin. People do need their artefacts, don't they? Pilgrims will walk barefoot for thousands of miles to gaze at the skull of an apostle, even when they know there's five other churches claiming to possess the self-same head. St Andrew appears to have had eighteen legs, judging by how many churches claim to possess his shin bones. I'm just helping people keep the faith.'

I can't find my voice. Can't make sense of what I'm seeing, what I'm feeling.

'This is difficult, isn't it?' he asks, scratching at his beard. 'You probably have so many questions. You'd no doubt love to interrogate the pair of us and find out what you've been entangled in. Trouble is, your mind isn't working correctly right now, is it? You're afraid. The different glands in your brain are releasing all manner of chemicals and they're encouraging you to run or to fight and in that state you're hardly able to ask pertinent questions, which must be horribly frustrating.'

'Everitt,' I say again. 'He led me here.'

Talbot shrugs, eyebrows sliding upwards. 'It's possible. I've trouble enough knowing whether I believe in saints and demons without throwing in the spectre of restless spirits.' A grin spreads across his face like flame as he applauds his own little joke. 'A spectre! Oh, they just come to me, they really do.'

I look past him. Glare at Peg. 'You let him do this to your husband?'

Peg looks to Talbot, who waves his hand as if shushing a child. 'Which part do you mean, Claudine? The flaying? Really that was a joint effort. It's a laborious process and one really does need a helping hand to do it properly. Have you ever tried getting a wellington boot off when the sole is covered in dirt? Multiply that by ten and you're not even close. But if you're referring to the poor gentleman's death, I think we can chalk it down to unnatural causes. Is that a sensible term, I wonder? To die of fright, for the heart to stop and the brain to rupture itself as an act of self-interest? Imagine a mackerel closing its own gills so it doesn't have to experience the horror of being devoured by the shark.'

'You've skinned him,' I whisper, looking down to the floor. 'Skinned all of these creatures...'

'Omelettes and eggs, I'm afraid,' he says, placing the lamp down on the little workspace. It illuminates glass bottles full of floating, bulbous, misshapen things; illuminates sheaf upon sheaf of crinkled skin, laid out like swatches of fabric. 'The disciples understood this. Saul too. Peter, Paul, Thomas, Judas – they witnessed Jesus perform his party tricks for themselves. It wasn't difficult for them to have true faith. It's the poor sods who had to take their word for it that deserve a little more credit, don't you think? I mean, imagine it. Some chap tells you that his dead mate was the son of God and that he could raise the dead and turn a couple of fish into a banquet? And you're supposed to take it as gospel and risk crucifixion just to help spread the word?

'Saul was a pragmatic man. He might have had his own conversion on the road to Damascus, but I reckon after being run out of town by non-believers he quickly learned how to pull a coin from behind a doubter's ear and give the credit to God. The church is founded on well-intentioned deceits – you must know that. Some of the most revered saints were deceivers, Claudine. Do you really think that the relics venerated in churches belong to the actual saints? Many a sensible bishop plucked a shin bone from a pile and said it belonged to a martyred apostle. People need physical proof to cling to – something tangible that they can hold and venerate and press to their breast. It's all very well trying to visualise a benevolent deity sitting on a cloud surrounded by worshipping angels, but most people lack the imagination to keep faith in Father Christmas past their seventh birthday. I make it easier for them. I help people who wish to believe, to believe.'

I press my teeth together. Bite down until I taste blood. 'Jethro,' I say. 'You made all this happen, didn't you? His death, the deaths of those poor men...'

'Martyrs, child,' he says, smoothly. 'That's how history will remember them. If anybody's to blame it's your brother. And Everitt too, of course. Some memories are best left buried. He had to go digging around in there, didn't he? Had to retrieve some recollections that had no business coming to the surface.'

I force myself to meet his gaze. 'His suicide attempt – when he was young. You did that, didn't you? All the years he suffered, they were down to you…'

Talbot raises a hand, shushing me and shaking his head. 'You have a very poor opinion of me, Claudine. I could almost be hurt to be so mercilessly pre-judged. If you've got it in your mind that I bumped your brother over the head and dumped him in a grave, please, put your mind at ease. No, Jethro jumped from the church roof entirely of his own volition. Admittedly I'd fed him the drugs that allowed him to believe he was going to step onto the palm of God, but it's hardly my fault if God didn't show up, is it?

'Besides, he'd been suffering horribly in the months before it happened. You saw it yourself. His mind was pulling itself apart. He was seeing things, hearing the voice of God, of the saints, of Lucifer. He was becoming rather tiresome company, if I'm honest, though it was best to keep him near so he didn't do either of us any mischief. I almost convinced him that he'd imagined what happened at the churchyard. Almost.'

I can feel an icy sweat glistening on my brow. I'm cold inside my bones. I have to force myself to focus on his words, to try and make sense of what he's saying. Behind him, Peg is staring at the side of his face, utterly enraptured. Talbot follows my gaze. Grins.

'Peg has always been a woman of appetite,' he explains, closing an eye and leering at her, then at me. 'Fell for a gentleman by the name of Sam. Used to leave her poor long-suffering husband at home while she met up with him for all sorts of pleasures of the flesh. Found herself in the little stone outbuilding at the church in Little Mercy one cold night in November. Stumbled onto something she shouldn't have seen. I really didn't have a great deal of choice. Grave robbing is hardly something one wants to be associated with and Sam really did give me quite the scare. If it helps, he didn't suffer. I thought Marguerite here had succumbed too. I really did knock the daylights out of her. Gave me a horrible start when she sat up and tried to kiss me.

'She'd seen, Claudine. Seen Sam's spirit walk into this vessel – to take up residence among the legion within me. I'm home to so many wandering spirits that I've no reason to doubt her. I'm a Matryoshka doll, I think: home to so many smaller and smaller souls. Sam is in here and that permits Marguerite to continue to live. The thought of his absence was too much, you see. So she went home to poor dull Everitt and lived a good life and looked forward to the moments when she could feel Sam's nearness, his soul working through my flesh.

'It broke her heart when Everitt tried to cheapen their union and to suggest that I was some kind of charlatan. Jethro told him what he saw, you see. All the memories started coming back. He told his friend Everitt about the young woman in the graveyard and the man whom they laid in the grave of Nicolas Hobekinus. Everitt wasn't a stupid man. He'd harboured doubts for thirty years. He confronted her. Confronted me. So I told him the truth and the knowledge of it killed him. Mysterious ways and all that jazz. We'll make use of him, of course. Give it a century and people will start to venerate him as a saint. So it shall be with your brother. With Beccelm and Cissa and Enoch. And the church will continue. Faith will continue. God remains. I remain. I make saints, Claudine. I am the intercessor. I am Father and Son and Holy Spirit.'

I look up at the mess of Everitt's remains. I think of the pale figure who moved silently around the house; who led me here, to this place, this now. I feel the rage rise in me like flame.

'You convinced my brother he was the resurrected St Guthlac,' I say. 'You convinced the others they were his acolytes. Does that make you St Bartholomew?'

He looks briefly offended. 'Claudine, please, there's no reason to be so vicious. Of course I'm not Saint Bartholomew. That would be madness. Dragging your brother's soul back from the lip of hell? Me? I'm an academic, Claudine. I don't do physical labour.'

'So who are you?' I ask. 'What's it all for? Why do you do these things?'

He opens his arms, palms up. Looks at me as if I'm simple – as if the answer should be obvious. 'I'm God,' he says, gently. 'You don't have to kneel or anything. I'm not expecting a big song and dance. Maybe a thank-you, once in a while. He had to spoil things with his conscience and his doubts. What choice did I have? Enoch was always the most loyal of the believers. He did as he was instructed. Took a couple more for his trouble. I think he might even have taken your life too if Jethro hadn't used his last breath to pray for you. I wonder what his cult shall be like in the years to come? Will his symbol be the blade? Will he be the patron saint of knife sharpeners and bridge divers? What strange creatures, you mortals be...'

I feel a sudden icy draught swirl around my legs. I watch my breath rise from blue lips; a swirl of vapour that writhes and twists and reshapes itself in the suddenly sparkling air. I feel a sudden agony in my temples; a surge of nausea licking at my throat, my balance shifting, the world contracting so that for an instant it seems as if the two robed figures are far away, viewed through a porthole on angry seas.

'Claudine,' says Peg, stepping forward. Her face twists, the colour leaching from her skin. Beside her, Talbot looks momentarily bewildered. He stares into the silvery swirl of air around my face and narrows his eyes. Something like fear takes his features in its fist. I see his eyes widen, the tendons in his neck suddenly elongating, his jaw protruding, twisting, as if an electrical current were passing through his body.

I feel the nearness of something greater than myself. Feel a surge of something wondrous and terrifying. Snap my head towards the light. The lids on the jars of ammonia have all become unscrewed. They lie upon the workbench like little silver offering bowls. The vapour of the toxic chemical rises up, fills the air, twists the balance of our fragile minds. I'm high, I realise. I'm being poisoned. We're all being poisoned...

I remember my brother at the kitchen table. Remember him filling my head with trivia, with nonsense, with useless facts. I remember him telling me that ammonia, when ignited, becomes a lake of fire.

Talbot turns his head to follow my gaze. His eyes are

bulging. Behind him, Peg is clawing at her throat. Next to her – half formed, insubstantial – is Everitt. He stares at me. Closes his eyes. Nods, once.

I grab for the oil lamp. Close my hands around its glassy surface. Lift it high.

'No!'

I smash it against the wall and turn to face the pair of them. There is a brief moment of perfect silence. And then the air becomes a river of flame.

Epilogue

**THREE DEAD AS FIRE DEVOURS HISTORIC
COUNTRY HOUSE**

By Julie Crawford

THREE people have been confirmed dead after fire tore through a remote country house.

This newspaper understands that the property was recently linked by police to the spree killings in London. The historic house stands next to the near-derelict cottage owned by local man and stabbing victim Jethro Cadjou.

Resident Marguerite Goodall and her husband Everitt, 66, are among those who lost their lives in the fatal blaze. It is understood that controversial academic and theologian, Struan Talbot, 60, was the third man. His publishers last night tweeted a heartfelt tribute to the much-loved writer.

A fourth occupant of the property is understood to be in a stable condition in hospital. Firefighters called to the scene said that the individual's escape was 'nothing short of miraculous'.

*

Claudine closes the laptop. Shuts her eyes. Rolls onto her side. She finds the use of the word 'stable' a little comical. The psychiatrist who assessed her last night, and again this morning, believes the opposite to be true. She's in no position to be questioned by the police; he's made that clear. She's suffered something close to a complete mental collapse. She may have been suffering with a raft of undiagnosed personality disorders for some time. Post-traumatic stress disorder is the top of the list but there are plenty more to be worked through. She's going to be transferred to a specialist facility as soon as it can be arranged. The police, eager to talk to her about the origins of the blaze, will just have to wait their turn.

Claudine does not question the validity of the prognosis. She doesn't believe herself to be unwell, but neither did Jethro. Neither did Everitt or Struan or Enoch. And all were insane, in their own way. She is willing to believe that she might be mad. But she doesn't feel insane. She feels more powerful, more capable, than at any point in her adult life.

She rolls onto her back. She cannot seem to discern that which is imagined, and that which she truly sees. She thinks of Billy Dean, eyelids taped closed; tubes coming into and out of him, his soul hanging in that place between life and death. A woman sits at his bedside, holding his hand. She reads to him from time to time. She's Fran, and she loves him, and he loves her back. Claudine thinks she might like to nudge him one way or another – to tip the scales between life and death. There's a decency to him, she's sure of that. But there was that punch. She might feel a new connection to the Almighty, but she has yet to learn the art of forgiveness. She fancies that she could reach into the vision and pinch his tubes shut. She doesn't do so, but she fancies that she might yet change her mind.

It all makes sense to her, now. Since the cellar, since the flames, there are no unanswered questions. She even understands Struan Talbot. He was no more than a narcissist, an arrogant megalomaniac who used scripture to manipulate those more biddable than himself, and who came to believe his own lies. If he ever truly believed himself divine, it was always more demon than God. He only kept Jethro alive for all those years so he would have a believable patsy if the gaze of the authorities ever began to linger upon him. And yet even as he laid plans to avoid earthly consequence, he was taking lives in his search for Heavenly reward.

He practised his rituals upon forgotten men and women, drew apostles from the streets and promised them salvation, taking their lives as much for his own pleasure as to summon the ancient spirit that dwelled in the murk of the Fens. He subverted the godliness of St Guthlac's teachings. He saw proof of his own righteousness with each new revelation – grew more saintly in the eyes of those who followed him each time he gave communion to those who walked barefoot and bleeding to his church. Jethro only told him of his sister's pregnancy so that his mentor could share in his joy. Instead, Struan saw a chance to twist scripture to his own will. Jethro could be the risen Christ and Esmerelda's spirit the Holy Ghost: Talbot himself the Almighty in a gross perversion of the Holy Trinity. Claudine can't help but think he deserved more pain as he died.

She feels Jethro in the corner of the room. He's holding

a child. Stroking the infant's hair and smiling that same lopsided smile. Esmerelda grins. Glows.

Claudine puts her palms together. Crosses herself like somebody out of practice. For an instant her memory is full of flame, full of the lake of fire that devoured Peg and Struan and Everitt's flayed corpse. For a moment, she remembers the hand that reached out to her and led her, untouched, past the two burning, screaming figures. She couldn't see their face. They were light and heat and love and they carried her safely into the welcoming arms of the eternal Fen. That's where the firefighters found her. Untouched. Untainted. Sanctified.

When she prays, it is in no tongue known to man.

About the Author

D.L. MARK spent more than fifteen years as a journalist, including seven years as a crime reporter with the *Yorkshire Post*. He writes both haunting psychological suspense and twisty historical thrillers. Mark is also the author of the DS McAvoy series (as David Mark). He lives in rural Northumberland with his family.

Follow D.L. Mark at @davidmarkwriter
and www.davidmarkwriter.co.uk.